THE SECRET LIFE OF A LADY

DARCY MCGUIRE

Boldwood

First published in Great Britain in 2024 by Boldwood Books Ltd.

Cover Design by Head Design Ltd

Cover Photography: Shutterstock and iStock

A CIP catalogue record for this book is available from the British Library.

Paperback ISBN 978-1-83603-532-9

Large Print ISBN 978-1-83603-531-2

Hardback ISBN 978-1-83603-530-5

Ebook ISBN 978-1-83603-533-6

Kindle ISBN 978-1-83603-534-3

Audio CD ISBN 978-1-83603-525-1

MP3 CD ISBN 978-1-83603-526-8

Digital audio download ISBN 978-1-83603-528-2

Boldwood Books Ltd
23 Bowerdean Street
London SW6 3TN
www.boldwoodbooks.com

To my writing group: Linda, Heidi, Jon, and Jill, I wouldn't be here without you!
And to Derek, my forever.

1

BELGRAVE SQUARE, LONDON, AUGUST 1847

Hannah Simmons held the ledger in her hand, fingers tingling with excitement at being so close to identifying the killer.

Secrets never revealed themselves easily, but Hannah would discover the evidence she needed. Her record was impeccable. Tonight would be no different, and none of the powdered toffs below would be any the wiser. Except the guilty party, of course.

Shadows danced and wavered, taunting Hannah as she squinted at the meticulously perfect script. More light would be much appreciated but she dared not risk a second candle.

Claws of desperation scraped along her nerves, tightening her muscles. She had been gone too long. She might be an inconsequential speck of brown muslin tossed amongst the glittering lords and ladies of the beau monde, but someone was bound to notice if she didn't return soon.

While adept at lying, inventing a viable reason for being nose-deep in Lord Geoffrey Bradford, the Earl of Sussex's financial records would be a challenge, even for Hannah. But she refused to leave empty-handed.

Even in the dim light, Hannah could make out intricate carvings in the mahogany bookshelves of cherubs chasing each other. An odd choice for such a sombre room, but Lord Bradford was known for his eccentricities.

His horrific moustache, for one. Enough to make any young miss shudder.

As if she had time for such delicate behaviour. She snorted. A lady's companion cresting the dark side of four and twenty was made of sterner stuff. Especially one with her particular training and skillset.

Best crack on with the task at hand.

She could say with certainty the Earl of Sussex was a fastidious bookkeeper, but a killer? She couldn't answer the question. Yet. Her mission demanded she find evidence before reaching a conclusion and exacting justice.

The clock ticked ominously in the corner. The longer she rifled through his desk, the greater risk of discovery.

So quit faffing about.

She turned another page. Her heartbeat quickened at the name written in neat, even print.

I found her!

Before she could copy down the information, the study door creaked open.

Quick as a whip, Hannah pinched the candle wick, extinguishing the flame. She ducked behind the desk, holding her breath. With any luck, it was just a nosy footman or a scandalous liaison.

The brightness in the hallway briefly highlighted a man's silhouette before he shut the door with a deafening click, plunging the room back into darkness.

Blazing hellfire!

Hannah didn't have time for interruptions. But the mystery man piqued her curiosity. A footman would carry a candle to light the way. Perhaps one of the gentlemen below was meeting a lady, or one of the servants was thieving from Lord Bradford. Regardless, Hannah couldn't wait around to find out. Nor could she pop out from behind the desk and create any kind of plausible excuse for her presence in the study.

Time to make a quiet exit.

A consummate professional, Hannah did not get caught. Ever. And this dunderhead, whomever he was, wasn't changing that. Quietly gathering up her skirts, she found the blade tied high on her thigh, just above the ribbon holding her hose in place. She slipped the knife free, taking comfort in the familiar heft. Hopefully, she wouldn't need the blade, but it never hurt to be prepared.

Rising from her crouched position, she paused. He couldn't see much in the dark room, and the brown material of her simple dress kept Hannah hidden in the shadows. While she preferred to fight, in this instance, flight was a cleaner exit strategy.

Bay windows were spaced evenly along the outer wall of the study. She could sneak behind one of the curtains shrouding the windows. They were on the second floor, but she could shimmy out if there was a ledge. It wouldn't be the first window she used for escape, nor the last.

A floorboard creaked to her left. Hannah moved to the right. Her leather boots, far too comfortable for fashion, slid silently over the thick rug as she inched closer to the wall. Reaching out her hand to avoid colliding into the cherub-carved bookcase, Hannah's fingers followed the grooves in the wood leading her to freedom.

The stranger paused in his movements. She held her breath.

Damnation!

Had he heard her? Impossible. Hannah moved like a ghost. Her training ensured that.

Her fingers met the soft, velvet curtain.

Huzzah!

Something large and solid crashed into her before she could pull the heavy material aside and slip behind it. She tumbled to the ground, her dagger flying from her hands and bouncing on the rug.

The sneaky bastard had tackled her. Hannah's arms and legs tangled with far more muscular limbs.

'Who the devil are you?' His gravelled voice sent unexpected shivers through her. Not fear, but something akin to it. The man gripped her around the waist, rolling with her so she landed underneath him. His body, harder than a tempered blade and bloody heavy, pressed against hers. An unfamiliar warmth bloomed low in her belly.

'Bollocks!' Hannah hissed before taking inspiration from the curse. She twisted, seeking space to ram her knee between his legs. Missing her mark, she hit him somewhere on his inner thigh.

The man grunted as he thwarted her second attempt to smash his bollocks by twisting his torso away and straddling her with his legs, pinning her pelvis to the ground with his own.

Hannah recognised his skills as a fighter too late. Before she could aim for his vulnerable parts – eyes, throat, belly – he shackled Hannah's wrists in his large hands.

Pulling her arms over her head, he lifted his upper body away to see her.

Well, this is ridiculous. I'll never live this down if the duchess finds out.

They were both breathing hard from their struggles, a task

made imminently more difficult for Hannah by her corset. She was acutely aware of his body pressed against hers. While she should be pulling away, her body wanted to arch into his. Highly alarming.

The curtain had been pulled open in their struggles. A beam of moonlight illuminated his face. Thick curls fell over a wide forehead, and shadows didn't hide the slight bend in the bridge of his nose. Hooded eyes narrowed in appraisal. Handsome was too gentle a term for such severe features in a face not easily forgotten.

Lieutenant General Robert Killian, Duke of Covington.

Bugger!

A decorated war hero and honoured guest of Lord Bradford's dinner party, he was also a man she had been explicitly told to avoid.

Lieutenant General Killian was dangerous. To her and the mission.

'You're a woman!' His voice registered shock, but he didn't release her.

'Last time I checked, yes.' Hannah bit her lip. She probably shouldn't have said that. To a duke, no less.

'What in the devil is going on here?' Lord Killian's dark-green eyes looked almost black in the moonlight as recognition sharpened his gaze.

'Good evening, Lieutenant General.' Hannah tried for an innocent smile. After all, she hadn't been caught doing anything specifically nefarious, merely found in the wrong place at an odd time. Men rarely suspected women of truly devious behaviour. The pontificating idiots didn't think the fairer sex smart enough to be treacherous. Thank heavens she'd kept her fighting skills hidden. Hannah could act the innocent fool and dupe the duke.

She softened her voice to a breathless whimper. 'Goodness, but you frightened me. Release me, Your Grace, and we can conduct this conversation from an erect position.'

Lord Killian's jaw ticked as his lips hardened in a determined line.

For the second time in as many minutes, Hannah regretted her impetuous tongue. He was a duke accustomed to doing as he pleased, and they were alone in a rather compromising position. She didn't need to go putting ideas into his head about the erectness of anything.

His deep voice rumbled through her like a caress, intimately soft. 'You didn't seem frightened while attempting to knee me right in the... what was the charming term you used? Ah yes, "bollocks", I believe. You display some unusual abilities for a lady's companion, Miss Simmons.' He didn't release her hands or attempt to stand.

Bloody hell! He knows my name.

Which meant he paid attention. To her. Not good.

I can fix this. I just need to remind him of my insignificance.

A simple smile would suffice as an acceptably diminutive response. But something about the man goaded her. 'I only did what any woman would when attacked, Your Grace. Perhaps it is your behaviour that deserves censure, and not my own.'

'Really?' The duke leaned closer, inhaling sharply.

Dear God, is he sniffing me?

And why did that cause a flutter of excitement? Most irregular and completely unacceptable. Hannah ignored the strange rush of heat spreading from her belly along her limbs. 'There is nothing unusual about me, I assure you. Now, if you would please get off...'

The insufferable man raised a condescending eyebrow. 'On the contrary, Miss Simmons. I find you shockingly unique.'

Damnation.

Unique things were noticed. Not good.

Hannah cleared her throat. 'Quite honestly, I'm flattered, Your Grace. But let me reassure you, I'm completely common and very easily forgotten by someone as grand as you.' When all else failed, appeal to a man's vanity. It was usually a successful trick. Though the tart edge to her voice sounded more insulting than flattering.

She shouldn't let the man provoke her. Yet, inexplicably, she wanted to pit her will against his and see who emerged the victor. Completely untoward.

What is wrong with me tonight?

'I remember everything, Miss Simmons.'

Hannah rolled her eyes. 'I see male hyperbole is still alive and well.'

'You dare to doubt a duke?'

'I dare to doubt you. What kind of duke pins a lady to the floor and refuses to release her? Hardly gentlemanly behaviour.' Despite her efforts to remain calm, her awareness of their position became increasingly acute.

His hands were rough and warm around her wrists. His heavy body created friction in peculiar places, quickly morphing into pleasurable tingles. The scent of bergamot blended with whiskey, mint, and leather in a distinctly masculine aroma.

Blast and bother. Now I'm sniffing him.

Judging by the tick in his jaw and the flex of his fingers around her wrists, he noticed.

'Dukes rarely behave like gentlemen.' The darkness in his gaze deepened, and a thrill of fear stiffened Hannah's spine.

He was a powerful man. She had given him a considerable advantage. To free herself now would require incapacitating him which she could easily manage, but questions would be asked if the duke was found unconscious and bleeding in the study.

Serves him right for being so gallingly obtuse.

Thankfully, he relieved her of having to make a choice. As quickly as he tackled her, Lord Killian released her wrists and rose, gripping her hands and pulling her upright. While he still stood too close for propriety, at least his body no longer pressed against hers.

'I should go.' Hannah backed toward the door.

'What exactly are you doing in Lord Bradford's study in the first place, Miss Simmons?'

Hannah raised her brows in mock innocence. 'One might ask the same of you, Your Grace.' She let the silence sharpen between them like a blade. Just before it cut, she shrugged, breaking the tension. 'I was looking for the retiring room and became lost.'

'Liar.' Lord Killian's gaze pierced through her.

'Ladies don't lie.'

'Ladies don't use "bollocks" in conversation either.'

'That depends entirely on the lady.' Hannah narrowed her eyes. 'What were *you* doing here, Your Grace?'

'Rather bold of you to question a duke, Miss Simmons. Should I be impressed or infuriated?'

'Neither. In fact, I think it prudent we forget this entire incident.' She turned and unlatched the door.

'Are you in the habit of telling dukes what to do?' His voice was devoid of inflection.

'Hardly, sir. I'm rather in the habit of avoiding dukes altogether. Something I shall endeavour to accomplish with more success in the future.' She glanced over her shoulder at him, his plains and edges illuminated by the moonlight. He really was a dashing figure with wide shoulders, powerful legs, and a trim waist.

Devils are always dashing.

'You seem a woman accustomed to success, Miss Simmons.

But something tells me your luck is about to change.' His lips curled in a suggestive smile, transforming his face entirely from arresting to devastatingly handsome.

A gauntlet had been thrown. One she couldn't resist.

'I create my own luck, Your Grace.' Before she could stop herself, she winked. Turning in a swirl of brown skirts, she slipped out of the study and shut the door behind her.

Bloody hell. I shouldn't have done that.

She'd blundered this mission. The duchess would not be pleased. Neither would the Queen.

* * *

Lieutenant General Robert Killian, Duke of Covington, honoured war hero, leader of men, killer of tyrants, and spy for the prime minister, was well and truly flummoxed. Outfoxed by a diminutive woman in brown muslin who wielded a knife. He bent to pick up the incriminating blade from where it had landed under the couch.

'Who exactly are you, Miss Simmons?' he whispered into the empty room. A dark chuckle rumbled from his chest. He was barking at the moon if he expected any answers in the hollow spaces of Lord Bradford's deserted study. But she had been looking for something before he interrupted her. Which was precisely why Killian was there himself. It was a capital place to search for evidence.

But what on earth was a lady's companion doing looking for evidence?

He walked over to the desk, now illuminated by silver moonlight. An abandoned candle still smoked on the marble tabletop, emitting a pleasant blend of smoke and beeswax. He picked up the candle, walked briskly to the banked fire, and used a burning coal to light the wick.

Returning to the desk, he studied the open ledger: a column of neatly printed names with numbers adjacent. Wages, judging by the amounts. One name jumped out at him like a striking snake.

'Why is Miss Simmons interested in the wages of Lord Bradford's household staff? And why would she pause on this page?' The room remained annoyingly silent, refusing to reveal its secrets. Killian shook his head, baffled by the mysterious motivations of the intriguing woman. When was the last time a woman had drawn such interest from him?

He should return to the drawing room. A prospect far more enticing when he thought of Miss Simmons. She had been in his vicinity all evening yet managed to escape his notice.

Fascinating.

There was more to this wallflower than copper hair and the intoxicating scent of orange blossoms and vanilla. His sixth sense urged him to pursue her. The same silent voice that had saved him from innumerable perils during the Anglo-Afghan war. The voice prompting him to follow loose ends, thereby thwarting three assassination attempts on Queen Victoria in the two years since his military retirement. The voice whispering to him now about the petite woman in a dull, brown dress.

Miss Simmons is far more complex than she appears.

He had no desire to sip port and smoke cigars with the men invited to Lord Bradford's dinner party. Nor did he wish to join the ladies at their whist tables, but he wouldn't mind another verbal sparring match with the prickly lady's companion. Or a tumble on the carpet.

Absolutely not.

Killian was not immune to the charms of the fairer sex, but it had been years since his body reacted to a woman with such fierce and demanding need. That was troubling enough, but his lack of control was even more concerning. He almost pressed his advantage when she was trapped beneath him. Unconscionable. He was a man of honour, or at least, a man desperately trying to reclaim his honour. Taking liberties with an innocent woman was unacceptable, especially when those liberties had not been requested.

But if she were to request them...

Impossible. He would not ruin a woman who had no hope of becoming more to him than a passing pleasure. While her protector, Lady Philippa Winterbourne, was among the most wealthy and powerful individuals within the beau monde – even rumoured to be friends with the Queen – Hannah Simmons was a commoner. The idea of a liaison with her was laughable. And yet, when he exited the study and clipped down the winding staircase, a thrill of unexpected anticipation propelled him into the drawing room.

'Killian! Where did you wander off to, eh?' Lord Geoffrey Bradford's words emerged from a cloud of fragrant cigar smoke. He sported an obscenely lustrous moustache that he was prone to stroking like a sleek cat. 'Bothering my maids, you rogue.' The older gentleman burst into rasping laughter that ended with a coughing fit.

'Hardly,' Killian answered, joining his host and Lord Cavendale, Duke of Landington. The two men were congregating near a massive hearth at the room's far end. The hot, summer evening precluded a fire. Killian was grateful the windows had been opened to usher in a cool breeze. It did little to dispel the miasma of fragrances emanating from the ladies in the room. Lavender, rosewater, and lily warred with one another much as the women battled for attention from the eligible bachelors in their company. Killian's wealth, title, and military record made him a highly coveted prize amongst the ladies. He shuddered at the thought.

Alfred Cavendale, Lord Cavendale's eldest son, joined the trio of men. 'Lieutenant General Killian, I was surprised to hear you were attending tonight. Shouldn't a man with your military reputation be off leading innocent men to their deaths in some godforsaken land? Oh, but you've retired, haven't you? A stroke of luck for future solders.' Alfred's grip was firm as he shook Killian's hand, and his gaze narrowed with scorn.

Killian ground his teeth together, refusing to allow the rage to surface. He deserved Alfred's contempt after failing to save the man's brother.

'Alfred.' Lord Cavendale's brows drew down in stern censure.

Alfred turned away from his father and sipped his glass of whiskey.

Lord Cavendale's focus shifted to Killian. His eyes softened. 'Please accept my apologies on behalf of my eldest. Alfred has never understood the harsher realities of war. While Patrick was fighting for his country, Alfred was wasting his time and a good deal of my money at the gaming hells showing his wastrel friends how bad he is at bluffing, weren't you, boy?' Lord Cavendale's lips turned down as though he tasted something sour.

Alfred continued to stare at the barren fireplace, but Killian saw the younger man flinch at his father's words.

'Age has taught me much. Cruel and terrible things happen to us, and sometimes there is no one to blame.' Lord Cavendale's gaze speared Killian, seeing more than Killian wanted to reveal. 'Least of all the courageous few who take on the burden of leadership.' He tipped his chin at Killian, a silent gesture of affirmation.

Lord Cavendale's kind words only intensified the flames of guilt licking at Killian's soul. He doubted Patrick's father would feel the same way if he knew the truth. Patrick Cavendale had died broken, bloodied, and disfigured in a stinking pit while Killian remained untouched by the enemy soldiers who had held them captive. He had failed Patrick. He had failed all of his men, and the shame consumed him. Killian glanced again at Alfred.

Goddammit, he looks like his brother.

But where Patrick had been an eager young man, his brother was far more arrogant and bitter.

What should Killian expect after the sudden loss of Alfred's younger brother? Alfred's undisguised derision was completely justified. In some ways, his hatred was easier to bear than Lord Cavendale's forgiveness, as Killian deserved the former and would never be worthy of the latter.

Despite the cool breeze washing in from the open window carrying a sweet scent of hyacinth, sweat gathered and trickled down the small of Killian's back.

'Lieutenant General, I say, are you quite alright?' Alfred raised a brow and lifted his chin, managing to look down at Killian though he was several inches shorter. 'You've gone quite pale.'

Killian swallowed the disgrace rising like bile in his throat. He straightened his posture, surreptitiously wiping away perspiration from his upper lip and gave Alfred a curt nod.

Lord Cavendale and his surviving son were the only reasons Killian hesitated to accept this mission. Facing the family of a soldier he had so horrifically failed threatened to unman him. Unfortunately, when the prime minister asked a favour, the only acceptable answer was, 'Yes, sir.' And surely Killian deserved this penance for a sin he could never hope to absolve.

Lord Cavendale jumped in, saving Killian the need to respond. 'I was just speaking to Bradford about your work in the House of Lords, Killian, trying to get the Wounded Soldiers Relief Bill passed this session.' Lord Cavendale turned his back on his son and clapped Bradford on the shoulder. 'We're rather impressed, aren't we Geoffrey?'

'Ah, yes.' Lord Bradford nodded at Killian. 'Jolly good of you to keep the fight up for our boys who've come back from the war so broken.'

Before parliament recessed for the summer season, both Bradford and Cavendale had put pressure on several of their cronies in the House of Lords to back Killian's proposed law.

Killian tipped his chin down. The Wounded Soldiers Relief Bill was the least he could do for the men he had failed. He didn't deserve anyone's praise.

Lord Cavendale laid a heavy hand on Killian's shoulder, inadvertently dropping ash from his cigar on the inky blackness of Killian's jacket. Acrid smoke choked Killian. He needed to get away from these men and all the memories they were stirring up.

Killian cleared his suddenly tight throat. 'We all do what we can. Speaking of soldiers, Major General Drake looks like he could do with some rescuing from the whist tables.' He tipped his chin in the direction of the gaming tables. 'Perhaps I should lend a hand to a brother in arms. Excuse me, gentlemen.' Retreat was sometimes the best option as courage failed him once more.

Brushing the ash off his shoulder, Killian strode across the drawing room, taking deep breaths through his nose, focusing on the steady rhythm of his heartbeat as he traversed the polished, parquet floor. Control was a tenuous strand he clung to with a death grip.

The ladies were bunched together at the whist tables like a bouquet of wildflowers in multihued dresses. Major General Drake stuck out like a thorn amongst the petals. A massive scar cut through his face, enhancing his monstrous appearance.

As Killian strode closer to his friend, he couldn't stop his gaze seeking out Miss Simmons. She sat several paces away from the other young ladies. Perched on the edge of a hardback chair set against the wall, she wouldn't be expected to join the titled ladies as they played cards. Lady Philippa Winterbourne, the Duchess of

Dorset, reclined next to Miss Simmons on a chaise, flicking her fan like a cat might flick its tail.

If the seemingly demure lady's companion was trying to fade into the background, she couldn't have chosen a more advantageous spot than adjacent to the duchess.

While the ladies at the whist table were a garden in bloom, Lady Winterbourne was an exotic hothouse orchid. A renowned beauty, despite her years, she drew the attention of any man with breath still in his lungs and blood pumping through his veins. Jet-black hair with a few streaks of silver was piled high in an intricate coiffure, contrasting starkly with the simple chignon worn by Miss Simmons. Lady Philippa wore a tailored gown of silk and lace, resplendent in deep tones of black and purple, while Miss Simmons was draped in a shapeless dress the colour of the earth. Yet it was the plain Miss Simmons, not her glamorous patroness, who captivated Killian.

Leaning closer to Lady Winterbourne, Miss Simmons whispered something low, her mouth barely moving. Killian was caught by the full shape of her lips.

No one in the drawing room would guess the dowdy lady's companion kept a wicked blade somewhere on her person. Or that she swore like a man and fought like a hellion. They wouldn't know she smelled of citrus and cream. He wanted to pass by the whist tables and stand next to Miss Simmons. Close enough to feel the heat of her. Close enough that she couldn't ignore him. But that was beyond the pale. He was a gentleman. He never broke the rules of propriety. Unless he were in the heart of battle where no rules existed beyond survival.

He called upon years of discipline to force his steps away from Miss Simmons and toward his friend at the whist table.

Lord Drake saw his approach. 'Ladies, I hate to unbalance our numbers for the game, but I believe Lieutenant General Killian and I have important matters to discuss.' He stood hastily, nearly knocking over his chair as the table shuddered.

Rich laughter erupted from one of the women. 'By all means, take your leave, sir. There's no chance of you winning here.'

'Indeed,' he gritted. He towered over the women, executing a bow of military precision before facing Killian. 'Dear God, man. Please tell me you've come to rescue me.' Drake spoke under his breath as he shook Killian's hand. 'That woman,' he nodded toward a lady skilfully shuffling cards, 'is a harridan, for certain.'

Killian followed his friend's gaze. The woman in question looked to be firmly on the shelf. She had flaming red hair in a riot of curls. Her figure was too generous, and her features too bold to be considered beautiful. Still, her voice was pleasantly low, and mischief sparkled in her chocolate eyes as she leaned over to speak to the pale blonde lady sitting nearest her at the table.

'Things must be desperate when you seek rescue from such a bountiful gathering of feminine grace and beauty.' Killian smiled at his old friend.

'Hardly.' Drake touched his scar in a habitual gesture. 'More like a gathering of feminine spikes and daggers. I can't believe I let you drag me to this dinner party. I could be sitting in front of my fire, sipping whiskey in blessed silence.' As a counterpoint to Drake's words, the ladies broke into loud laughter.

'You've spent too long sitting in front of your fire. You're getting fat and lazy.' Killian glanced at his friend's flat stomach and shook his head in mock disgust. 'The prime minister needs us to ferret out a killer, and that's exactly what we shall do. Have you no sense of duty left?'

'None. It was stripped from me along with my dignity and any possible happiness.' Drake stretched his lips into the semblance of a smile made gruesome by the pulling of skin and scar tissue. The stark resentment in his glare belied any humour in his words.

Anger and depression were constant companions for soldiers returned from war. Especially those who experienced the kind of torture Killian and Drake endured in Afghanistan. Killian's torment was of the mind, Drake's was of the body, but neither had healed without being irrevocably altered.

Killian knew inactivity and brooding was food for the fire that would consume him. Activity and distraction afforded some relief from the constant memories. He suspected it was the same for Drake. At least this mission would give them something to focus on beyond the monsters in their past.

'I believe there is another player on this field.' Killian nodded his head toward Miss Simmons. 'A fellow detective, perhaps.'

Major General Drake shifted his body and glanced in the direction Killian indicated. 'A woman? Are you mad?'

'She was snooping in Lord Bradford's study just now. And she had a knife on her.'

'Those hardly signify as reasons to assume she is investigating a crime. You can't possibly expect a woman to have the skills necessary for such dangerous work.'

'Perhaps. It's just a feeling I have.'

'Feelings only cloud judgment. When feelings become involved, your logic and intelligence fly out the bloody window.' Drake twisted his neck, popping the vertebrae. 'Whatever feelings you have left are best kept buried deep in the blackness, Killian. You know this well.'

'Instinct then. Surely, we can still trust that.' Killian glanced again at Miss Simmons. Her face was tilted down, but her eyes were focused on him. The air in the room grew impossibly thin, stretched tight by unseen hands. She hastily returned her gaze to Lady Winterbourne, and the spell broke like glass in the flames.

'Facts. Facts can be trusted.' Drake rocked back on his heels.

'Then facts we shall find.' Killian forced his attention back to his friend. He clapped his hand on Drake's shoulder. 'Facts leading us to the killer.'

Despite Drake's warning, Killian had a feeling Miss Simmons would play her own part in this dangerous game of discovery. And he looked forward to it.

2

Hannah wiped a bead of sweat trickling from her temple to her cheek. Lady Philippa combed through her dishevelled hair. They had just completed a rousing training session with rapiers, cudgels, daggers and throwing knives, leaving both women winded.

'Tea?' Philippa asked.

'That would be lovely,' Hannah replied.

The duchess walked serenely to a bell pull and tugged.

Mr Stokes appeared. His upper lip curled in a dismal expression of distaste as he somehow straightened his already military posture. In the ten years since Hannah's arrival, he had not warmed to her, but she was in good company.

'Yes, Your Grace?' His sonorous voice rumbled in the cavernous ballroom they converted into their training arena.

Lady Philippa once explained to Hannah that Mr Stokes never recovered from losing Lord Winterbourne. He struggled with a woman being the master of the house. Apparently, Stokes had mentioned this to Philippa. Repeatedly.

And so, the battle of wills between the butler and the duchess commenced.

'Oh, there you are, Stokes. I thought you must be napping. Old age can be such a heavy burden to bear. Miss Simmons and I would like tea, please. You know how we prefer it.'

Stokes exhaled through his prodigious nose.

'Sometime today, if your poor old bones can manage it.'

'It would be my pleasure, Your Grace.' His tone could have frozen the Thames.

'We shall be in my private sitting room.'

'Of course. Shall I have Cook include refreshments? Perhaps some stewed prunes to assist with your digestive troubles?'

Philippa's mouth hardened into a tight smile. 'Just the tea, Stokes.'

'Certainly, Your Grace.' Stokes spun and walked away.

'Horrid man. One day, I shall use him as target practice.'

Hannah tried to hide her smile. 'I doubt he would move fast enough to make the effort worthwhile.'

'Hmmm. But it would still be fun. Shall we?' Philippa led them out of the ballroom, up the stairs to the family wing, and into her private suite of rooms.

Both ladies settled themselves in the cosy sitting room. Large windows let in the late-afternoon sun and a fragrant breeze played with the sheer curtains.

A maid entered with a tea tray setting it down and curtseying before closing the door softly behind her. The staff knew Philippa preferred to pour her own tea. It allowed the duchess privacy.

'Shall we discuss your unfortunate encounter with Lieutenant General Killian?' Philippa leaned forward, filling two delicate porcelain cups painted with sprays of bright purple violets. She handed one cup and saucer to Hannah before claiming her own.

Hannah knew the teapot was full of more whiskey than tea.

She took a bracing sip and let the spirits burn down her throat. 'I suppose we must.'

'I specifically recall telling you to avoid him at all costs.'

Hannah carefully placed her teacup on its saucer. She soaked in the soothing shades of cream and sage decorating the sitting room before responding. 'Yes, Your Grace. You did.'

'Don't "Your Grace" me, Hannah. We don't stand on pretence.'

'Sorry, Philippa. And I'm sorry about last night.' Hannah shook her head. There was no excuse for her behaviour in the study. She should never have let the man provoke her. She couldn't understand *why* she behaved so impulsively.

Philippa raised a jet-black eyebrow. Her keen gaze lingered on Hannah.

It was disconcerting. Philippa saw altogether too much.

'You've grown accustomed to the shadows, Hannah. But even creatures of the dark long for sunlight's warmth. Perhaps this is why you allowed him to see you.' There was a small rip in the seam of Philippa's shoulder where Hannah's blunted rapier had caught in the fabric. Her maid would not be pleased. 'We can use this to our advantage. Keep his focus on you and away from his own investigations.' Philippa tapped her fingers thoughtfully on the armrest.

Alarm bells rang in Hannah's head. 'Keep his focus on me? Isn't the whole point for me to move amongst the beau monde unnoticed?' It was imperative Hannah remain a ghost hiding among shadows. Ghosts didn't experience the thrill of joy or the pain of grief. They could thwart evil without fear of consequences. Because ghosts were already damned.

Philippa pursed her red lips. 'Lieutenant General Killian is one of the prime minister's private detectives. The Queen indicated both he and Major General Drake attended Bradford's dreadful dinner party last night for a singular purpose. They were on a mission for Prime Minister Russell. Chances are, they're focused on the same man we seek.'

Hannah sat forward. 'Why would the Queen have us looking for a killer if the prime minister already assigned this case to Lord Killian and Lord Drake?'

Philippa erupted into laughter. 'Prime Minister Russell trusts in the House of Lords to hold this gentleman accountable for his crimes. The Queen does not share his confidence.'

'Does Prime Minister Russell know Queen Victoria has dispatched her own investigators?'

Queen Victoria had no qualms establishing her own agenda. But to actively work against the prime minister seemed rather bold, even for the rebellious Queen.

'There are many things happily ignored by men like Prime Minister Russell if it doesn't suit their purpose. The corruption in his government, for instance. Do you know how many peers have been tried in the House of Lords since this new century began?'

Hannah knew, but she kept quiet. Her patroness was not looking for an answer but rather a platform from which to preach.

Philippa's dark eyes flashed with passion. 'One. One man. The sodding Earl of Cardigan. And do you know what happened to that man?'

Again, Hannah remained mute.

'He was acquitted. Do you know why he was acquitted?'

Hannah pressed her lips together and waited.

'A technicality. Some stupid discrepancy in the terms of the charge. Do you really think we can gather enough evidence to convince all the bloody peers in the whole sodding House of Lords to convict one of their own?'

Hannah opened her mouth, then paused.

'Speak your piece, Hannah. You know I hate it when you stay silent.'

'I don't think they would convict one of their own. And I was only staying silent because you wanted to vent your spleen.'

Philippa blinked slowly. 'A duchess does not vent her spleen, Hannah. She expresses her opinions with eloquence and vigour.' She poured herself more tea before continuing. 'But you are correct. They shan't convict one of their brethren even if his guilt is proven. Queen Victoria is well aware of this, which is why she has assigned us to the task. We must find the blackguard and hold him accountable for his crimes before those bloody men get involved and ruin everything.'

'Exactly. Which is an excellent reason to keep Lieutenant General Killian as far away from us as possible. Drawing his focus to me will not benefit our cause.' The idea of capturing Lord Killian's attention inspired an unfamiliar need for Hannah to retreat rather than attack.

Philippa's full mouth curved into a wicked smile. 'Hannah, you forget. Men become incredibly stupid when their tackle gets involved. If he's busy chasing you, he won't have time to pursue this killer.'

Imagining Lieutenant General Killian's tackle had Hannah sipping too deeply from her tea. She spluttered, covering her mouth with her hand.

'Are you quite alright?' Philippa placed her cup and saucer on the table. She joined Hannah on the couch, patting her roughly on the back.

Hannah nodded her head but couldn't speak around the burn in her throat.

'You aren't worried, are you? About Lord Killian?' Philippa asked.

'Of course not.' Alcohol roughened Hannah's voice.

'You've fought men as big and skilled as Lieutenant General Killian. Don't be intimidated by his military credentials. I know how capable you are. I dare say you are even more deadly than me. You must develop more confidence in yourself.'

'I'm confident in fighting him, but that's my point.'

Philippa's brows drew down, and she cocked her head. 'I don't understand.'

'You aren't asking me to fight him.' Hannah wished the room wasn't so warm. She must still be heated from their sparring, or perhaps it was the whiskey. 'You're asking me to entice him. To flirt with him. I...' The words died on Hannah's tongue.

In a rare gesture of comfort, Philippa reached out and took Hannah's hand in her own. 'Ah. I see. You don't think you know how. Or are you frightened?'

Hannah hated admitting any weakness, but she couldn't lie to Philippa. 'Yes. To both.' Hannah bit her lip. Worse than the fear was the burgeoning desire. To draw his interest. To capture his undivided attention. It was madness.

Philippa exhaled heavily and squeezed Hannah's hand. Her perfume was a heady blend of jasmine and something darker. 'I remember the night you came to me ten years ago. The night your mother was murdered. The night you stood up to a monster. The rumours I heard about your mother's lover, Lord Smythe, were not pleasant. I've never asked, but often wondered if he didn't hurt you in... other ways.'

Hannah's shoulders tightened. 'No. This has nothing to do with that night.' She refused to revisit what happened with Lord Raymond Smythe, the Baron Ragnor. Just hearing his name filled her with rage and revulsion so bitter, it burned like bubbling tar on her skin.

This was not an issue they ever discussed.

'I know your mother chose men who were not... kind. Including my husband.' It was another topic best left buried in the past. Hannah's father was Philippa's husband. It was the reason Hannah now lived with Philippa. While many women would feel jealousy and anger toward their husband's by-blow, Philippa had felt responsible to care for Hannah. To provide a home and vocation for her. It defied logic unless you understood Philippa.

Hannah's memories of her father were opaque from age, but she remembered some things. The smell of cloves. Rich laughter. The way her mother would glow when he came for his bi-weekly visits. But during her time with Philippa, Hannah learned the gentle man she remembered from early childhood had another face not so benevolent.

Philippa straightened her shoulders. 'Not all men are like the ones your mother chose. I'm sure some are quite nice. While no man has ever appealed to me, it's highly possible one might appeal to you.'

Hannah had wondered about Philippa's inclinations. It was another topic best left hidden. But on the streets of London, where Hannah did most of her work, she had seen many things in the shadowed corners of White Chapel, Wapping, and St Giles. In the darkest parts of London, damned lovers had a certain freedom not found in society's bright lights. But even there, it was dangerous for two men or two women to be caught in a moment of passion.

If joy and pleasure could be found between consenting adults, Hannah didn't understand the fuss about whether those adults shared the same anatomy. But she worried about Philippa's safety if her suspicions were true. Thankfully, her patroness seemed to prefer a solitary existence, so Hannah kept her nose out of it.

Apparently, Philippa felt no such qualms about delving into Hannah's intimate life.

'Are your jitters an indicator of... curiosity for the dashing Lieutenant General?' Philippa narrowed her gaze.

Hannah toyed with a loose button on her dress. Her heart thundered. 'Don't be ridiculous.'

The night she failed to save her mother from being murdered by Lord Smythe, the night she struck out into the cold, damp, London fog with a letter clasped to her chest, blood soaking her dress, and a single destination in mind, she put to rest any dreams of a normal life. She hadn't been strong enough to save Cynthia, but with Philippa's help and years of training, Hannah had honed herself into a powerful weapon capable of protecting other innocents.

But weapons were built for destruction, not desire.

Hannah had no interest in the distractingly attractive, potentially dangerous, devilishly wicked duke. None whatsoever. 'Lieutenant General Killian is *not* dashing. He tackled me, Philippa. I have a bruise on my hip because of him!' Hannah's voice pitched perilously high.

'Mm. Yes. Not many get one over on you. Isn't that interesting.'

Hannah scoffed. 'Well, it won't happen again.' Because she would squelch this ridiculous need to be noticed by a man who infuriated her. It was stupid to imagine any kind of attraction between herself and a duke. Preposterous.

'Are you sure there aren't parts of him that interest you?' Philippa raised both eyebrows, her lips tilting in the hint of a smile.

'Parts of him?' Hannah's eyes widened. This entire conversation was madness. 'Exactly what parts are you talking about? He's not a pistol I can break into pieces, clean, and then put back together.'

Philippa scrunched her nose. 'I'm making a hash of this. I'm just saying, you are four and twenty. Given your mother's situation, I'm sure you are aware of the particulars between a man and a woman.' Hannah's mother had been a professional mistress.

Hannah had seen far more than any child should, though her mother had always protected her. Indeed, Cynthia died fighting for Hannah's safety.

'I'm not some ignorant fool.'

'Yes, but we've never discussed the tenderness one might feel towards, er, another.'

'Did you ever feel tenderness for Lord Winterbourne?' Distracting Philippa from her line of interrogation was becoming desperately imperative. Hannah was willing to latch onto any topic. Even the forbidden ones.

Philippa's mouth hardened. 'Decidedly not. He quickly realised any inclination of affection he had toward me was best abandoned. In truth, I encouraged his unfaithfulness. We were happiest when apart, so we strove to maintain distance.'

'Was he so terrible?' He used to always bring Hannah lemon drops when he came to visit because he knew they were her favourite. But one couldn't always trust kindness.

'The man I knew was very different from the one who visited you and your mother.' Philippa rubbed her finger against her thumb rhythmically. A clear sign she was upset.

Hannah's stomach churned. She hated the stain of her birth. A bastard child. Knowing her father was Philippa's husband added another sticky layer of guilt to the weight Hannah carried.

Philippa shook her head. 'That was badly done of me, Hannah. I didn't mean to speak ill of your father.'

'Please. You have done nothing badly. I am more grateful to you than I could ever express.' Disgrace tasted like ash in Hannah's mouth. She did not deserve the lavish life Philippa provided, so she must never stop striving to earn her second chance.

Philippa brushed the whole awkward conversation away like a

pesky gnat. 'Let's get back to the point. Namely, your interest in Lieutenant General Killian.'

The woman was impossible!

'I am *not* interested in him.' Hannah's voice rose with exasperation. 'Besides, what could I do even if I were interested? Flirtation ruins reputations.' She shook her head, resolute. 'I wouldn't dare bring such shame on you. Not after everything you've done for me. I am not a creature built for love.'

Whiskey-laced tea steamed in Philippa's cup as she brought it slowly to her lips and sipped again. She held Hannah's gaze. 'All creatures deserve love, Hannah. And no woman should feel shame for her desires. Men certainly don't. If you wish to explore physical intimacy with a worthy partner, I'd never think less of you. Besides, I'm too wealthy and too well connected to care much about the opinions of others. Most people are dolts. Their judgements are irrelevant.'

Hannah exhaled. While she knew Philippa was wrong about *all* creatures deserving love, her words were an unexpected boon. Love was out of the question, but desire? Perhaps one day, she might be tempted to indulge her curiosity and see what all the fuss was about. Especially knowing she could pursue a dalliance without risking her place in Philippa's house or her patroness' esteem.

'Thank you. As marriage is not my goal, I always assumed my options were considerably limited in that arena. Perhaps with the right man, I might want to... well, anyway. It doesn't matter because Lieutenant General Killian is *not* the right man. He's far too...'

'Potent?' Philippa's eyes sparkled with mischief.

'Inappropriate. He's a duke and I'm... well, me. I wouldn't have the first idea how to flirt with him.'

'I'm going to tell you a secret about men. Prepare yourself as it will shock you.'

Hannah straightened her shoulders and nodded, ready for any helpful advice.

'All men are fascinated... with themselves. Just keep the conversation focused on him.'

'That is a revelation.' Hannah rolled her eyes, leaning back into the soft cushions of the love seat. 'I thought you were going to be helpful.'

Philippa patted Hannah's hand. 'Don't fret. You'll be fine. I have complete faith in you.'

Hannah sighed. 'I appreciate your vote of confidence, but I still don't think it's wise to draw Lord Killian's notice.' Nor did she trust herself to remain invisible in his presence. 'Let's stick to our original plan. After my discovery last night, I can prove Sarah Bright was a servant of Lord Bradford's until two weeks before her body was found. The ledger shows her last wages were paid on that date. It clearly links her to him. Or at least to his house. He could easily be our killer.'

'Fine. We shall carry on as planned.' Philippa placed her tea back on the saucer and stood. She walked to the bell pull and tugged. 'He could be our killer, but it's not enough. We must be sure of his guilt before exacting judgment. There is another avenue of inquiry I want you to explore. I received a message from the Queen.'

Hannah nodded for her to continue.

'Apparently, Sarah Bright's father is a handloom weaver. I want you to have a little chat with Sarah Bright's parents. Perhaps they can shed some light on the last two weeks of her life.'

Hannah stood. 'Well, if the Queen commands it, I'd better be off.'

'May I share a piece of advice with you before you go?'

Hannah paused, her hand on the door handle. 'Of course.'

'If you aren't going to distract Lieutenant General Killian, then you really must stay out of his way. Prime Minister Russell does not choose his detectives for their stupidity or clumsiness.' Philippa's cobalt eyes held a warning. And concern.

Hannah smiled. 'Don't worry, Philippa. I'll stay well out of his way. Trust me.'

Lieutenant General Killian's sharp green gaze flashed in her memory, and heat flooded her cheeks. He wasn't for her, but when she remembered the feeling of his weight upon her, his hard hands holding her still, something in her belly clenched and her skin tingled.

She reached up to feather her fingers over her first scar, ten years healed. Hannah's soul was steeped in damnation for failing to protect her mother. But at least there would be justice for girls like Sarah Bright. Sacrificing the fantasy of love was a trade-off she could accept.

3

Of all the people Killian expected to see traipsing along the filthy streets of Bethnal Green, Miss Simmons was among the last. Yet there was no mistaking her proper posture, the gleam of her copper hair in the fading light, or her quick and purposeful stride.

'What the devil are you up to?' Killian murmured.

He kept a safe distance and stayed in the shadows. The anaemic sunlight was quickly admitting defeat to crowded brick buildings tumbling over each other in their quest to blot out the sky. Noxious sludge made a slow track down the centre of the dirt street. Three children sat on a stoop, huddled together and playing a game with five stones. Their clothes were stained and threadbare, and only the eldest boy had shoes. The smallest of them was a girl with wispy hair so blonde it looked silver in the waning light.

Killian knew he was throwing a thimble of water into the blazing fire of poverty, but he still fished in his pockets and gave each of the children a half-crown. The little girl broke into a gap-toothed grin, and his heart cracked. The older boy ran off, probably to alert his friends that a dozy toff was handing out money.

Killian would be swarmed with urchins if he didn't get a move on. Besides, he couldn't dally if he intended to keep up with Miss Simmons's blistering pace.

He had a sneaking suspicion he knew precisely where the prim little woman was heading. Sarah Bright's parents lived in one of the many ramshackle buildings crowded along the narrow street. Killian would bet his favourite stallion Miss Simmons was on the same trail he followed. 'Sneaky, infuriating woman. How did you get her family's address?' She was an enigma he couldn't decipher. And if there was one thing Killian couldn't resist, it was an unsolvable puzzle.

Wind whipped down the street, bringing the foul scent of rotten garbage and raw sewage. Soon the rain would pelt the ground in a summer storm, intensifying the noxious aromas and flooding the street with even more refuse.

Miss Simmons ducked down an alley, and Killian followed. The narrow passage opened into a cramped courtyard with several houses smashed together. Miss Simmons took stock of the doors, striding to the second stoop and knocking loudly. She turned around, almost spying Killian before he ducked behind a dilapidated, wooden structure. Based on the stench emanating from between the sagging planks, it must be the shared privy for everyone living in this small courtyard. Killian repressed a gag.

The state of London's poor was deplorable. Killian was determined to focus his attention on revamping the New Poor Laws once he passed the Soldiers Relief Bill.

With Miss Simmons beating him to Sarah Bright's family, Killian found himself at loose ends. He couldn't very well follow her in. Mayhap he should leave and come back on a different day, but Killian didn't feel comfortable abandoning Miss Simmons in this part of London. Bethnal Green wasn't quite as dangerous as Whitechapel or St Giles, but the western end was notoriously rough. With darkness fast approaching, best for a man to keep his pistol primed and his sword close at hand.

Killian spent twenty awkward minutes watching the sky for rain and avoiding the suspicious stares of a large variety of cats patrolling the area. A rather hefty tabby was growing bolder by the moment and had gone so far as to swipe at Killian's boot.

'Oi, are you the cove who wus 'anding out 'alf-crowns?' A boy of eight or nine with more dirt on his body than clothing stood in front of Killian. He had the hardened stare of a man in the cherubic face of a child.

'It seems doubtful.'

'Wot you doin' standing by the privy? You barmy or summink?'

Killian frowned at the boy. 'If I were a mad man, you would have to be rather brave or rather stupid to come and ask me for money. Which is it?'

'Me mum and dad live 'ere. Me three younger sisters and baby brother. It's my job to protect 'em, innit? Can't have some loony nutter lurking round the shitter.'

'So, it's brave then?'

The boy shrugged and scratched his arm. 'Well, an' if you really were the cove givin' away 'alf-crowns, I'd be a right idiot not to ask for my share. Oi, cat, piss off.' The boy kicked a rock in the general direction of the tomcat, who hissed but sauntered away with his tail flicking behind him.

'So, brave and smart, then?'

The boy assessed Killian with unblinking eyes too large for his small face. 'Depends on you, don't it?'

Killian laughed despite himself. He reached into his pocket and pulled out a guinea. 'You don't happen to know who lives in that house two doors down, on the left?'

The boy's eyes widened at the gold coin. He turned and

glanced down the shadowed street, then looked back at Killian and squinted. 'Wot's it to you?'

'There's a family there. They had a daughter named Sarah Bright.'

The boy's mouth tightened, and his slight shoulders hitched up. Suspicion narrowed his gaze. 'Why you askin' 'bout Sarah?'

'You knew her?'

The boy glanced at the guinea in Killian's hand. He bit his lip, then frowned. 'I'm not telling you anyfink unless you tell me why you want to know.'

'Brave, smart, and honourable. You will make a fine gentleman one day.'

The boy's cheeks reddened in the last light of day. 'I ain't no gentleman. I'm no coward neither.'

'You certainly aren't.' Killian held the gold coin in his open palm. 'This is for your loyalty to Sarah Bright.'

The boy snatched the coin quicker than a striking adder. He bit the metal and used a broken thumbnail to scratch at the surface before nodding his head in approval.

'I'm trying to find the man who killed her.' Killian hunkered down to the boy's level. 'I could use the help of a brave, smart lad like yourself. If you think of anything that might help me, you can leave word at the Crown and Bull. Do you know where that is?'

'Course I do. That's where all the toffs in London go to drink their beer, innit? They wouldn't let me in there.'

'They will if you give them my name. Lieutenant General Killian, Duke of Covington.'

''Caw. You're a duke *and* a Lieutenant General? You ever kill someone?'

'Only when I had to.' He wished he could have added that he'd never killed any innocents. But he fought in a war. Innocents died on both sides. They always had and always would. 'There might be more guineas in it for you if your information helps me find my man.'

The boy carefully closed his fingers over the coin. 'Wot will you do when you find 'em?'

'I'll make sure he's charged for his crimes and faces judgment.'

The boy glanced behind him again, then broke into a cheeky grin, displaying a prominent gap in his front teeth. 'I think I'll help that lady instead.' Killian followed the boy's gaze in the deepening shadows of early evening as Miss Simmons emerged from the doorway. 'She says she'll kill 'em. 'Ooever he is, he deserves to die, don't he? For murdering my sister.'

* * *

Hannah missed her dagger profoundly. Thankfully, she had a pistol strapped to her thigh, a replacement dagger on the other side, another blade in her left pocket, and several throwing knives secured to various parts of her body. One did not come to Bethnal Green of an evening without appropriate accessories.

Still, it wouldn't pay to dally. Sarah Bright's parents had given Hannah much to ponder, and she needed to speak with Philippa. This could alter the course of their inquiry.

Sarah had been a shining success story in the Bright family's impoverished lives. She was fifteen when she got her job at Lord Bradford's and seventeen when the dockworker found her body in a casket in the shipping yard. Scratch marks on the inside of the coffin indicated Sarah was alive when the monster put her inside.

Sarah's parents didn't expect justice for their daughter. But her brother, a boy of nine, with ancient eyes and the gap-toothed smile of a cherub, made Hannah promise to exact vengeance on Sarah's killer right before he scurried out the front door.

'And how the bloody hell am I going to do that?' Hannah

questioned aloud as she pulled her cloak tight against the damp cold.

Early evening had quickly shifted into full darkness. Hannah would have to walk twenty minutes west towards St Paul's Cathedral before she had any hope of finding a hackney cab. Quickening her pace, she shifted her gaze from the street to the shadowed alleys. The hair raised on the back of her neck. She was being followed.

She had spotted the gentleman when exiting the courtyard of Sarah Bright's house. He matched her pace as she clipped past another alleyway in her leather boots. Hannah rolled her shoulders back and reached into the clever slit sewn into her skirts. She could easily reach the pistol holstered against her thigh. It was primed and ready.

Five men emerged from the shadows in front of her, complicating an already less than ideal situation.

'Drat.' Six men in total. She would have to fight fast and dirty. The chances of her dress being irrevocably soiled were high. She liked this dress. It was a pity.

'What's a quality piece of muff like you doing down 'ere?' The leader established himself by taking a point position. His four friends spanned out behind him.

Hannah would eliminate him first. Hopefully, the others would be discouraged from further mischief if their leader went down hard.

'Minding my own business, sir. I would encourage you gentlemen to do the same.'

'Oi lads, she's got a mouth on 'er, this one. I like my ladies with a bit of fight in 'em. Makes the whole thing more fun.' The leader's hand snaked down to his crotch where he rubbed himself. One of the men behind him laughed, a high-pitched giggle that skated cold fingers down Hannah's spine.

'You won't like the way I fight, sir.' Hannah wrapped her fingers around her weapon. She cocked the pistol in its leather holster and gauged the distance between herself and the leader.

He grinned at her, his stained and broken teeth barely visible in the moonlight.

'Leave summink for us.' The bruiser behind him shouted to a chorus of male laughter.

The leader took a step closer.

'I think it best you turn around and leave, sir. This is the only warning I'll give you.' Hannah narrowed her gaze. Fear wanted to run riot, but she clamped down on the useless emotion, focusing instead on things she could control. Her breathing. Her finger resting on the trigger. Her body position. She slid her leg back, widening her stance and increasing her balance.

The man spat into the street. 'That's rich, that is. A little piece of fluff like you warning us? Hah!'

'Have it your way.' Hannah pulled the pistol from her skirt and fired it, aiming low. The loud report echoed in the night. A puff of smoke erupted, filling her nose with the acrid scent of gunpowder.

The man spasmed and shrieked before collapsing in a bloody heap. The bruiser directly behind him swore loudly.

'Really, gentlemen. There's no need for such language.' Hannah quickly tucked her gun away in her skirts and retrieved her dagger from her pocket.

It was a shame there was no easy place for a woman to hide a sword. Using a short blade required drawing the enemy in for close combat. These men smelled foul from a distance. She doubted their scent would improve with proximity.

Hannah flicked her gaze to the fallen man before eyeing the remaining four in front of her. 'Your fearless leader seems to have taken a turn for the worse. Might I invite you to dissipate, or do you need further encouragement?' She wielded the dagger and flashed her teeth in a vicious smile.

'Caw blimey, she killed 'im.' The bruiser edged forward and nudged his leader with a scuffed boot.

The leader, who was now bleeding into the street, groaned.

Hannah cocked her head to get a better look. Her bullet had found its mark, right between his legs. 'Doubtful. I hit nothing vital. As long as he doesn't bleed out, and there's no infection, he'll likely recover. Shall we bid each other good night?' Hannah kept her voice calm.

'I rather think you gentlemen should take her advice.' The gravelled voice behind her sent shivers of recognition through Hannah's system.

The Duke of Covington.

'Blast and bother,' she muttered.

What on earth was he doing in Bethnal Green? And why was he following her? Had she known it was him, she would have handled the five idiots in front of her differently. She certainly wouldn't have displayed her skills so boldly. This was exactly what she wanted to avoid. A ripple of irritation washed over her. What was it about him that had her constantly making mistakes?

She should let the Lieutenant General take the lead. Fall back and be the damsel in distress. But everything in her recoiled at the thought. Hopefully, he would stay out of her way. Knowing men, it wasn't likely. Hannah exhaled loudly.

The murky light afforded by the moon illuminated the remaining men. Bruiser One and Bruiser Two had the broad shoulders and lean build of actual fighters. Fat Man was more mass than muscle, and Skinny Man was thin enough to make Hannah wince.

Bruiser One strode forward. 'I reckon we can take this piece of skirt and her poncy friend, eh boys?'

Hannah registered the singular sound of metal scraping free from leather. Lord Killian had drawn his sword. Awfully kind of him, even if his chivalry was unnecessary.

'Stay back, Miss Simmons. I will protect you.'

Hannah stifled a laugh. She didn't take orders from anyone. Except Philippa, of course. And the Queen.

With a grunt of command from the new leader, the would-be assailants surged forward. Hannah sighed. Men could be so predictably stupid.

Instead of retreating as she should have done, Hannah attacked. Bruiser One had no time to react. She rushed forward, swiping low with her blade, slashing across his thigh, severing muscle and tendon. She spun and sliced again where his arm met his body. He bellowed like a wounded bull and landed hard on the dirty cobbles, his leg and arm rendered useless.

She glanced at the duke, but instead of fighting, he was staring at her, his mouth parted, eyes wide.

'Where did you learn to fight like that?' His rough voice made her shiver. Something inside of her unfurled like a flower in sunlight.

Dear God, am I preening in front of him? Stop it this instant!

But she couldn't help herself. Hannah shrugged. 'Oh, you know. Here and there.' She listened to the footsteps of Bruiser Two as he circled to her left but kept her gaze on Lord Killian. 'Behind you.'

The duke spun around and used the hilt of his sword as a cudgel, crashing it against Fat Man's temple. Fat Man fell onto the wet street with a massive slap of flesh against stone.

Hannah turned her attention to Bruiser Two. With a flick of her wrist, her throwing knife rested in her palm. She flung it before he could lunge forward. It lodged neatly in his left eye.

Bruiser Two screamed in horror. He fell to the dirty cobblestones, clawing at the metal.

Skinny Man looked at his fallen comrade then back to her.

'Bloody 'ell.' He took a halting step backward.

'I did warn you.' Hannah held the dagger in front of her and smiled again, brushing a stray curl from her eyes with her free hand.

The idiot lowered his head and charged like a bull. Hannah held still until he was almost upon her. Lord Killian shouted a warning just as she crouched low. Skinny Man's knees crashed into her shoulder. She pushed up. Using his momentum and her strength, she toppled the bastard over. He landed flat on his back with an explosion of air. Hannah leapt on him, her dagger to his throat.

'Why do men never listen?' she asked, pressing the blade against his neck hard enough to draw blood. Skinny Man's eyes widened, and a tear tracked down his filthy face.

'Please, don't,' he wheezed.

Hannah glanced over her shoulder. Surely the duke would be repulsed by such a brutal display of violence from a woman. Lord Killian stood frozen, his sword at the ready. But it wasn't revulsion flashing in his eyes. And that shouldn't fill her with pride. She returned her gaze to the wretched man beneath her. 'The next time a woman issues a warning... pay attention.' She stood and stepped away. 'Leave. Now.'

Skinny Man scrambled to his feet, his hand pressing against the shallow wound on his throat.

Before he could run away, Hannah called out to him. 'Wait!'

Skinny Man turned, his face twisted with fear and shame.

She reached into her purse and pulled out a coin. 'Take this, and get some food in your belly, for goodness' sake.'

Lord Killian and Skinny Man gave her twin stares of astonishment. Hannah shook her head in exasperation and strode over to the man, pressing the coin in his dirty hand. He flinched away from her but pocketed the shilling before scuttling into the dark night.

'What the bloody hell just happened?' Lord Killian looked at the four wounded men strewn about the street, moaning in various tones of distress.

'Weren't you paying attention?' Hannah raised an eyebrow. 'I defeated four idiots. You managed to take down one. If we're counting.' She wiped her blade over her ruined skirts. 'We should probably follow the example of that gentleman and leave post haste.' Hannah tucked her dagger back into her pocket. 'Damnation. These stains will never come out.' She sighed and shook her head before taking her own advice and quickly walking westward. The sound of boots striking pavement informed her Lord Killian was following close behind.

He caught up to her and gripped her arm, turning her to face him. 'Who the devil are you?'

Hannah was caught off guard by his scent. Bergamot, leather, and soap with the faintest hint of mint.

He leaned closer. She could see the stubble on his cheek. Would it be rough against her fingers? Shocking thought. She pushed it away and ignored the flush of heat.

'I'm Hannah Simmons, Your Grace, or did you forget? Surely not, as I distinctly recall you saying you never forget anything.' Hannah tried shaking free of his grip, but it only tightened. 'I'm in a bit of a rush, sir. It's not safe for a lady to be on these streets after dark, or so I've been told.' Her bravado had been yet another mistake. Why in the blazes did she feel a need to show off in front of this man?

Lord Killian leaned even closer, the warmth of his body

seeping through her layers of clothing. His gaze caught on the scar along her left cheek before lowering to her lips.

'As a gentleman, I'm duty-bound to accompany you safely home, Miss Simmons.' He stepped back and gallantly offered his arm.

Hannah froze. When presented with numerous scoundrels intent on bodily harm, she knew exactly how to react. But a gentleman offering her his arm? She was confounded.

'I don't think so, sir. I am far safer on my own.' With that, she swirled and walked briskly away, not looking behind her to see if he followed.

4

'She took down four men? Are you sure?' Drake furrowed his blonde brows and sipped carefully at his scalding coffee.

They sat at a favourite coffee house, popular amongst Killian's set even at such ungodly hours as nine in the morning. Sturdy wooden tables were pushed close together to allow more patronage as boys scurried back and forth with brimming cups of hot, black liquid.

Killian's laughter held no mirth. 'Am I sure I watched her shoot one man in the bollocks, attack another with the skill of a trained assassin, throw a dagger into a third man's eye as easily as one might apply jam to toast, then send the fourth away with a shiny new shilling? Yes. I'm quite sure.'

Drake shook his head. His closely cropped hair was so light, it glinted silver in the sun streaming through the window to their left. The scar running diagonally across his face from temple to jaw, bisecting his eyebrow and cutting over his nose, made him look dangerous. Because he was. 'It makes no sense.'

'That a woman could be trained to fight as well as a man? I think it makes tremendous sense. Men never look at women beyond their own interests. They are beautiful decorations appreciated as periphery distractions. We assume they are harmless. Which is exactly what she wants us to believe. But she's more dangerous than most men I know.'

Drake raised a judgmental eyebrow. 'I know women are far from harmless, but are you seriously proposing Miss Simmons, a lady's companion, is actually some highly trained, deadly agent?'

Killian knew it sounded preposterous. But he'd seen her skill with his own eyes. 'I am not proposing anything. I'm stating facts. She knew the address of Sarah Bright's family. She took down four men with a pistol and a blade. And the only time I saw her hesitate was when I offered to escort her home.'

Drake nodded his head and tapped his fingers on the table. 'Well, then. Our way is clear.'

Killian waved over a serving boy to order another cup of coffee. 'I don't follow.'

'Well, isn't it obvious?' Drake leaned back in his chair and crossed his arms over his barrel chest. 'You must court the wicked Miss Simmons.'

All the air was sucked from the room. Killian took a large gulp of his fresh coffee and scalded a layer of skin from his tongue. 'Pardon?'

'Didn't you say the only time she seemed flummoxed was when you offered your arm? She is unnerved by you. The best course of action is to keep this devious detective close at hand, where you can monitor her every move. How better than by courting her?'

'Now, that is a ludicrous plan.' But the idea was more appealing than Killian wanted to admit. Which was alarming in the extreme. Marriage was an expected reality for him, but not an immediate one, and not something he anticipated with anything close to pleasure.

His parents had an uncommonly happy union with a tragic end. They died together in a carriage accident when Killian was in Afghanistan. Killian didn't find out about their deaths until his return. As years dulled the pain of his loss, he appreciated they died together. Neither would have done well without the other. But he held no such illusions of a love match for himself.

War stripped him of his honour. The man remaining had nothing but a head full of nightmares and a chest full of regret. Allowing a woman into the hidden places where his shame lived, where the horrors of war echoed in emptiness, would only end in her revulsion and his inevitable undoing.

He would marry a lady with the right pedigree and age to produce heirs. He owed his father the continuance of the dukedom, and he would not shirk that final duty. But while Killian hoped for cordiality with his wife, he would not allow intimacy. To grant someone access to his inner self, as his parents had done for each other, was impossible. She would only find ash and shadows amongst the echoes of what had once been a decent man.

'I can't court Miss Simmons. I am obligated to carry on the dukedom with a lady from an established family.'

Drake shrugged. 'I'm not suggesting you actually marry her. God, man. No. I'm just saying you woo her.'

Killian shook his head. 'That wouldn't be fair to her. If I publicly pursue her only to break the relationship, her reputation wouldn't survive the backlash.'

'And this matters how?' Drake sipped his coffee.

'The beau monde loves scandal. They would tear Miss Simmons's reputation to shreds.'

Drake swept Killian's argument away like a rotten odour. 'If she truly is working against us, your actions will be justified. And if she is just an innocent woman, another scandal will emerge soon enough, and they'll forget the whole affair. The peerage is nothing if not fickle. Besides, Miss Simmons is protected by her connection with Lady Winterbourne, and that's not about to change because you jilt her. You may actually fall in love with the chit and make her your duchess.' Drake's loud laughter filled the rowdy room. 'Can you imagine?'

The most infuriating thing was, he could. A woman steeped in her own darkness might understand his. But it was madness.

'No, my fancy doesn't run so wild as to believe I could fall in love with any lady, least of all Miss Simmons. But I won't underestimate her either.'

Drake nodded his head. 'That almost sounds like admiration.'

'Hardly. And your plan is fatally flawed. You forget that to court her, she must first accept my affections. That will never happen with Miss Simmons.'

'You saw the woman attack four men on the streets of London.' Drake shrugged. 'Imagine if that information got out. I sincerely doubt Miss Simmons wants to see her name splashed about in the papers. Blackmail her.'

'I'm looking better and better in this scenario. First an inconstant rogue, then a blackmailer. How could she possibly refuse me?'

Drake's humour evaporated like mist. His broken lips pulled down in a scowl. 'It doesn't matter, Killian. This whole conversation is farcical. Miss Simmons is not a rogue detective, and under no circumstances should you court her. I only said that to highlight how ridiculous your theory is about her.' He stood, wiped his mouth with a napkin and threw it on the table. 'I'll take my leave. We still have a real murder to investigate.'

'What is your next course of action?' Killian raised an eyebrow at his friend.

'Resolutely endeavouring to avoid any more social functions with you.'

Killian smiled. 'Well, don't try too hard. The Somersets are hosting their annual ball Thursday next. Several esteemed members of society will be in attendance, all of whom could be our potential killer. I expect to see you there.'

Drake rolled his eyes. 'Being your friend is a thankless task, Killian.' He turned and strode out of the crowded coffee house, his limp almost imperceptible as he wound through the tables.

Killian knew he was right. Miss Simmons moved with the same lethal grace displayed by all trained killers. Which meant someone taught her. Someone directed her. But who?

Courting her was a novel way to draw her closer and discover her secrets. Drake may have been joking, but Killian was deadly serious. Still, could he force Miss Simmons's hand in such a despicable way? For Queen and country, he must.

Killian sipped the last of his coffee, the bitter taste lingering on his tongue.

* * *

Tea was a soothing drink, but whiskey was better. Unfortunately for Hannah, Philippa had strict rules about when to imbibe. No spirits before noon. One mustn't become a sloppy Poppy. And so, Hannah contented herself with an overlarge measure of cream and three sugar cubes for their morning tea.

She and Philippa were in the main sitting room on the ground level. It was a tasteful space decorated in dramatic shades of pomegranate and chocolate. The dark colours would overwhelm if not for the massive windows letting in buttery summer sunshine along with views of the street. Crystal vases filled with white and magenta chrysanthemums sweetened the air.

Hannah rested her teacup on its saucer and took a bracing breath. 'I must speak with you about last night.' Once again, she must confess to Philippa her extravagant behaviour. But more importantly, she needed to share the evidence garnered from Sarah Bright's family.

Philippa was wearing a deep-purple day dress with black lace frothing at her neck and sleeves. Since her husband's death, Philippa only wore colours varying a few shades lighter than black. The beau monde believed it a mark of true devotion to Lady Winterbourne's departed husband. Hannah knew it was because Philippa's pale skin, black hair, and cobalt eyes were set off by dark hues. But there was no point in muddying public opinion with something silly like facts.

Her patroness was the perfect picture of beauty and refinement. By contrast, Hannah's grey dress was the essence of a dreary wallflower. A strategic choice. Hannah liked fading into the background. Which is why her behaviour the night prior was so inexcusable. And baffling. And not to be repeated. Ever.

'Don't keep me in suspense. What did you learn from Sarah Bright's parents?'

Hannah took a moment to organise her thoughts. 'Several things. Sarah visited them shortly before her death. Apparently, she wanted to tell them about an exciting job prospect. She had an interview for a new position in a different house.'

'Whose house?'

Hannah scrunched her nose and shook her head.

'She didn't say.' Philippa homed in on the biggest problem.

'No. She didn't. But she was excited about the opportunity.'

Philippa sat forward, her teacup halfway to her crimson lips. 'So perhaps Lord Bradford is not our most likely candidate for the killer. Drat. I was hoping he was guilty of something more nefarious than an obnoxiously large moustache.'

Hannah frowned. 'This is serious, Philippa.'

'Yes, and so is that moustache. A serious disaster.'

Hannah rolled her eyes, but Philippa only shrugged, brushing off Hannah's attempt to criticise her.

'You said you learned several things. What else?' Philippa asked.

Hannah sighed. 'Sarah always wore a necklace her mother gave her. It would have been worth a significant sum. She said Sarah was never without it. A gold chain with a flower pendant. A lily. But when they found her body, there was no necklace recovered.'

'Mm. Well. I suppose if we find some nobleman wandering around wearing a lady's necklace, we'll have our man.'

Philippa was right. It was damn little to go on. Hannah controlled her frustration. 'I was thinking the killer may have sold it. We could look at the pawnbrokers near Bethnal Green. I know it isn't very helpful, but sometimes even the smallest piece of evidence is important.'

Philippa rolled her eyes. 'I suppose.'

Hannah's tea cooled on the table. She couldn't avoid her poor behaviour from the previous night any longer. 'Philippa, I have more to share. I don't think it will improve your mood.'

Philippa raised an eyebrow. 'Does this have something to do with a certain duke?'

Hannah squirmed.

Philippa snorted. 'I'm intrigued. Do continue.'

There was a knock on the door, and Stokes entered. His posture was so rigid Hannah wondered if he was physically capable of bending over. 'Your Grace, there is a guest at the door.'

Hannah sat up straight. Philippa sipped her tea. The clock ticked away several seconds. Sometimes, Philippa liked to make Stokes wait for her reply.

Stokes hated this particular game. He lifted his chin a fraction higher.

'Who is the guest, Stokes?' Philippa finally asked.

'Lieutenant General Killian, Duke of Covington, madam.'

'Speak of the Devil.' Philippa smiled.

Panic surged through Hannah. She stood up, then abruptly sat back down. 'Dear God. What is he doing here? Philippa, what is *he* doing *here*?'

Philippa pursed her perfectly pigmented lips and carefully placed her tea on the table. 'I've no idea. But there is one way to find out. Show him in, Stokes. And have Cook send up more tea and some refreshments.'

Stokes stood frozen. This was his retaliation. If she made him wait, he would do the same for her. It was all rather petty, but Hannah guessed they both enjoyed themselves on some level, or one of them would have quit the game by now.

'Show him in, Stokes.' Philippa shouted across the room, then continued in a normal tone to Hannah, 'Poor old dear must be going deaf. It's common in one so decrepit. Such a shame.'

'It's just, shrill tones are often difficult to discern, Your Grace.' Stokes nodded once before slowly turning and walking out of the sitting room.

'God! That man! One day, I shall give him the sack. I really will.' Philippa scowled at the door before smoothing her face into an impassive expression.

'Philippa, please focus. Lord Killian is here. In our house. Your house. Whatever. What on earth—' Hannah was interrupted by Lord Killian's arrival.

He wore a morning coat of dark green that brought out the same colour in his eyes. His unfashionably long hair curled at the high white collar of his shirt. He was obscenely masculine and distractingly out of place in a room full of fresh blooms and delicate furniture.

Hannah's heart beat so loudly, she was sure they all heard it.

'Lieutenant General Killian. What a pleasant surprise. It is early for social calls. To what do we owe such an unexpected visit?' Philippa rose and extended her hand to Lord Killian. He strode across the room and took her fingers in his gloved hand, bowing cordially.

'I apologise for the abruptness. There is a matter of great urgency about which I must speak with you. Privately.' Lord Killian glanced briefly at Hannah before returning his gaze to Philippa.

This is not good!

Hannah pressed her lips together and focused on Lord Killian's cravat. The knot was simple and severe, just like the man.

'There's nothing you can say to me that Hannah can't hear, and I wager there's quite a lot you're planning to say that directly impacts her. Or have I missed my mark?'

Lord Killian's mouth quirked at the corner. 'You are as perceptive as you are beautiful, Lady Winterbourne.'

Philippa's smile flashed harder than the diamond pendant sparkling at her throat. 'Flattery will get you nowhere, Lieutenant General Killian. But don't let me stop you from the attempt.'

Heat rose from Hannah's chest, over her neck, and into her cheeks. She would bet her favourite pistol he was here to tattle on her. Beastly man.

'I would like permission to court Miss Simmons.'

Well. That was unexpected.

What could he possibly be thinking?

Lord Killian kept his gaze focused on Philippa as if Hannah's opinion meant nothing in the matter. Which gave Hannah a moment to collect herself before letting the anger build.

The sheer arrogance!

'I have no wish to be courted by anyone. Least of all you.' Hannah's voice was strong, even if her stomach was full of bees buzzing in a frenzy.

Lord Killian clenched his jaw, the only indication he'd heard her. 'Lady Winterbourne, are you sure you wouldn't prefer to discuss this privately?'

Oh, that just beats all.

Hannah rose from the couch and walked to Killian's side. 'Are you a complete imbecile? I'm the one you should be asking, and I already gave my answer.' She was tempted to shove him just to force his attention toward her. But she didn't trust herself not to punch him in his pompous *(gorgeous)* face.

'I think Lord Killian has a point. This is a private conversation.'

Hannah turned to Philippa, her mouth parted on a shocked inhalation. 'Excuse me?'

Philippa softened her smile when she faced Hannah. 'A private conversation between the two of you. I shall take my leave.'

Hannah put her hand out to stop Philippa. 'Wait, please stay. Neither of us needs to leave. It's Lord Killian who should be excusing himself. I have nothing to say to him.' Panic clawed at her throat. She couldn't breathe. What could he be plotting? Certainly not a marriage proposal.

'I'll see you at luncheon.' Philippa leaned closer and lowered her voice to a whisper. 'If you end up killing him, please try not to get blood on the couch. We just had it reupholstered.' She squeezed Hannah's hand.

'This is completely untoward.' Lord Killian's eyes widened, and lines bracketed his mouth. Hannah took perverse pleasure in knowing he was equally uncomfortable. 'I have come here to seek your permission to court Miss Simmons, Lady Winterbourne. Surely, after such a declaration, you don't mean to leave us together alone, unchaperoned?' Lord Killian stepped away from Hannah, moving to block Philippa's exit.

Philippa smiled. 'Why not? I have no doubt Hannah will conduct herself as a proper lady. And as an honourable gentleman, you wouldn't dare press an advantage.' Philippa swept around him to the door. 'If you do, Hannah will remind you of your manners. She can be quite convincing.'

Killian stretched his neck and took a deep breath. 'This is not how things are done, Lady Winterbourne. If she had a father, I would discuss this with him. As you are her patroness, I have come to you. A young lady does not choose who will or will not court her.'

Hannah ground her teeth together and tried not to scream.

Philippa laughed. 'This is why men's opinions should be confined to cigars and card games. Hannah is the only person capable of choosing her future happiness. As such, she is the one you must appeal to. Good day, sir.' Philippa turned and walked out, closing the door behind her.

Insufferable man!

The very idea that he would swan into Philippa's morning room and arrange Hannah's entire life without her permission or input was infuriating enough to have her hand itching for the hilt of a dagger.

It was so much easier to fight men than converse with them. But needs must.

In any conflict, a direct path was usually best. Shut him down quickly and efficiently without unnecessary fuss. Hannah smoothed her skirts and tried to keep her voice calm. 'Lord Killian, while I am flattered by your proposal, I must decline.'

There. That was clear, precise, and polite. She should win a prize for decorum.

'I do not accept your answer.'

Bastard!

The man was impossible.

'You must. It is the only answer I will give.' Hannah walked to the wall where the bell pull hung. She would get Stokes to come with his ramrod-straight spine and escort Lord Killian out of the sitting room and out of her life.

Lord Killian beat her to the decorative rope and grasped her arm, turning her towards him. 'Perhaps I can convince you otherwise.'

This close, his eyes were not fully green but rather an intriguing hazel. Striations of brown and blue intermingled with deep jade. The scent of starch from his shirt tickled her nose. She looked away from his eyes only to stare at his mouth. His bottom lip was fuller than the top, and he pressed them together in a firm line. He had a freckle just to the upper left corner of his mouth. It was a delicate mark on such a masculine face.

'If you value the use of your fingers, I suggest you release me, immediately.' Hannah pulled back and was disappointed when his hand loosened and slipped from her arm. It would have been lovely if he gave her a reason to slam the heel of her hand into his solar plexus.

'I am quite invested in my fingers, Miss Simmons.' Killian's gravelled voice stroked along her senses. She almost shivered.

'Then use them to open that door and walk away. You cannot convince me of anything, Your Grace. You are wasting your time.'

Killian smiled, but it didn't warm his eyes. 'I could always try charm. But I think blackmail is more expedient, don't you?'

Hannah swallowed. Of course, he would use her bravado against her. 'You disappoint me, sir. I can only assume you are speaking of last night.'

'A lady under the protection of the Duchess of Dorset shooting one man in the street, cutting another down with a dagger, and a third with a throwing knife? Pretty salacious stuff, wouldn't you say?'

'I'm hardly a lady.'

'That's not what you keep telling me. If you're not a lady, then what are you?'

Just a woman.

Hannah pressed her lips together. Such honesty might damn her. A woman garnered no respect in a man's world and often became an easy target.

She gathered her thoughts before responding. 'I'm not the kind of lady you're accustomed to encountering. You plan on splashing last night's events throughout the beau monde? Please. No one will believe some drab old lady's companion capable of squashing a spider, let alone attacking four men.'

'You are neither old nor drab, Miss Simmons. But you raise a valid point.'

'Precisely.'

'When I tell the prime minister about your impressive deeds, it will only be one man that you vanquish. I will have managed to take down the other ruffians with my expert skills.'

The prime minister? Blasted hell!

Prime Minister Russell would surely tell the Queen. Her Majesty would take a decidedly dim view of Hannah's carelessness in being seen, especially by one of the prime minister's men. Hannah didn't make mistakes. At least, she hadn't made them until she met the blockheaded Duke of blasted Covington.

Lieutenant General Killian would not ruin her reputation with the Queen.

Hannah laughed, hoping he didn't notice her panicked notes of hysteria. 'The prime minister will never believe you.'

'The prime minster has utmost faith in me.' Killian leaned infinitesimally closer. Her heart rate and the temperature of the room simultaneously increased. 'I will sing your praises as a modern-day heroine. Will that garner you favour amongst the peerage? Probably. Will questions be asked about why a young lady was alone and unchaperoned in an area as dangerous as Bethnal Green? Presumably. Will it bring you enormous attention and make it impossible to disappear? Most assuredly.'

'Bastard.'

He backed her against the papered wall. 'Careful. Words like that could get you into trouble. A man would be called out to duel for such an accusation against a duke.'

'But I'm not a man.'

Lord Killian's pupils dilated. 'No. You certainly aren't.'

'Besides, I would best you in a duel of pistols or swords. You can't intimidate me, sir.' Her voice was husky, and a drip of perspiration trickled between her breasts. Breasts that had become unaccountably heavy. And when did her nipples decide to develop extra nerve endings as they tightened and chafed against her corset?

He startled her, reaching up and tracing an escaped curl from her chignon with his gloved finger. The whisper of soft leather danced along her skin. 'Is that a challenge?'

'That's a fact.' Hannah's breathing was too fast. Bergamot and leather invaded her senses. Heat from his body engulfed her, and something electric crackled in the air between them. She was in the eye of a terrible lightning storm, both dangerous and exciting.

'Perhaps I can't intimidate you with threats. But charm? That's another story.' He leaned closer, his body not quite touching hers. Their breaths mingled as his fingers explored her cheek, pausing at the scar. She hated that it made her self-conscious. 'You feel safe with violence, but softer emotions terrify you, don't they, Miss Simmons?'

Yes.

'No.' When faced with danger, Hannah always attacked. And this moment was laced with peril.

She put her hands flat on his chest and shoved him hard. He stumbled backward, almost catapulting over the back of the couch before regaining his balance. Hannah squared her shoulders and tucked the traitorous curl behind her ear. 'You *do not* terrify me, sir. You don't know me, and you certainly don't wish to court me. What is your game?'

5

Killian recovered quickly despite the strength of her shove. Dark satisfaction in unnerving the indomitable Miss Simmons eased his bruised pride at almost landing arse over teakettle on Lady Winterbourne's patterned rug. Her impressive shields hid a vulnerable core. What possible forces created such a contradictory woman? Killian was determined to find the answer.

But perhaps distance was advisable. Something about the woman made him want to lunge forward when he should hold back. If he was going to win a battle of wills against Miss Simmons, he needed to keep a cool head and let logic, not lust, lead the way.

Killian loathed manipulation and despised blackmail. But at least he could be honest with Hannah about his motivations. And for reasons he did not wish to examine, he didn't want to lie to her. He tugged down his vest and sat on the overstuffed chair opposite the couch. 'You are correct, Miss Simmons. Courting you is not my primary goal. Finding a killer is. But you know that because you are seeking the same man, aren't you?'

The confounding woman pursed her lips and shrugged her shoulders.

'You refuse to answer?'

'You don't seem particularly amenable to my answers, Your Grace.' Miss Simmons curled her lips in the imitation of a sweet smile. She had a dimple in her right cheek, just below the scar.

Killian had noticed the pearl-coloured crescent marking her otherwise smooth cheek the night before. Questions burned about how she sustained the injury. And if the person responsible for hurting her had suffered, or if Killian could still exact punishment on him. But his thoughts were getting off track.

'Fine.' Killian wished he could remove his gloves and loosen his cravat. The room was insufferably warm. 'Your admission is irrelevant. I know we are focused on finding the same culprit. What is less clear is who you are working for and why.' He raised his eyebrows in a question.

Miss Simmons remained stubbornly silent.

'You won't tell me. But I will find out, Miss Simmons. According to a certain young master Bright, while I seek justice for the crimes this gentleman committed, you plan to kill him. Murdering a murderer? Hardly honourable.'

'That depends entirely on your definitions of justice and honour, Lord Killian.' Miss Simmons walked around the couch and sat on the edge of the cushion. Deep pink flowers were stitched into the material and her agile fingers worried at the pattern, the only betrayal of her nerves.

Killian wondered how many blades were hidden underneath her skirts. A man could spend hours scouring every inch of her body to discover her weapons. He shifted in his seat, willing his libido to behave.

Force wasn't working. He would try logic. 'Accepting my offer could be as beneficial to you as it is to me. If we work together, there's a far greater chance we'll find this man.'

Miss Simmons sighed and glanced out the window behind him. 'I don't need your help.'

'But you do need my silence. If I expose your actions from last night, you will gain notoriety amongst the very group of nobles you hope to infiltrate. Hardly beneficial to your mission.' It was a powerful argument. She could not dispute his reasoning.

She narrowed her eyes in undisguised loathing, pinning him with her glare. 'You haven't answered my question. How does pretending to court me bring you any closer to finding this man?'

Killian smiled and leaned back in the chair. 'What's that delightful saying? "Keep your friends close and your enemies closer."'

'Sun Tzu. You've read *The Art of War*?'

Killian's eyebrows winged up, and he inhaled sharply. '*You've* read *The Art of War*?'

Miss Simmons shrugged once more. 'Don't look so surprised.'

'The only copies I've found are written in French.'

'*Oui*.' Miss Simmons was a multilingual little minx with violent taste in literature.

'So, you shoot men in the street, carry blades in your pockets, and are versed in *The Art of War*? Truly, Miss Simmons, you are a fascinating woman.' He rose from his seat. 'But are you brave enough to accept my offer?'

'I'm far from fascinating, Your Grace. Let me see if I understand your motivation. You wish us to pretend a romantic interest to keep an eye on me. Presumably, I will reciprocate by keeping my own eyes on you.'

'Precisely.' Killian held his breath, waiting for her answer.

She rose from her seat. Killian's breeding forced him to stand with her.

'I don't think it requires courage to accept your offer, just an acute sense of confidence. Because despite what you think or how closely you watch me, I will find Sarah Bright's killer first.' Miss Simmons walked to the door and paused. Killian joined her, stopping a few feet away. Distance. Distance and decorum were key.

'I accept your proposal on one condition.' Miss Simmons eyes were the colour of amber garnet when they caught the light.

Killian's tongue must be broken, for he couldn't form words. Instead, he gave a curt nod for her to continue.

'In public, we will conduct ourselves as any courting couple might, but privately, there will be no such flirtation. No false charm. This is a business deal between two opposing forces. Let's not pretend otherwise. Do you agree to my terms?' She stuck her hand out to shake.

Killian grasped her small hand in his larger one, wishing again he could remove his gloves and feel her skin against his. She had the firm grip of an equal. When he squeezed her hand and shook, her shoulders relaxed. Until he brought her fingers to his mouth and pressed a kiss against her knuckles. While he wore gloves, she did not. Her bare skin brushed against his lips. He relished her gasp. 'I don't believe it possible to pretend charm with you, Miss Simmons.'

She pulled her hand away, her lips hardened in a tight frown as she opened the door. 'Finding Sarah Bright's murderer first and killing him before you can save him from his fate will be the greatest of pleasures, Lord Killian.'

'The satisfaction of finding Sarah Bright's murderer first and delivering him to the House of Lords where he will experience true justice shall only be eclipsed by the pleasure of your company, Miss Simmons.'

'Bastard.'

'I'm beginning to appreciate your expansive vocabulary. You say the sweetest things when you're angry.'

'You haven't glimpsed the spectrum of my rage, sir.'

'Something for me to look forward to, then. The Somerset's annual ball is Thursday next. I shall come for you at six. One can only hope you own a ball gown in shades other than brown or grey.'

He felt the heat of Miss Simmons's gaze and it warmed him as he walked away.

* * *

Buggering bloody bollocks!

Eight days had passed since his invitation. The Duke of Covington was arriving within the hour to escort Hannah to the Somerset Ball. A firing squad would be preferable.

'Hannah, if you keep frowning so fiercely at poor Betty, she'll think you don't like her handiwork.' Philippa smacked Hannah with her fan.

'Ow!' Hannah put down the blade she had been polishing and rubbed her arm. 'Sorry, Betty. You are doing a wonderful job.'

Betty was new to the household and studying to be a lady's maid. Hannah liked her immensely, though the fifteen-year-old was as naïve as a lamb and hopelessly lacking in confidence.

Hannah tried to force her freshly reddened lips into a smile as she spun the blade on the table.

'You really are becoming quite the lady's maid, Betty.' Philippa nodded approvingly at the young woman, who blushed so fiercely, the tips of her ears turned crimson.

'It's me who should be thanking Your Grace for this opportunity. It's ever so kind of you.' Betty's clever fingers twisted another curl into Hannah's complicated coiffure. 'Miss Delacroix's recipe for lip salve is wonderful. I never would have thought to tint it with beet juice, but Miss Simmons's lips look ever so natural.'

Her mouth was lusciously red. No less than a million pins held Hannah's hair together. Each one dug into her scalp like angry daggers, but the effect was rather magnificent. Her shining, copper hair was piled high, decorative jewels glittering throughout the mixture of braids and curls. Delicate tendrils spiralled around her face. She felt both vulnerable and elegant.

Every time she imagined Lord Killian seeing her like this, her belly dissolved into a thousand butterflies. It shouldn't matter what he thought. This whole courting business was a load of tripe. He knew it. She knew it. But how did she get her stomach to understand and stop flipping around like an eel caught in a bucket?

Hannah returned her attention to Philippa. 'I wasn't frowning at Betty. It's this evening. And the expense you went to on my dress. Silver is such an incredibly dear colour, Philippa.'

'Yes, so very close to grey, which I know you prefer.' Philippa smiled.

Hannah rolled her eyes, though she couldn't help noting how the material sparkled in the candlelight. 'I will enjoy knowing I didn't follow Lord Killian's order. But this gown has far too much material in the skirt and not nearly enough anywhere else. I mean, look at these.' She gestured to her chest. The dress was cut in a low scoop neck, exposing Hannah's shoulders and a generous amount of her modest cleavage. 'Not to mention these sleeves. I can't lift my arms higher than my shoulders.' She picked up the knife and tried to swipe it in a diagonal slash. The sleeves of her gown cut into her limbs, constricting her movement. 'What am I supposed to do if someone attacks me? I might as well tie myself up and save them some time. I mean, really.'

Philippa's rich laugh was low and melodic. 'You aren't usually prone to such histrionics. What's the matter, Hannah? Nervous about spending an evening on the arm of Lieutenant General Killian?'

Huffing out a breath, Hannah reached into the specially designed pocket to deposit her weapon with one hand, while she fingered one of the jewels dangling from her ear with the other. 'Please. I'm worried about losing one of these earrings. They are actual diamonds, Philippa.'

'I know. They're mine.'

She must sound like a petulant child to the duchess. 'I'm sorry. Thank you for lending them to me. They are stunning. I'm just not used to...'

'Showing your beauty? No. You've always been more comfortable hiding behind your dowdy disguise.'

'By fading into the background I'm free to go anywhere, hear everything.' And no one noticed her. She didn't have to worry about anyone looking beneath the surface at what lurked in her depths. Nothing good lived in those dark waters. There were no boundaries she wouldn't cross to protect those she loved, even if her efforts failed to save them. She was almost as monstrous as the men she hunted.

'Are you sure that's the only reason you like to be invisible?'

Hannah caught Philippa's piercing gaze in the mirror. Hannah swallowed the words that almost escaped. Words of fear. Words of shame. Ten years wasn't long enough to forget what happened the night the baron had noticed Hannah. That evening ended in bloodshed and death. Hannah had failed her mother. She was supposed to be her mother's champion, but she hadn't stopped the baron from murdering Cynthia Simmons. Failures didn't deserve to wear priceless baubles and dress in fine frippery.

Stokes knocked on the door and pushed it open. 'The Duke of

Covington has arrived. He is waiting in the entry.' His gaze scanned over Philippa and stalled on Hannah.

'Have you forgotten something, Stokes? Like how to blink?' Philippa raised an imperious eyebrow at her butler.

Stokes cleared his throat. 'No, Your Grace. Miss Simmons, you look quite ready for a ball.'

'I don't think she needs your help ascertaining her readiness, Stokes. Tell the duke we shall be down in a moment.'

'Yes, Your Grace. Although I'm happy to make him wait if you need more time to ready yourself.'

Philippa blinked slowly as everyone in the room held their breath. 'I'm quite prepared for the evening, Stokes.'

'Of course, Your Grace. I hadn't realised the newer fashions were quite so garish.' He clipped his heels together and spun, exiting with a noticeable spring in his step.

'Dreadful man! Betty, let me know if you hear of any butlers looking for a new position. We might have a vacancy.'

Betty looked horrified at the entire exchange. Hannah turned to the maid. 'Thank you so much. You've done a marvellous job.'

Betty nodded, her white cap bobbing frantically. 'You do look ever so lovely. And you, madam. Breathtaking, I assure you. I hope you have a wonderful time.' She dipped a curtsey to Hannah, then Philippa before scurrying out the door.

'That girl can't stand up to the mice in the cupboards.' Philippa shook her head, black hair shining in the candlelight. In contrast to the silver of Hannah's dress, Philippa was draped in hues of midnight and crimson, enhancing the blush of her cheeks and the blood-red stain on her lips.

'I can't remember ever being so sweet. Can you?' The binding of Hannah's corset tightened as she took a shallow breath. Melancholy settled over her like a shadow in the flame.

'You are going to be wonderful tonight. You will dazzle the

duke, but you will also blend into the pomp and frippery of the beau monde. I think you'll find when one is surrounded by jewels, even a diamond can fade into the background, Hannah. Come. The duke is waiting.' For any other woman, Philippa's words would sound like an insult. But for Hannah, it was a message of hope.

She stood, feeling the weight of her skirts as she followed Philippa to the door.

The duke might be waiting, but Hannah wasn't sure she was ready.

She held her head high and took slow, measured steps down the wide staircase, the rustle of her skirts sounding like leaves in the wind.

He was watching her. She didn't have to look at him to know. The burn of his stare heated her exposed skin. She couldn't meet his gaze. Not yet. She would lose her nerve. Instead, she stared at the train of Philippa's gown.

Hannah reached the bottom of the stairs and he was waiting, his white-gloved hand extended. Finally, she raised her head, looking into Lord Killian's eyes.

It was a terrible mistake.

Scorching fire blazed there. Incendiary. Mesmerising. She was caught like a fluttering creature. Fascinated by what could engulf her.

'Miss Simmons, you look quite enchanting.' He pressed his lips against her fingers. The firm warmth of his mouth seeped through the thin silk of her glove. She remembered the last time he kissed her hand. Soft lips brushing over bare skin.

'Bloody hell,' she whispered.

Heat was replaced by a spark of humour in his eyes. 'You say the sweetest things, Miss Simmons.'

6

Lady Winterbourne and Miss Simmons sat on one side of his carriage while Killian reclined opposite them. It was a dark evening, and the women's faces were masked in shadow. He couldn't keep his gaze from straying to Miss Simmons. Her copper hair caught the passing streetlamps and shone like a flame in the heart of winter. She was stunning. The shimmering silver of her gown set off the rich colour of her hair and smooth perfection of her skin. Her seamstress was the very Devil, knowing precisely what to expose and what to keep hidden to drive a man insane. Killian danced on the edge of chaos.

At least Lady Winterbourne's withering glares tempered his imagination and kept him from doing something rash.

There were so many ways a man could seduce a woman in the small confines of a carriage. If only there wasn't a chaperone present. And if only that chaperone wasn't the terrifying Duchess of Dorset.

When they reached the Somerset's estate, a long line of carriages waited to offload the sparkling lords and ladies.

'I must confess, I am not a frequent attendee of Lady Somerset's Ball.' As conversation starters went, it wasn't scintillating, but he was preoccupied wondering how soft Miss Simmons's skin would be against his mouth. Whether her scent of vanilla and orange blossom would be stronger at the pulse point of her throat.

Lady Winterbourne speared him with her gaze. 'Something we have in common, Your Grace. Though my husband was frequently in attendance. He couldn't pass up an opportunity to play cards with his cronies. He knew your father, I believe. I was very sorry to hear of your parents' accident.' Her voice softened when she mentioned his parents.

Killian sat straighter in his seat. 'Yes. It was a shock.' It always surprised him how the gaping wound reopened with the slightest provocation. Though years had passed, grief was still raw and vicious.

'They seemed truly in love.' Lady Winterbourne looked out of the carriage window as they passed under one of the lamps set around the drive. The flickering light highlighted her striking profile.

'Yes. They were very happy together.' Had Lady Winterbourne been happy in her marriage? She painted the picture of a devoted widow, but something in her tone seemed haunted.

'Is that what you hope for in marriage? A love match like your parents?' Miss Simmons asked.

Killian swung his gaze to her. She pressed her lips together as if wishing the words had not escaped.

He felt the added weight of Lady Winterbourne's regard, and both women stilled, waiting for his answer. When did his cravat become so tight? 'Don't paint me as a romantic, Miss Simmons. You will be disappointed. I plan to marry a woman of impeccable breeding and immense dowry, as all dukes do. We shall provide the dukedom with heirs, then I imagine we'll spend the rest of our lives happily pursuing separate interests.'

'That sounds very lonely,' Miss Simmons murmured.

'A capital plan,' Lady Winterbourne declared simultaneously.

Killian repressed a smile. 'Don't misunderstand me. I hope we'll be cordial to one another. But one does not need love to find a partner.'

'And often, partnerships are better off without love.' Lady Winterbourne removed a fleck of lint from her skirt.

'It's all so very mercenary. Breeding, check. Dowry, check. Heir, check. As a woman of inconsequential parentage and miniscule means, I count myself quite lucky.' Miss Simmons's sharp words bounced off the carriage walls. 'I have nothing to fear from dukes seeking dowries.'

'You have everything to fear from this duke,' he muttered to himself before saying loud enough to be heard, 'One might say your situation is just as lonely as mine.'

She blinked, and Killian immediately regretted his words.

He softened his tone. 'But you are correct, Miss Simmons. With your particular set of skills, I imagine you have little to fear from anyone.' The image of her wearing *that* dress while holding a blade to the throat of a vagrant flashed through his mind.

Lady Winterbourne snorted. 'All women have something to fear from men, Lord Killian. Especially powerful idiots with more money and titles than brains in their heads. Oh, look. We've arrived.' She turned toward the door as the carriage trundled to a stop.

The duchess did not wait for Killian to exit and assist her. She alighted immediately after the door was opened and the step was set. Gliding over the cobbled path with the grace and poise of a swan on a serene lake, she left Killian and Miss Simmons in her wake.

Killian climbed out of the carriage and held his hand for Miss Simmons. She hesitated.

'It's much easier than shooting a man, Miss Simmons. You simply reach out and grasp my hand.' He smiled.

'Quite the contrary, Your Grace. Shooting a man only requires the twitch of a finger. Exiting a carriage is infinitely more treacherous in these blasted skirts.' Miss Simmons kept her eyes downcast as she took his hand.

Her grip was firm and steadying in the oddest of ways, as though she supported him. A ridiculous notion. He didn't need support from anyone.

'That dress is treacherous in a multitude of ways, least of all to my concentration,' Killian whispered, his lips scandalously close to her ear. He was rewarded with the fascinating transformation of her skin warming from pale pearl to shell pink.

'Do not tease me, Your Grace.' Her voice lowered.

'I would never tease you, Miss Simmons.'

Her lips twitched, and she tilted her head to glance at him as they followed Lady Winterbourne up the massive, stone staircase leading to the front doors of the Somerset's gothic mansion. Columns rose like giants on either side of them. Footmen lined the walk holding lamps.

A vast array of women in beautiful dresses surrounded them. Bright orange, dew pink, deep purple, blood red. None of them compared to Miss Simmons in shades of moonlight. She had ascended from the shadows to sparkle in the heavens. He could feel her nerves thrumming through her fingertips as she gripped his arm. But Miss Simmons was a brave woman in battle or at a ball, both of which often felt similar to Killian. She lifted her chin and threw back her shoulders even as her fingers dug deeper into his skin.

Courageous warrior, readying for combat.

But he didn't want to fight. They were opposing forces seeking the same goal, yet he wished they could put down their weapons tonight and just be a man and a woman.

Which was impossible, of course.

The eyes of the beau monde were upon them as they passed through the front doors and were announced. The crush of lords and ladies made it almost impossible to slowly circulate through the ballroom.

A novel feeling was growing within Killian. He had pursued women before who inspired a sense of possessiveness, but not like this. Every gentleman who stared at Miss Simmons's décolletage, every lord who gave him a wink of approval, every pompous ass who hovered near her inspired a frightening rage within him.

'Your Grace, if you continue to clench your jaw so tightly, I'm worried you might crack a molar. It's not often you find a gentleman with such nicely arranged teeth. It would be a shame to ruin yours. Unless you're overly fond of soup, I suppose.' Miss Simmons turned to face him.

He forced himself to relax. 'Doesn't it bother you? The way all these buffoons are leering?'

She smiled, wit sparkling in her blue eyes. 'What bothers me more are the ladies staring daggers at me. Men are easily distracted by the next shiny thing. But these society mothers and their daughters will never forget the night the Duke of Covington lowered himself to escort a dowdy lady's companion to a ball. You'll be drowning in cards from all the dregs of the peerage who never thought to reach so high as a duke.'

Killian was momentarily distracted by her argument. 'Dear God, surely not?'

Hannah's laughter was low and pleasant. 'You've only yourself to blame. I have no sympathy for you. Suddenly our deal doesn't look so wonderful, does it, Your Grace?'

The orchestra began to play the opening waltz. If she was

going to hold his feet to the flame, he might as well enjoy the moment. 'May I have this dance?' Killian extended his hand.

Miss Simmons's eyes widened, and her mouth parted. It was a look he never imagined seeing on her face. Sheer terror.

'I don't... that is, I've never... I think perhaps some punch instead?'

Of course!

Miss Simmons had never danced at a ball.

But does she want *to dance?*

The question burned in his mind.

Her gaze flicked to the couples gathering on the dance floor, and Killian had the distinct impression she did.

'I think some fresh air would be welcome.' Killian took her arm and steered her to the back of the ballroom where French doors opened onto a terrace.

This early in the evening, everyone was still desperate to see and be seen. The terrace was deserted and would not be in use until later when the women had drunk enough ratafia to be coerced into making bad decisions. The sickeningly sweet liquor was a favourite of most ladies. As its alcohol content was high enough to souse a lush, the men were happy to provide it, even if most would not be caught dead drinking the mixture.

Killian escorted Miss Simmons to the edge of the terrace. She pulled free of him and took several steps away before spinning back, her silver dress swirling in a perfect circle of decadent silk. 'I don't think we should be out here alone.' Miss Simmons raised a hand to her throat as if suddenly aware of how much her dress revealed.

'You're afraid.' Killian wanted to provoke her with his words. A spitting mad Miss Simmons was far preferable than this frightened one.

'I am not.' Miss Simmons dropped her hand to her skirts, reaching into a pocket that doubtless held some kind of weapon.

Ah, there's the warrior.

Killian raised both of his hands in surrender. 'No need to attack, Miss Simmons. If you're not frightened, are you curious?'

'I'm neither. Why would I be?'

'I'm not sure. A sixth sense that I have. Makes me think maybe you are a bit of both. Frightened *and* curious.' He watched her throat constrict as she swallowed. She broke eye contact with him, and it was all the confirmation he needed. 'I'll tell you what, I make a solemn vow that you have nothing to fear from me, Miss Simmons. Not here. Not now.'

A dry laugh escaped her lips. 'When a gentleman escorts a lady to a deserted location, it's rarely from altruistic motivations.' Her hand remained in her pocket.

'An astute judgment, but I will not press my advantage. I know when it comes to you, a man has very little advantage at all.'

'Then why are we out here? Alone?'

'You've never danced at a ball.' It was a statement, but he waited for her to confirm his guess.

She raised her chin and blinked.

I'm correct, then.

Killian took a tentative step closer. 'I want to dance with you. But I don't want you to feel watched by them.' He flicked his chin toward the windows.

She kept her gaze on him. But her lips trembled. This fearless fighter looked ready to run. And Killian wanted to know why.

'I don't know how to dance.' It was a difficult admission for her. Killian knew it by the hesitation in her voice. 'It's not something a woman like me would ever need to know. Lady Winterbourne offered to have an instructor come, but I always declined.'

'Do you want to dance?'

'I just told you, I can't.'

'No. You said you don't know how. That's not the same. I'll show you. If you'll let go of the dagger in your pocket long enough for a waltz.'

Miss Simmons narrowed her gaze. 'It's a muff pistol.'

'Of course. Will you?' Killian extended his arms in a dancing frame, which felt frighteningly vulnerable with no guaranteed partner. Not to mention the risk of a bullet from the lovely Miss Simmons. But it was also monumentally important for her to have control of this moment. He knew this truth even if he didn't know why.

She looked at his arms, then his face. Slowly, she removed her hand from her skirts. 'I won't be very good.'

'Well, that should be a novel experience for you. I wager you're usually quite good at anything you put your mind to.' He stopped himself from smiling by sheer force of will. 'Be brave, Miss Simmons.'

She huffed out a breath. 'Oh, please.' Brusquely walking towards him, she stopped just short of his arms.

He reached for her, guiding her hand to his shoulder, pulling her close. 'You put your hand here. And here.' Slowly, he caught her other hand, her palm resting against his. 'And I will put mine here.' He let his right hand settle at her waist. Her scent surrounded him, sharp and sweet.

The evening was cool, but he only felt the warmth of her body against his. Her skirts brushed his legs.

'What now?' Her voice had grown husky.

The strain of music was muted but he could still find the count.

'Now, we dance.' He pulled her forward as he stepped back. She stumbled at first and stiffened. 'Follow my lead, Miss Simmons. Feel the beat of each step. It's not dissimilar to fight-

ing. You read my movements and counter them with your own.'
She glanced up, and the absolute clarity of amber in her eyes,
like the finest of whiskeys and just as intoxicating, captured
him.

He felt the moment she relaxed. Her body flowed into his.
They were one being, moving together to the layered vibrations of
violin and cello, wind and heartbeat.

* * *

Hannah was acutely aware of three facts. Lord Killian's body was
hard everywhere she touched him. He moved with lethal grace.
And he lied when he told her she had nothing to fear from him.
She had everything to fear. The man was dismantling all her care-
fully constructed walls and threatening the very boundaries of
her heart.

The music stopped, and their bodies stilled. His hand tight-
ened on her waist.

Hannah had never kissed a man.

That's not true. The baron kissed me.

Hannah shoved the memory away. Nothing about that
horrible night was similar to this moment with Lord Killian. She
wouldn't let the past poison her present.

She had never desired intimate contact before. Until now. Her
mind burned with questions, and her gaze caught on his mouth
as she contemplated what it might feel like to have his lips pressed
against hers.

'I should very much like to kiss you, Miss Simmons. I wonder
if you would allow it or if your hand might find its way back to the
pistol?'

Hannah licked her lips. Lord Killian pulled her closer, his
chest pressed against hers. She moved her hand over his shoulder,

feeling the contrast of his stiff collar and soft cravat before tangling her fingers in his thick curls.

'Miss Simmons, you test the strength of a man's resolve.' His voice was a gravelled growl in the dark night. 'May I?'

The request undid her. He didn't take. He asked. And she didn't want to refuse him. A thrill of anticipation tripped down her spine. Her skin tingled in the strangest places. The inside of her wrist, the back of her neck, the tips of her breasts.

She pulled his head closer. He seemed surprised she would take the lead. Killian resisted for a fraction before manoeuvring them both to a shadowed corner. In a shocking display of intimacy, he removed his gloves and shoved them in his pocket.

'I want to feel you.' His voice was raw. His words caused something within her to loosen and melt. He pressed her back against the balustrade, the cold stone creating a counterpoint to his heat. Bare fingers traced over her scar.

She wanted this. To know what it felt like. Just for a moment. To be lost in sensation.

Killian pressed his lips against hers. Firm and warm. He tasted of whiskey, mint, and something singular. The man himself. He pulled back for a moment, and she caught her breath. Rough fingers brushed against her skin, his thumb grazing her bottom lip.

'Jesus, you are so sweet,' he whispered.

His lips found hers once more. The shocking wetness of his tongue as he tested the seam of her mouth startled Hannah. Sparks cascaded along her overly heated skin. When he licked more insistently, she opened her mouth, and his tongue touched hers in a silken slide of sensation.

Shifting his body, he leaned harder into her. The friction of her corset against her breasts was a revelation. He pushed his muscled leg between hers, creating pressure at the juncture of her thighs. A sweet pulse emanated from her core. She moaned as his hands flexed around her waist.

And then he was gone, her skin suddenly abraded by cool breeze.

Hannah blinked twice before the haze cleared. Lord Killian stood a few feet away, breathing hard and running a shaky hand through his hair. 'I apologise. That was badly done.'

Hannah laughed despite herself. 'If that was badly done, I'm not sure I could survive having it done well.'

'I promised I wouldn't press my advantage.' Killian jerked his gloves from his pocket and shoved his hands into the leather.

'You didn't.' Hannah couldn't explain the rush of frustration filling her, but it throbbed in her blood, creating a hollow ache low in her belly. She wanted to continue kissing him. But he had moved away from her like she was a flame, and he feared being burned. His rejection embarrassed her. Maybe she had done something wrong. Hannah hated being incompetent. Even in this.

She squared her shoulders. 'You wanted to kiss me, and I wanted to be kissed. I find it hard to believe this is your first dalliance with a young lady. Are you always so quickly plagued with guilt?' The sharpness in her tone cut through the crisp evening, but the wave of anger felt good, powerful. So much better than the echo of need pulsing through her veins.

Her ire sparked a twin fire in Killian. He closed the distance between them, slapping his palms against the stone railing on either side of her hips, pinning her. 'Are you always so free with your favours? That was your first kiss, if my guess is correct. Wasted on a gentleman with no intentions of acting honourably.'

Hannah threw back her head and laughed, the caustic sound hurting her throat. 'Yes, that was my first kiss.' At least the first one intentionally given. 'And pray tell, how can I be free with my favours if I've never shared them before?' Hannah chose to focus on his irrational argument over her embarrassing confession. 'But I suppose now I have kissed a man, I can continue sharing my favours with whomever I like, whenever I like. They are mine, after all.'

'So, in one night, you would slip from an innocent to a lightskirt?'

She leaned nearer to him, narrowing her gaze, ready to attack. 'I've never been innocent, just inexperienced. Men are so quick to paint women as whores. Yet we cannot earn the title without significant help from you. If you feel bad for kissing me, that is your problem, not mine. I won't share your shame. I enjoyed it. If the fancy strikes, I may enjoy it again. Just not with you.'

'I wasn't calling you a whore.'

'Lightskirt? Whore? Are they not the same?'

He exhaled, a gust of warm air caressing her cheek. 'I'm sorry. I don't know why I said that. I only meant you shouldn't waste yourself on someone like me. Of course, you are free to kiss whomever you choose.'

Hannah's investigative instinct awakened, dulling her anger. 'Someone like you? A duke? A hero? Why are my kisses wasted on you, Lieutenant General?'

'I am no hero. My blood might once have been blue, but it runs black with the sins I've committed, Miss Simmons,' he whispered, his lips almost touching hers. The buttery leather of his gloved fingers stroked her neck.

Only a wicked woman would be seduced by such words. Hannah felt herself falling into the midnight of his voice. He was a wizard, weaving a devilish spell of darkness and vulnerability.

'Well, then. It's lucky I won't be kissing you again, Your Grace.'

'Are you quite certain?' He moved away from her mouth, his warm breath teasing the sensitive skin just behind her ear. 'If you refuse to feel guilty, then neither will I.' Her world was about to catch fire in the heat he created. 'You won't kiss me again? Is that a promise?'

'Yes,' she breathed.

'I wonder, can I make you break it?'

She swallowed her need as he nibbled along her neck from ear to shoulder. Perhaps she hadn't been so terrible at kissing. He seemed very intent on reengaging in the behaviour. But she'd already told him she wouldn't kiss him again. Which was highly annoying. Because everything in her demanded she do just that.

'Will you kiss me if I kiss you here?' He pressed his mouth against her collar bone. 'Or perhaps here?' His words brushed the hollow of her neck a moment before his lips. 'What about here?' He nipped along her jaw. 'Here?' He feathered kisses over her scar, along her cheekbone, ending at the corner of her mouth.

Hannah was drowning in need and frustration. On a strangled cry, she buried her hands in his hair and held his face still. 'Damn you, Robert Killian.' His name felt strange on her lips, but then she was tasting his mouth, rubbing against him, plunging into his depths, and revelling in the scrape of his teeth against her tongue.

He held still for a moment before taking control.

Hannah knew the desperate need coiled within him mirrored her own. He was a predator poised to strike. But she was no help-less prey. She met him as an equal on the battlefield of desire, and it was glorious. He lifted her up on the balustrade, splitting her legs and pushing between them with his narrow hips.

Her skirts separated them with layers of silk and cotton, but the ridge of his evident need pressed against her like steel. His fingers gripped her bottom, pulling her closer.

This was madness. Total anarchy. Her body was staging a revo-lution against her mind. Everything was moving too fast. Panic sparked and warred with desire. Her arrogance and need had led her down a path she wasn't ready to walk.

'Stop. We must stop.' She placed her hands flat on his shoulders and pushed away. Her breathing was erratic. She only felt this way after an intense fight.

'We will. Soon.' He pulled her back, kissing her gently this time, his mouth light and playful.

She almost let herself be swept away, but if she sank now, she feared she might never resurface. 'Now. We must stop now.' It would be so easy to lose herself in the frenzy. She couldn't. She wouldn't. He was the enemy. But she struggled to remember why.

Killian froze, a groan escaping his lips. She felt his muscles shaking as he eased her down from the stone railing. 'Of course.' Pressing his forehead against hers, they stood silent. The only sounds were their mingled breaths, a nightingale singing its evening song, and the echo of a waltz floating on the wind.

'Will you accept my apology this time? Surely, you are owed one,' his rough voice was strained.

Boisterous laughter and male voices burst onto the veranda. Lord Killian took measured steps away from her, putting the proper distance between them, but his gaze was no less explicit than his mouth had been moments earlier.

Hannah ran a shaky hand down her skirts. 'You deserve my thanks, not my forgiveness. You stopped when I asked.'

'I will always stop when you ask. Although next time, I hope you won't.'

'There won't be a next time, Your Grace.'

'Liar.' Lord Killian's mouth curved in a rogue's smile, and moonlight flashed in his eyes. If the Devil was made to tempt, then Lieutenant General Robert Killian was Lucifer in a dinner jacket.

The men moved closer to Hannah and Lord Killian's hidden corner. The duke crooked his arm in an invitation. 'Shall we return to the ball, Miss Simmons?'

Hannah cautiously placed her hand on his arm and willed herself to be calm. 'Yes, I believe that would be best.' Her body vehemently disagreed.

* * *

A carefully orchestrated spark could so easily catch the wind and flame into an uncontrollable inferno. Killian reminded himself of this fact in a harsh internal lecture as he escorted Miss Simmons back into the ballroom, joining Lady Winterbourne near the refreshment table.

He had never let desire consume his rational mind. Not until this night. All thoughts of the investigation turned to vapour when his gaze caught on the vulnerable juncture of Miss Simmons's graceful neck meeting her strong shoulder. He wanted to sink his teeth into her skin and mark her. It was barbaric. And unforgiveable. And dear God, he needed to regain control of his lust.

'Exactly where have you two been?' Lady Winterbourne raised a perfectly shaped brow.

'Just taking a stroll on the terrace.' Miss Simmons's skin was still flushed. She looked quite beautiful in the blaze of candlelight.

'I'm sure.' Lady Winterbourne stared at Miss Simmons for two blinks, then turned her gaze to Killian. 'Your friend, Major General Drake, is just there.' She indicated with her fan. 'Perhaps you should go and say hello.'

Killian wasn't used to being commanded by any woman save the Queen. Lady Winterbourne reminded him of Her Majesty. It would be intriguing to put them together. There were only two possible outcomes. The women would join forces and achieve world domination or pit themselves against each other, creating total annihilation. Either way, it would be awe-inspiring to watch.

'An excellent suggestion, Lady Winterbourne. I shall take my leave for the moment.' He nodded to them both. Hannah's gaze lingered on him, dipping to his lips. He wished he could sweep her back onto the veranda. Kissing her had been the single most erotic experience of his life, and every sinew of his being ached for more. More of her skin, more of her scent, more of her sharp wit and sweet taste. More of her.

Miss Simmons was far more dangerous than he anticipated. His attraction was problematic, but more troubling was his growing admiration. She was an intriguing contradiction of strength and vulnerability, lethal skill and fragile innocence. The more he learned about her, the greater his fascination grew. Like an opium addict only falling more deeply entangled with every inhalation.

Distance was key. Killian turned and wound through the crowd toward Drake, refusing to look back. He could not lose focus on the investigation.

'Hello, Killian. Looks like you took my advice.' Drake nodded to where Hannah and Lady Winterbourne sipped punch and whispered to each other. The women near them kept a wide circle, likely too intimidated by Lady Philippa to dare approach. 'I must say, being courted by you agrees with the young lady. Whether or not she could kill someone is debatable, but that dress is certainly murdering the concentration of several men, you included.'

'It's lucky I know how deadly you are with duelling pistols, or I might be tempted to call you out for such comments.' Killian tried to smile but feared it was closer to a snarl.

'Stand down, Lieutenant General. I have no interest in competing for Miss Simmons's favour. I learned my lesson well.

There's a reason cupid shoots arrows. Love is far more fatal than your Miss Simmons's hypothetical knives.'

'She isn't my Miss Simmons, her knives aren't hypothetical, and we have more important matters to discuss than homicidal cherubs.' Unfortunately, nothing felt more important than getting back to her. Killian clenched his teeth. He could still taste her, and his body demanded more. But it wasn't just desire coursing through him. He felt driven to discover her secrets. How had a woman like Miss Simmons learned to fight with the fierceness of a trained killer? Why was she fearless in battle, but terrified of dancing at a ball? And how in the devil did she get that scar?

Drake tipped his glass in the direction of Miss Simmons. 'So, you still expect me to believe the woman presently tripping over her own skirts is actually a highly skilled operative.'

Killian glanced at Hannah. She was indeed caught in her dress, grabbing the nearest lady's arm to maintain her precarious balance.

'God, it's that woman from Lord Bradford's dinner party. Something or other Whittenburg. No wonder Miss Simmons is falling all over herself. She's attempting to escape that harridan.' Drake shook his head.

Before Killian could move to assist Hannah, the two women left the ballroom together.

'Probably going to the necessary. Funny how they always go in packs. Makes a man wonder what they're up to in there. Probably scheming about the next hapless chap they plan on duping.'

Killian refused to engage in Drake's bitter diatribe against women. 'Can we please get back to the subject at hand?'

Drake drank again. 'I've had a message from the prime minister. He received important information from Lord High Chancellor Hardgrave.'

A tingle of premonition feathered over Killian's senses. 'And?'

'There are more.'

'More what?' Sometimes Drake could be wilfully mysterious. Killian found it incredibly annoying. Drake knew it.

Drake glanced around him, then leaned closer. 'More dead girls in caskets.'

'Shit.' Killian's premonition transformed into an oily weight of dread in his belly.

'Yes. Exactly.'

'Is he sure?'

'Very sure. They were found in France. Questions have been asked of our government. Rather uncomfortable questions with no clear answers.' Drake rocked from heel to toe, surveying the couples swirling around the dance floor.

A gentleman wearing a bright-purple coat with a canary-yellow waistcoat stumbled out of the crowd, crashing into Killian. The overdressed peacock carried a goblet of wine that nearly spilled.

'Terribly sorry. Looking for a lovely little woman wearing,' the man swirled his arm in a large circle around his head, sloshing wine onto his shoulder, 'pink feathers in her hair. Told me to meet her by the stairs, then she disappeared.' He broke into a braying laugh.

Drake stepped away from the soused idiot. 'She is not here.'

The drunk dandy draped an arm over Killian's shoulder. Given their height difference, it was quite a stretch for the man, whose balance was already compromised. 'Ladies do take pleasure in being chased, wouldn't you agree?'

'In my experience, a woman only runs when she wants to escape.' Killian shook off the man's arm and stepped aside. The dandy stumbled, spilling the remainder of his wine over his bright-blue shoes.

'Bugger. Just bought these shoes.'

Drake looked down without moving his head. 'I wouldn't consider it a loss.'

'Perhaps we should continue this conversation somewhere less populated.' Killian raised his brows at Drake. The scarred man nodded his assent, and they left the fop to fumble on his own.

Skirting around the edge of the ballroom toward the doors leading to the main hallway, Killian didn't have to look behind him to know Drake was following. Despite their years away from the battlefield, they could still move as a unit.

Killian trailed two older gentlemen into a billiard room. Instead of following the men to the crowded table, he drifted to a dark corner. Drake removed a cheroot from his pocket. He used a candle to light the fragrant cigar.

'Did the French give us any information?' Killian asked.

Drake puffed several times before answering. 'Three women have been discovered so far. Two in Calais and one in Boulogne. All of them in caskets. All of them dead. But based on the marks inside the coffins, they were alive when the sick bastard nailed them in. The French don't know what to make of it.'

'All three women were from England?'

Drake shook his head. 'The caskets were abandoned, so there is no way to know for certain what ships brought them to France. But their government believes they originated from London. The bodies were in advanced stages of decay. Impossible to identify. But they were all young, somewhere between thirteen and twenty.' He winced. 'The similarities to Sarah Bright's case can't be ignored.'

'Fuck.'

'Yes. Exactly.'

'Is it possible they aren't connected?' Killian knew the answer, but he wanted Drake to confirm his suspicions.

'Anything is possible. But it stretches the imagination to think four dead girls, all found in caskets, all alive when they were nailed in, are not somehow connected.'

Killian nodded. 'Did Prime Minister Russell give us any instructions?'

'Yes.' Drake puffed on his cheroot. 'Find the killer. Fast. Apparently, the Lord High Chancellor has a vested interest in the outcome. He fears it will further strain our relationship with France. He is putting significant pressure on Russell to find the responsible party.'

'There could be more than one killer, maybe working together. With this many dead girls found in two different countries, we might have multiple murderers.'

'Or one very depraved soul. I don't know. Because Sarah Bright is the one body we can identify, she's our best lead. I spoke with her family.' Drake angled his body away from Killian to watch the men at the billiard table.

'Without me?'

'You were busy chasing the skirts of a femme fatale.'

'I was going to follow up with the Bright family. If Miss Simmons hadn't interrupted me that night, I would have already interviewed them.' He hated feeling incompetent. Drake should not have had to complete the task assigned to Killian.

Drake waved Killian's excuses away with his cigar smoke. 'And if gold coins spilled out of the Devil's arse, I'd be a rich man.'

'A delightful metaphor.'

Drake smiled. 'Thank you.'

Killian tried to shrug off the weight of his guilt. 'Did they tell you anything?'

'Yes.'

He took a steadying breath, the smoke and whiskey making

his stomach churn. 'Damn it, man. Stop being so elusive and tell me.'

Drake's laughter scraped against Killian's nerves like sand against skin. 'That's the rub. They told me I should ask Miss Simmons. She promised to kill the man responsible for Sarah's death. Sarah's parents aren't talking to anyone else.'

'I told you. Miss Simmons is much more than she seems.'

'Or she is just a woman making promises she can't keep. A common occurrence with the fairer sex in my experience. It doesn't alter the fact that we know bugger-all about any possible leads.'

'Shit.'

'You've said that already.'

'Fuck.'

'You've said that too. Their son did say something to me when I was leaving.'

'What's that?' Killian could only imagine.

'He said to tell the nutter hiding by the shitter that he'd still come see him at the Crown and Bull if his coin was good. Any idea what the lad meant?'

Killian smiled. 'I might have an idea.'

'Well, until he shows up, see if you can weasel anything out of the lovely and highly annoying Miss Simmons.'

'Easier said than done. She's impervious to intimidation and highly volatile with charm.'

Drake raised an eyebrow. 'Careful there, Killian. Women are masters of weaving webs to ensnare us. Don't forget, she is not our ally. She's making a difficult case even more trying. I suppose that's a woman's skill, isn't it? Complicating what should be a simple matter and making our existence as dismal as they can?'

Killian shook his head. 'Nora really ruined you, didn't she?'

Faster than Killian could track, Drake flicked his cigar away and grabbed Killian's shirt. Drake's face hardened and his lip twitched. 'Don't say her name. Ever. Again.'

Killian swallowed. 'I meant no harm, Drake.'

Drake's breath sawed in and out of his lungs. His fist gripped tighter. Killian tensed, ready for the blow that was sure to come. But then his friend blinked, his pupils dilating. He shoved Killian away, running a shaky hand through his hair. 'I didn't mean... I shouldn't have... shit.'

'As you pointed out earlier, I've already said that.' Killian straightened his waistcoat. Both men stood silent as the fraught moment dissipated. 'I overstepped. I'm sorry. Let's forget the whole thing.'

Drake bent to pick up the cigar where it smouldered on the wood floor. Killian almost missed his murmured words. 'I wish I could forget.'

'You will, Drake.' Killian patted his friend's granite shoulder. 'Give it time.'

Drake re-lit his cheroot and took several puffs. When he turned back to Killian, his eyes were still wild, but he had recovered his mask of civility. 'Time is something we don't have. Speak to Miss Simmons, Killian. See what she knows. The longer we take, the more girls will die. Of that, I'm certain.'

Killian wished he could refute Drake's words. But he had never been comfortable with lies. Especially the ones he told himself. 'Then I best not waste a moment.'

7

Hannah had ripped a petticoat. It dragged behind her as Miss Whittenburg led them to the ladies' retiring room.

Bloody blazes! No one needs this many layers.

'Don't worry, Miss Simmons. We'll have you fixed in a trice. I don't know why we must wear a thousand petticoats, do you?' Miss Whittenburg's voice was pleasantly low.

Hannah laughed, her face reddening. 'I'm not usually so clumsy. If you hadn't been there to steady me, I'm sure I would have landed in a heap.'

'Well, we wallflowers need to stick together.' Miss Whittenburg pushed open a massive door and Hannah followed her through the room. Panels of soft pink and seafoam green silk draped the walls. Several dressing tables with attached mirrors were scattered about for women to use as needed. Miss Whittenburg helped Hannah gather her skirts to sit on the ornately gilded chair. Several maids rushed over to assist.

'I'm sorry to be such a bother.' Hannah flinched when the maids flipped up her skirts to find the torn layer. What if they discovered the dagger tied to her thigh? Or the pistol tucked in her pocket? Or the throwing knives hidden in the cleverly designed pleats of her sleeves? Or the extra dagger stuffed in her unfashionable boots?

Miss Whittenburg leaned down, peering into the mirror behind Hannah. Her ample bosom almost spilled out of her dress. 'Dear Lord. My hair is a mess.' She reached up to tuck a fiery red curl back into her elegant twist.

Another lady entered the room wearing an ice-blue dress, emphasising her pale skin and crystal eyes. Freckles covered the bridge of her nose. Hannah couldn't help but note how slight she was. Even with her corset, her shape was almost that of a boy's. She walked towards them with her hands extended to Miss Whittenburg.

'Millie! I saw you making a quick exit from the ballroom and thought I would join you.' She clasped Miss Whittenburg's hands and pulled her close for a brief hug.

'You look beautiful, Ivy.'

The delicate woman snorted. 'I look like a plank of wood in silk and lace.'

Miss Whittenburg stepped back. 'Balderdash!'

Hannah tried to hide her surprise. How refreshing to be around women who spoke so plainly.

Ivy turned and faced Hannah. 'Miss Simmons, isn't it? We met briefly at Lord Bradford's dinner party.'

Hannah cleared her throat. 'Yes, Miss Cavendale. I remember.'

Miss Cavendale smiled, her eyes crinkling at the corners. Ladies of the peerage rarely noticed Hannah, but Ivy's keen gaze assessed Hannah astutely.

'Petticoats and heeled slippers never play well together. Oh, but you aren't wearing slippers. What... comfortable-looking boots.' Ivy's brilliant smile almost covered her surprise at Hannah's unconventional footwear peeking beneath horsehair and cotton. She might have succumbed to a fancy dress, but Hannah would never suffer to wear the torture devices most women called dancing slippers. Certainly not for Lieutenant General Killian.

Miss Whittenburg nodded. 'You are clever, Miss Simmons. Men traipse around in trousers and boots, oh-so-comfortable. Here we are, squeezed into corsets, suffocating in petticoats, expected to glide like swans in slippers that pinch our toes and rub our heels. I admire you.' Miss Whittenburg exposed dimples when she grinned.

It was impossible not to like these women, so Hannah didn't try.

'Please, you must call us Ivy and Millie. And we shall call you... what shall we call you?' Ivy asked.

'Hannah.' Heat crept from her chest to her cheeks. Ladies of the peerage never asked for the intimacy of her name. This was so different. Their interest was equal parts flattering and confounding. With so many secrets to keep hidden, friendship was a dangerous endeavour Hannah avoided. But friendship with these women might be worth the risk.

'After surviving that dreadfully dull evening together at Lord Bradford's, I believe we've earned the right to be friends, don't you?' Millie returned her gaze to the mirror and pinched her plump cheeks until they turned rosy. 'Of course, when a man spends so much time on the care of his moustache, he has little resources remaining to create an interesting dinner party.'

'Millie! You are terrible.' Ivy's large eyes widened further. 'Lord Bradford isn't as bad as all that.'

Millie shrugged before using a pot of beeswax on the table to gloss over her eyelids. 'Or perhaps I'm just honest. Do you remember that horribly pompous military man... something or other Drake?' She shuddered, then pressed her lips together hard before opening them with a popping sound. 'With men like that around, I'm grateful to remain a wallflower.' The red curl she had tucked away escaped again, bouncing next to her cheek. 'Damnation. This hair! It hates me. Or perhaps it is possessed. Can hair be possessed? I must convince Father to let me hire a lady's maid. Your curls are fabulous, Ivy. How is your new girl working out? Didn't you steal her from Lady Bradford? I'm surprised she invited you to her dinner party at all.' Millie winked at Ivy.

Ivy quirked her mouth in a frown. 'I don't know what you mean. I don't have a new lady's maid.'

'Truly?' Millie cocked her head. 'Lady Bradford told me one of her maids was taking a new position in your household. What was her name... Light, White...'

Hannah's heart thundered in her chest. 'Bright? Sarah Bright?'
Dear God, no.

Could Sarah's new job have been with the Cavendale family?
Damnable luck!

She was just beginning to like Ivy. Must she now treat her as a suspect?

Millie grinned, her chocolate eyes sparkling in the candlelight. 'Yes! That was it. Bright. Clever of you to know.'

Hannah shrugged and concentrated on keeping her voice calm. 'A lucky guess. I hope she is working out for you, Miss Ivy.'

Ivy shook her head. 'But that's just it. I don't have a new maid. I'm not sure why Lady Bradford thinks we stole one from her household. I feel terrible. I should speak with her. There's been a misunderstanding.'

The vice around Hannah's chest eased. Perhaps it was just a mistake, which wasn't good for the investigation but far better for her budding friendship with Ivy and Millie.

'Maybe your father hired her as a house maid for Everly Manor,' Millie suggested while adjusting a feather in her hair.

'That is Ivy's country estate. Well, her father's estate,' Millie informed Hannah.

Bollocks! The vice tightened again.

Ivy reached over to help Millie, expertly tucking the feather into her friend's loose twist. 'I shall inquire with Father.' A shadow flashed across Ivy's delicate features but was quickly gone. She smiled brightly at Millie. 'Which reminds me, we're returning to Berkshire in a week. You must come and stay with us at Everly.' Ivy turned to Hannah. 'You are welcome to join, Hannah. Father would consider it quite an accomplishment to host someone as well respected as the Duchess of Dorset.'

'You mean powerful. I don't know how she convinced her husband to will his money to her, but I want to learn her secrets.' Millie raised a calculating eyebrow at Hannah. 'Do you think she'd tell us? Fortune and independence all at the cost of a husband. It's enough to make one consider marriage. Briefly.'

Hannah coughed. 'I think Lord Winterbourne was just very devoted to her.' The words tasted of a lie. He was devoted to her mother, not Philippa. Once that would have filled her with pride, but after ten years of living and working with Philippa, Hannah's feelings about Lord Winterbourne were much murkier. He loved her mother, and he loved her. But at what cost to Philippa?

Millie blinked slowly. 'Devotion. Yes. I'm sure that's what it was.'

Ivy pinched her friend's shoulder. 'Really, Millie. You will scare poor Hannah off, then she won't join us. Please do come, Hannah. I'm sure I could convince father to invite Lieutenant General Killian. I know he desires a closer acquaintance with your beau. And I think the Lieutenant General could be a good influence on my eldest brother, Alfred.' Ivy's crystal eyes sparkled in the candlelight with what might have been tears. 'He never recovered from losing Patrick. Grief is such a terrible thing, don't you think?' She blinked furiously before smiling a trifle too bright. It was the second time in as many minutes she masked her feelings with a smile. 'Your Lieutenant General would be a welcome distraction for all of us.'

Hannah's cheeks grew warm, and her pulse fluttered. 'I think you're mistaken. He is not mine.'

'Tosh! Obviously, the man is smitten with you.' Millie winked at Hannah. 'It's all the ladies can talk about.'

Hannah wasn't sure her cheeks could grow any redder, but she was about to find out.

'Millie! Honestly. You are too bold.' Ivy put a delicate hand on Hannah's shoulder and patted her. 'Please don't take offense, Hannah.'

'Pardon me for being honest. I saw Lord Killian watching you from across the ballroom when you were battling your skirts. I thought the curtains might catch on fire from all the smoulder in his gaze.' She waggled her eyebrows and shimmied her shoulders, her breasts jiggling with the motion. Millie laughed. 'I'd better be careful, or these girls will cause a scandal. Almost as big a scandal as you and Lord Killian.'

Hannah felt queasy. This kind of speculation was exactly what she hoped to avoid. 'I don't think he's smitten. I suspect he is doing this as a favour to Lady Philippa.'

'Just ignore Millie. She loves to stir the pot.' Ivy arched pale brows at Millie who stuck her tongue out in reply.

Hannah surprised herself with a giggle at Millie's silly expression, then slapped her hand over her mouth. She hadn't giggled since she was a young girl. The bubbling mirth in her belly was most alarming.

Ivy returned her attention back to Hannah. 'Lieutenant General Killian would never toy with your reputation by courting you without intentions of marriage. And if you must have a husband, you could do far worse than him.'

You shouldn't waste yourself on someone like me. His words haunted her.

Could a man whose blood runs black with sin understand the monster living in my dark centre?

She had neither time nor interest in answering such a question. He might be compelling in a contradictory kind of way. And he might do wicked things to her against a balustrade. He might dance like a dream and kiss like a devil, but that meant nothing. She was not interested in Lord Killian. Not for marriage or anything else.

Although, if she wanted a dalliance with the duke, Philippa had made it clear Hannah could pursue an affair. She would never bring disgrace on Philippa, but with the duchess's assurance of continued support regardless of Hannah's behaviour, her virtue only held what value she placed upon it. And there was no guarantee she would get another chance to answer lingering questions she had about desire.

In this instance, engaging in a physical liaison with her enemy might actually hold merit. She wouldn't have to worry about her heart becoming involved, and the duke was certainly not at risk of emotional entanglement. Their kiss on the balcony proved they shared attraction, even if they lacked trust. But that was also beneficial. She wouldn't have to pretend affection to satisfy her curiosity.

'Hannah, you look positively flushed. Shall I get you a cup of water? Perhaps some lemonade?' Ivy fluttered around her like a mother hen.

'No, I'm fine.' Hannah wisely kept her thoughts to herself. It wouldn't do to scare her new friends off with her illicit wonderings.

The maids had mended her petticoats without discovering her weaponry, thank heavens. Hannah resettled her overskirt in place. 'Thank you so much.' She smiled at them.

The two girls curtsied and bustled off to wait for the next dishevelled lady.

Hannah turned to Millie and Ivy. 'You are both imagining things between the duke and me. We barely know each other.'

'Men don't have to know a woman to want her. In fact, knowing a woman generally puts a damper on wanting them.' Millie tugged on the front of her dress, adjusting the fabric to cover as much of her ample décolletage as the silk could manage without splitting at the seams.

'Don't listen to her. Millie's had a rough go, but that doesn't mean all men are heartless, cold blackguards like Lord Franklin St George. It's such rotten luck he's best friends with my brother. Alfred's always been the victim of poor friendships.'

'Lord Franklin St George is a blackguard, your brother is far too trusting, and I have no wish to speak further on the subject.' Millie pinched her cheeks a final time, but Hannah didn't miss the quiver in Millie's chin. There was a story there Hannah wanted to discover. But she couldn't lose focus on finding Sarah Bright's killer.

'I shall send an invitation to the duchess for our house party. Please do come, Hannah.' Ivy looked at Hannah with the same wide-eyed expression a puppy employed to get its way. It was a devastatingly successful trick.

Hannah forced her lips to tip up in a smile. Would Ivy be so welcoming if she knew Hannah's sole purpose in joining the party was to potentially expose Ivy's father as a sadistic murderer? Doubtful.

'I would love to join, but I shall defer to Lady Winterbourne. My activities are limited to her interests.'

'Well, I'm sure you can exert some influence over her, Hannah.' Millie squeezed Hannah's hand. 'Now, mind your skirts, ladies. We're on the move.'

Hannah fell in step behind them. Philippa would most definitely accept the invitation to Ivy's house party. After hearing Millie and Ivy discussing Sarah Bright's possible position in the Cavendale household, turning down an opportunity to have such unfettered access to investigate their home was unthinkable.

A house party would give Hannah limitless opportunities to slip away and poke her nose into countless nooks and crannies where one might hide evidence of a murder. Her traitorous thoughts slipped to other things that might happen in the dark and empty rooms of the Cavendale's country estate. If Lord Killian attended, which he doubtlessly would, she might bump into him on a daily basis. Hannah's stomach fluttered.

An unexpected longing to be a normal woman with normal goals of love and marriage washed through Hannah like a rogue tide. But she pushed those thoughts back into the depths. To allow herself to get caught in a fantasy she neither wanted nor deserved was dangerous to her mission.

Her attendance at the house party was for a singular purpose. She would need to fade back into the shadows where she belonged. It was there the demons hid, and there, she would hunt a killer.

* * *

Killian looked for an opportunity to get Miss Simmons alone all evening with damnable success. She was avoiding him. But she couldn't avoid him forever. He breathed a grateful sigh when Philippa nodded to him, signalling her desire to leave. One did not argue with the Duchess of Dorset. Of that, he was certain.

As they trundled home in the carriage, Killian plotted his next move.

'Thank you for a lovely evening, Lord Killian.' Lady Philippa moved to the carriage door with an agility belying her years. Again, she did not wait for Killian, alighting as soon as the step was set. She swept up the stairs of her stone entrance and into the house before Killian could settle his boots on the pavement. Miss Simmons's patroness seemed determined to introduce a scandal into her household by leaving them alone. Killian would have to find some way of thanking her.

'Do you think she's trying to give us some privacy?' He enjoyed the feeling of Miss Simmons's hand in his, holding onto her even when she was safely down the carriage steps.

'Why would she want that?' Miss Simmons was nervous. She wouldn't hold his gaze.

Killian pulled her hand into the crook of his elbow and turned toward the house. 'Perhaps she means to encourage our little charade.'

'Philippa is not in the habit of encouraging farce. Unless it serves her purpose. And this does not, I assure you.' Her words were clipped as she tried to pull her hand free. 'I can walk myself to the steps, Your Grace.'

He put his gloved hand over hers, halting her escape. 'What kind of gentleman would I be to abandon you on the street?'

'The same kind who pins a lady to the floor, blackmails her, accuses her of being a lightskirt. Ringing any bells, Your Grace?' Her cheeks were flushed, and she swallowed.

He was ashamed of calling her a lightskirt, but nothing else. Killian remembered the first night they met with startling clarity. The feel of her small, lithe body beneath his. The thrill of confrontation sweetened by the heat of attraction. His body hardened and he cursed his lack of self-control. 'The last was a terrible breach of etiquette on my part. As for the rest, you can hardly blame me for acting like a duke. And you are no better, madame. The night we met, you were snooping around with a dagger in your pocket.'

'One I would very much like returned to me.'

Killian widened his eyes in mock innocence. 'And if I had it, you would see its return immediately. I imagine some lucky footman possesses it now. But allow me to redeem myself by escorting you to the door and showing you what a gentleman I can be.' He pulled her close enough to feel the swish of her skirts as they walked up the path.

Lady Philippa's house was impressive, boasting no less than six Grecian columns on either side of the stairs leading to the entrance. A grand oak door, wide enough for three men to pass through at once, stood open. The butler must have followed Lady Philippa into the house, for the entryway was empty.

Miss Simmons paused on the last step. He was one behind her. When she turned to face him, they stood almost eye-level. 'Do you recall our agreement? You who never forgets anything.'

The chill evening air embraced him as rain and coal smoke mingled with Miss Simmons's citrus and cream. London's weather was as inconstant as fate. Even in the heart of summer, it could turn frigid in a moment's notice. 'You refer to limiting our flirtations to the public arena. Yes, I remember.'

'Perhaps I might amend that arrangement.' She still wouldn't look in his eyes. Her gaze was firmly fixed over his left shoulder.

Killian leaned closer. He let his hand rest on her hip, curling his fingers around the curve of her waist. It was the same place he held her during their dance but standing this close on the front steps of her house, the position felt scandalously intimate.

'I've always considered myself open-minded to amending agreements when the reasoning is sound. What exactly were you thinking?' He didn't dare move for fear of unravelling the gossamer threads holding this moment together.

Her breath hitched and she bit her lip. Killian's entire body tightened. He hadn't wanted a woman so painfully since, well, maybe ever.

'I have no illusions of marriage. It is not my goal, nor my desire to be under the rule of a man.'

Killian cupped her cheek with his free hand and turned her head, forcing her gaze to meet his. He had no wish to marry Miss Simmons either, but something in him rejected the idea of a lovely woman being consigned to the lonely life of a spinster. 'Your view of marriage seems rather dim.'

'After your description of matrimony, I hazard our views on the topic align. For men like you, marriage is a duty you cannot shirk. For women like me, marriage is a yoke I strive to evade.' She tipped her chin, freeing herself from his grasp.

Killian blinked. He never considered how a woman might feel about marriage. He was rather more concerned with his own opinions on the subject. But now, he was forced to look at the establishment through a different lens. Her lens. For a fiercely independent woman like Miss Simmons, it was easy to see how the bonds of marriage would bring constraint rather than comfort.

Miss Simmons smiled at him. 'You look truly flummoxed. Have you never considered that a woman might not desire marriage?'

'I suppose I never gave it much thought. Marriage provides women with security and protection.'

'I don't need a man's security or protection. I provide that for myself.'

Killian frowned. His gaze caught on her scar, and he resisted the urge to press his lips against her cheek and test the contrast of textures. 'There are quite a few men who value the independence of being a bachelor. I suppose a woman could feel the same.' After consideration, there were far more reasons for a woman to wish for independence than a man. Very few women were ever granted the kind of freedom he had grown to expect. Lady Winterbourne, and by extension, Miss Simmons, were two of the rare ladies in his acquaintance who need not bow to the whim of a husband or father. It made sense she wouldn't want to give up that autonomy.

'Yes, it's truly remarkable how a woman can feel things just like a man, think as logically, fight as fiercely. Almost as if we were essentially the same.' Her smile faltered. 'I believe a woman's desires can also be of equal measure.'

Killian tightened his fingers around her waist. Their conversation had momentarily engaged his mind and distracted his body. But with one word from Miss Simmons, his senses realigned. *Desires.* Such a simple combination of vowels and consonants with endless possibilities.

'You have my undivided attention, Miss Simmons.'

'Perhaps, under the circumstances, you could call me Hannah.'

Something deep within Killian wanted to howl in triumph that she granted him such a familiarity. He leaned closer, his lips almost brushing her cheek as he whispered in her ear. 'Then, you have my undivided attention, Hannah.' Her name felt soft and sensuous in his mouth.

She pushed him back, and he reluctantly retreated. 'I would control the pace. And the, er, depths.'

He couldn't stop the rumble of laughter. 'Depths?'

'Lengths, then. I don't know. I would control how far we travel down this path.' She was back to looking over his shoulder.

'So, you suggest we continue our... flirtations, shall we say, in private. But you decide how fast and how far we go?'

She glanced at him and gave a curt nod. 'Exactly so.'

'Because while you don't plan on marrying, you do feel... desires.' Even saying the word made his cock harden further.

Enough light spilled out from the open door for him to see her blush. She turned away and stomped her foot in a display of frustration that had him biting his cheek to stop from smiling. 'Yes. I have desires. And I won't feel shame for that. As I said before, women are not so dissimilar to men, even if the rules placed upon us are vastly different. We have passions that run just as hot, yet we are given no freedom to express these feelings.'

Killian had never engaged in such an illuminating discussion. She was absolutely right. 'I owe you an apology, Hannah.'

She frowned at him. 'For what?'

'Earlier, I implied you were a lightskirt. You are not. Please forgive me.'

He loved surprising her. There was a unique sense of pride in knowing he momentarily derailed her wickedly sharp thoughts.

She tucked a stray wisp of hair behind her ear. 'Fine. You are forgiven.' Squaring her shoulders, Hannah tipped down her chin. 'I take this to mean you are disinclined to accept my amendment to our agreement. Please forget I broached the subject.' She stepped towards the door.

Killian caught her arm and pulled her back to him. He took her gloved hand and tugged at each finger before slowly dragging the silk over her skin, revealing her one inch at a time. When her hand was completely bare, he brought it to his mouth, turned it palm up, and pressed a kiss to her wrist.

Her pulse beat wildly against his lips. Her scent was stronger here. He inhaled her into his lungs. Pressing a second kiss to her palm, he revelled in her gasp as her fingers curled over his cheek. Killian trapped her hand against his face. 'I only mean that if we do this, I will not consider you with any less respect than I do now.

You have questions that deserve answers. How can I stand in the way of education? I would be honoured to embark on this journey with you.' He brought her wrist to his mouth again, this time scraping his teeth over her delicate skin.

Hannah's sharp intake of air had Killian groaning.

She pulled her hand back. 'At my pace.' Her voice was rough.

Killian tucked her glove in his pocket. 'Of course.' He now had her dagger and her glove. It was becoming quite the collection.

'And only as far as I'm willing to go. You stopped earlier when I asked. I expect you will continue to do so.' Hannah's pink cheeks darkened further to a beguiling rose.

'I shall endeavour to keep myself on the tightest of leashes.'

She nodded. 'Excellent. We have an accord. Well. Good night then, Lord Killian.'

'Just one thing.' He backed up a step.

Hannah lifted a single brow. A goddess deigning to grant him a boon.

'While marriage isn't either of our desires, if our explorations ever breach your boundary of innocence, I will make you my wife, Hannah. I may be damned, but I have not fallen so far as to become a libertine.' He had no wish to cage someone as wild and magnificent as Miss Simmons within an unwanted marriage, but enough of his father was left in him to recoil from ruining a woman, no matter the cost. 'I will not take advantage of a lady such as you without ensuring your honour remains intact.'

'I'm no lady, Your Grace. And my honour is not yours to worry about,' she said so softly, he almost missed it. Turning from him, Miss Simmons walked into the house, shutting the door behind her.

'Liar.' He spoke into the empty night.

He was in serious trouble.

8

Killian shifted in his saddle. He and Drake had been riding for hours. They would soon reach Berkshire. The weather turned on them when they passed Reading, and a summer storm made Killian wish for the comforts of his carriage. The country roads were turning into rutted lanes bogged with mud. Even on horseback, it was a dangerous slog through increasingly slippery terrain.

'Brilliant plan to ride to Everly Manor.' Drake glared at Killian from the back of his impressive stallion.

'We're almost there.' Killian hunched his shoulders as water dripped down his neck and into his collar. His trousers were covered in mud, and it would take all the hot water in Berkshire to thaw his bones.

'Can we revisit our conversation about Miss Simmons? You've seen her three times since the ball, and still you haven't gotten any information about Sarah Bright. One might assume your motivations are becoming rather separate from your mission.'

Killian regretted inviting Drake to join him. 'Assumptions make an ass of you, Drake.'

Although Drake wasn't wrong. The more time he spent with Hannah, the more time he wanted to spend. And it had fuck-all to do with Sarah Bright's investigation.

Despite Hannah's provocative amendment to their arrangement, his visits with her had been gallingly proper.

One thing was certain, Lady Philippa no longer topped his list of benevolent women. She must have had a change of heart since the ball. The duchess was taking her duties as chaperone in a stupidly serious manner. She kept her sharp gaze on him like a hawk. When Killian had finally stolen a moment alone with Hannah in the garden, the damned butler wandered into the rose patch with shears and a vase, sent on a mission by Her Grace.

Killian only hoped this house party provided him with opportunities to satisfy Hannah's curiosity before he expired from thwarted desire.

'I assume you have yet to discuss the particulars of Major Patrick Cavendale's unfortunate death with his family? You'll have a hard time avoiding his father and brother at Berkshire.' Drake winced as he manoeuvred his horse around a large rut in the road.

He never spoke of his leg injury, but Killian was there when the Afghanistan soldiers stretched Drake on the rack, dislocating his limbs in a sickening pop of ligaments. Killian knew Drake's body was covered in scars – the least of which cut through his left eyebrow – because Killian had been forced to watch every moment of his friend's torture. And yet, Killian emerged from that stinking prison unmarred. It was a special kind of agony to be spared from pain while the men he was sworn to lead and protect sustained horrific injuries on his behalf.

Killian was kept healthy and relatively well-fed while being forced to watch his men slowly decimated by torture, infection, starvation, and disease during their two-year imprisonment. It was almost more than Killian's mind could survive. Major Patrick

Cavendale had not been so lucky. The poor boy's sanity broke before his body. In the end, his death had been a mercy.

Shame tasted as bitter as hemlock, but it didn't change Killian's mission. 'Lord Bradford will be at the house party. He's still our best lead in this investigation. Besides, I can't avoid the Cavendales forever. Patrick's death is my responsibility. Had I taken command of the forces instead of listening to Major General Elphinstone...' Killian shook his head, rage and humiliation making him want to punch someone hard enough to feel his knuckles break. 'The whole affair was damned from the beginning. We never should have been there.'

'Elphinstone was an idiot. You are not.' Drake slowed his horse, and Killian matched the pace with his own. The scent of wet earth and sweet bracken surrounded them as raindrops pattered the ground. 'I carry the scars of war on my body, but I don't envy the burden you bear, Killian. Only a fool would believe you escaped the war unscathed.'

'I've never understood how you continued a friendship with me. I deserve nothing but hatred from you. When the very fires of hell were licking at your feet, I just sat there, useless. A weak coward.' The words tore something from Killian's soul. His throat was raw, his nerves exposed.

Drake stopped his horse as the rain fell around them.

An icy droplet slid down Killian's jaw like a frozen tear. In the waning light, it was impossible to read Drake's expression.

'You believe yourself a coward?'

Killian ground his teeth and pressed his lips together, refusing to let them quiver. He would not break down and sob like some pathetic schoolboy. He cleared his throat but didn't trust his voice. Instead, he dipped his chin in a quick nod.

'We don't speak of the war. After today, I never wish to again. But know this, Killian: none of us would have traded positions with you. Not a single man. You kept us alive in that reeking hole of a prison. Not once did you falter. Your stubborn belief that we would be rescued allowed us all to hope. Your refusal to break, when every single one of us would have, gave us the strength to endure. To live on, no matter what they did.'

'I did nothing.'

Drake's lips curved in a tight smile. 'You did more than you'll ever know.'

'It was my job to lead you, to keep everyone safe.'

Drake's harsh laughter cut through the drizzle. 'No one can keep everyone safe. But you can bring Lord Cavendale and his son a measure of peace. Tell them Patrick died honourably and leave it at that. It's bad enough we had to watch him go mad. There's no reason for them to know the details.' Drake spurred his horse on, cantering down the lane. His shouted words echoed back to Killian. 'Some burdens must be put down if you want to have the strength to carry on.'

That was Killian's mission now. To carry on. To find a killer. To atone for surviving a bloody war when so many better men died. But there was no room in the fragments of his heart for a beautiful woman who reminded him the world could still hold mystery and sweetness. So, he would seduce her, sate her curiosity, and indulge his desires, but he would not allow the broken, battled vessel of his heart to get involved. Even if the task seemed insurmountable.

* * *

Everly Manor was a grand estate sprawling over a vast expanse of Berkshire's fertile land and forest. The house itself boasted award-winning gardens, the largest ballroom in the parish, and some of the best hunting in the district. While it did not eclipse Lady

Philippa's country estate in size or design, it was nevertheless impressive.

In deference to Lady Philippa's title and position, the duchess had been settled in the grandest guest suite overlooking the front of the house. Hannah, by proxy, was shown to a very handsome room one door down from Philippa's.

Philippa and Hannah received a warm welcome by their hosts upon arrival, whereupon they retired to their rooms to refresh themselves and prepare for dinner. Betty was aquiver with nerves and anticipation with so many happenings below stairs. The girl's excitement bordered on frantic.

'There are ever so many people to meet. How will I remember them all? And it's so large! I'm sure to get lost. Will you be wearing your grey evening gown tonight or the brown? I knew I should have packed your silver dress, but you told me not to. Her Grace said I shouldn't listen to you about your clothes as you never take an interest.' Betty's eyes widened, and she pressed her lips together. 'Bother. I shouldn't have said that last bit.' Her pink cheeks flamed to crimson.

'Betty, it's fine. The grey dress will be perfectly adequate for tonight.' Betty was speaking faster than usual, and there was a sheen to her eyes, making Hannah worry she might burst into tears at any moment. 'I wonder if you should take a seat and collect yourself.'

Betty fulfilled Hannah's prophecy when her eyes filled. 'I've made a blunder of this. There's just so much flurry downstairs, and I don't want to disgrace you or the duchess, miss.'

Hannah placed her hands on Betty's shoulders and squeezed. 'You're doing fine. I'm sure being in a new place and learning the personalities of so many other servants is daunting. Don't worry. You'll be a credit to us, I know.'

Betty nodded, her cap bobbing as it was prone to do. 'The staff here aren't half so nice as back home. There was a boy in the stables who was right cheeky. He asked how a pretty girl like me wasn't married already.'

Hannah raised a brow. 'Did he? Shall I speak with Miss Ivy Cavendale about it? I don't want you being harassed.'

Betty shook her head. 'Oh, no, miss. I'm sure he meant no harm. A lad as handsome as him is probably used to all the girls fawning. But I set him right. I told him I was too smart to let some man tie me down. I don't answer to anyone except you and Lady Philippa, and that suits me just fine.'

Hannah didn't miss the way her maid's lips curled in a smile at the memory.

'So, this stable boy is handsome, is he?' Hannah couldn't resist teasing.

'Handsome won't buy you eggs in the winter. That's what my mum always told me.'

'She sounds like a very bright woman.'

Betty's voice grew soft. 'She was. A right gem was my mum.'

'Oh, Betty. I'm so sorry. I didn't realise...' Hannah could have kicked herself. How stupid for her not to know such a personal detail about her maid. The girl knew the most intimate particulars about Hannah's life, yet she knew nothing in return.

Betty turned to the wardrobe and pulled out Hannah's grey evening dress, laying it on the bed. 'No need to apologise, miss. Mum would have been proud of me, working in such a fine house, with ladies as brave and wonderful as you and the duchess.' She turned back around, all business. 'We'll get you out of your traveling clothes and ready for dinner, miss. You look wonderful in any dress, so it won't matter if yours is plainer than the others.' She bit her lip.

Hannah was saved from a response by a knock on her door.

Betty rushed to open it, and Philippa swept in wearing a stunning evening gown of cobalt overlaid with black lace.

'You aren't dressed yet.'

Betty's hands shook as she unbuttoned Hannah's dress. 'That's my fault, Your Grace. I'll have her ready in a trice.'

'Don't rush, Betty. A late entrance is so much more dramatic.' Philippa perched elegantly on a rose and gold chair in the corner of the room as Betty bustled around Hannah. 'Shall we review our strategy for the evening?'

Hannah lifted her arms, and Betty removed her brown travel dress. Hannah waited until the dress cleared her head before she answered. 'Certainly. We know Lord Cavendale, his son, and eldest daughter, Miss Ivy Cavendale, are in attendance. Miss Millicent Whittenburg will also be here. And of course, Lord and Lady Bradford. Philippa, you mustn't say anything about the man's moustache.'

Philippa laughed. 'Well, certainly not to his face, but you can't expect me to stay completely mute on such a ridiculous subject.' She wrinkled her nose and shook her head. 'Delacroix was able to find out from Ivy Cavendale's maid that Lord and Lady Hastings are also in attendance with their daughter.' Delacroix was Phillipa's lady's maid and was skilled at discovering information from the servants' quarters. 'Apparently, Miss Annabelle Hastings is pursuing Alfred Cavendale. Or at least, her mother is pursuing a son-in-law with Cavendale's pedigree and purse.'

'Quite the gathering. Which suits our purpose. It's always easier to disappear in a crowd.' Hannah stepped into her grey gown, and Betty began the arduous task of fastening the buttons along the back. Hannah shimmied her shoulders to help Betty adjust the dress. It was high-necked, terribly unfashionable, and far less revealing than the silver dress she had worn to accompany the duke. At least she could move her arms freely.

'I heard there'll be another gentleman in attendance. St George something-or-other.' Betty finished the last button and ushered Hannah to a chair so she could attack her hair with a brush.

Hannah cocked her head. 'Lord Franklin St George?'

Betty broke into a wide grin, her eyes flashing. 'That's the one!'

Betty dismantled Hannah's hair and brushed it out to begin anew. 'According to Sam, this St George character is best friends with Alfred Cavendale.'

Hannah caught Betty's gaze in the mirror. 'And who is this Sam? He wouldn't happen to be a handsome and cheeky stable boy, would he?'

Betty's mouth fell open for a moment before she snapped it closed. 'He, um, well, he sat next to me at dinner, you see.' Her hands flew over Hannah's hair. Deft fingers braided, curled, pinned and tucked the strands into a silky masterpiece. 'He had all kinds of funny stories. Kept the whole table in stitches, miss.'

Philippa shared a glance with Hannah. 'Just mind he doesn't charm you out of anything you want to keep, Betty.'

Nodding her head while her hands kept busy, Betty bit her lip.

'If you're quite finished, dear, we must head to dinner. You did a wonderful job with Hannah's hair. Elegant.'

Betty's cheeks flushed, and she carefully placed the last pin. 'You look ever so lovely, Miss Simmons.' She dropped a quick curtsey.

'Thank you, Betty.' Hannah smiled. 'Do keep your ears open for any word amongst the servants about a lady's maid who would have been employed here a few weeks back. Sarah Bright. Don't make it obvious, but if you find anything out, please let us know immediately.'

Betty nodded. 'Of course, miss.'

'Right, shall we make our entrance?' Hannah ignored the

sudden flush of heat at the thought of seeing Killian. She rose from the chair and waited for Philippa to precede her.

Philippa opened the door leading the way down the stairs to the drawing room, where the party was gathered for drinks before dinner.

Hannah noticed Lord Killian immediately. He stood next to the fire, sipping what she guessed was whiskey. His sharp gaze caught hers the moment she walked into the room. The left corner of his mouth curled in the hint of a smile.

Her stomach flipped uncertainly. Blood pulsed through her veins. Tingles of awareness sparked in her fingers, the base of her throat, and the apex of her thighs.

Damnation!

How could a half-smile from across the room make her body react so strongly? Her gaze locked on his lips. She remembered their texture, soft and firm, as he pressed his mouth to hers. It had only been a week since the ball, but it felt like eternity.

Since she made her scandalous proposal to Lord Killian, minuscule progress had been made. She confessed her proposition to Philippa the night she made it. For the first time in ten years, Hannah regretted being honest with her patroness. Philippa was all encouragement when she thought Hannah showed no interest in the Duke of Covington, but as soon as Philippa became aware of Hannah's arrangement, the duchess turned into a fearsome she-wolf guarding her cub. It was ridiculous. Hannah was not some innocent creature needing supervision.

Still, if something didn't happen soon, she would be needing a cold bath. At times, she worried she would melt from the smouldering thoughts consuming her about the devilishly handsome Lieutenant General.

The result of Philippa's sudden adherence to social conventions was three visits from Lord Killian culminating in nothing more scandalous than a brief kiss in the garden before they were interrupted by Stokes.

Philippa might think she was shielding Hannah, but her newly found protective streak only made Hannah more determined to follow her set course. She was a woman of four and twenty with no plans to marry. Philippa had given her permission to explore her passions, and if she wanted to engage in a physical affair, that was her prerogative. She had no expectations beyond that and no intention of involving her emotions. Therefore, no harm could come of her save the damage to her reputation if they were discovered. Philippa already said she didn't care about that, so Hannah's venture held little risk.

Hannah thought again of Killian's promise to offer marriage if he breached her maidenhead. It was equal parts ridiculous and infuriating. A man wasn't expected to marry all the women he bedded. Indeed, every gentleman in England would be a bigamist if that were the case. So why should such a demand of constraint be placed upon her?

His offer might stem from some ridiculous sense of honour, but no joy could be found in a forced union inspired by something as inconstant as passion and infuriating as obligation. Hannah wasn't even sure she wanted to take their explorations so far. But if she did, it would not result in marriage.

She was certain two missions would be accomplished by the end of the fortnight. Finding Sarah Bright's murderer and satisfying her physical desires for Lieutenant General Robert Killian.

She would start her second mission immediately.

Before Hannah could approach Lord Killian, Millie and Ivy rushed over in a flurry of pastel skirts.

Ivy reached out both hands to clasp Hannah's. 'I'm so delighted you're here, Hannah.'

Millie towered over her friend. 'What *are* you wearing? Did someone recently die? Should we be extending our condolences?'

Hannah looked down at her dress. 'No.'

'Millie! Ignore her, Hannah. You look lovely.' Ivy slapped her friend's arm.

'Your face looks lovely. And your hair. Your dress is dreadful.' Millie's gaze traversed Hannah's unfortunate dress.

Hannah stifled an unladylike snort at her friend's brutal honesty. 'I like my clothes.'

Millie frowned at Hannah. 'Dowdy dresses of a matron with no taste and very little income?'

'Millie!' Ivy hit her friend again.

'What? I'm being helpful. Hannah, how can you possibly seduce the delicious Duke of Covington when you're dressed like my least favourite governess? Ugh! Do you remember her, Ivy? She reeked of pickled onions. I swear she must have smuggled them around in her pockets.'

The butler entered the drawing room and announced dinner. Lord Killian approached as heat pooled low in Hannah's belly. She willed her hands to remain steady as he extended his arm to her.

'May I escort you to dinner?'

Millie raised an eyebrow several shades darker than her fiery hair, and Ivy covered her grin with a gloved hand.

Hannah cleared her suddenly dry throat. 'That would be lovely, Your Grace.' She placed her hand on his arm and breathed deep to catch the scent of bergamot and leather.

Killian dipped his head closer to her ear as they followed the group into the dining room. 'I have a favour to ask of you.' His voice was intimately low.

Hannah kept her gaze straight ahead by sheer force of will. 'I'm intrigued,' she murmured.

'Send your maid to bed before midnight, and keep your door unlocked.'

Hannah tightened her grip on his arm. 'That's two favours.'

'Will you do it? Please?' There was a desperate growl in his voice.

They reached her chair, and Hannah turned to face him. She nodded quickly before she lost her nerve. This was her opportunity. Time alone with Killian. But now he'd made the offer, anxiety and anticipation waged a war within her. Could she actually engage in a physical affair? Her body screamed a vehement *yes* even as her mind warned her of the consequences. But Killian was nothing like the putrid baron, nor any of the other dandies she watched from the darkened corners of ballrooms as they seduced the women of the beau monde. He was honest, and brave, and honourable. Even if his faith was misplaced in the House of Lords, and his stubborn opinions were wrong, and his views on love were irrevocably jaded.

Killian exhaled. His green eyes darkened as his pupils dilated. 'Good.' He turned and walked to his seat further down the table.

Hannah sat before her shaky legs gave out completely. *Dear Lord.* She was actually going to do it. She was going to seduce a duke.

9

Deciding what to wear for a scandalous interlude was damnably difficult when all of Hannah's clothes were made for economy of movement and a desire to be invisible. In the end, she settled for a clean cotton shift and her softest flannel robe. She huffed at her reflection in the mirror. It was nearing midnight. She had already sent Betty to bed, Philippa was undoubtedly sipping whiskey in her room, and Hannah was on the verge of needing smelling salts.

Toying nervously with the end of her braid, she pressed her lips together to bring some colour to her otherwise pale face.

'You can stop at any time. Quit being such a silly ninny!' She scolded herself in the mirror and almost missed the quiet knock. 'Drat!' she whispered before moving swiftly to the door.

Killian entered the room, closing the door softly behind him. He was wearing his suit from dinner, but he had removed his cravat and unbuttoned his shirt to reveal an inch of skin at his throat.

She backed away from him, feeling the unfamiliar zing of fear. Not that he would hurt her, but that she wasn't ready for this momentous step.

He leaned against the door. His eyes took in every detail of her with an expression nearing hunger. Hannah's blood flooded back to her face in a rush of warmth. Now she worried there was too much colour in her cheeks. She wasn't sure what to do with her hands, so she wrapped her robe tighter around her body and crossed her arms over her chest.

'Hello.' Hannah could have died. Of all the inane, stupid things to say. She bit her lip, wishing she could turn into a wisp of smoke and float away.

Killian smiled, his eyes flashing with wicked humour. 'Hello.'

He pushed away from the door, and Hannah found herself stepping backward at the same pace he moved forward. She kept an equal distance between them until she ran into the back of a loveseat near the small fireplace at the south end of her room.

'Are you nervous?' He asked an obvious question with an equally obvious answer.

Yes!

Hannah tipped up her chin and shook her head in a blatant lie. It was bad enough that her knees were knocking together, and a swarm of ants had taken residence in her stomach. She didn't need him to know how incredibly vulnerable she was in this moment.

He smiled again. The firelight played over his features, throwing his eyes into shadows, highlighting his prominent cheekbones and the laugh lines bracketing his beautiful mouth. He really did have ridiculously well-placed teeth which flashed at her when he spoke. 'I think we should sit first and talk.'

'Talk?' Hannah's pulse beat in her throat. Could he see its mad pace?

He closed the distance between them. Hannah stiffened. Looking directly in his eyes seemed too intimate. Too raw. Instead, she stared at his left earlobe. Ah, yes. Much better.

Lifting his hand, he traced her features from forehead to cheek to chin, where his fingers lingered. 'Look at me,' he commanded softly.

Hannah rarely responded well to being told what to do, but in this circumstance, she was adrift. A small part of her appreciated his authority. Also, there was desperation in his tone. Perhaps he was feeling a little nervous too. The combination of control and vulnerability was impossible to resist.

As she lifted her gaze, she noticed his eyelashes were obscenely thick, framing eyes more green tonight than hazel.

Leaning slowly closer, he pressed his lips to hers in a chaste kiss. 'I think it's important we talk first.'

Hannah swallowed. She took an unsteady breath and nodded. *First.* Such an innocuous word, yet laden with meaning. Because after talking, what would come *next*? Surely something quite extraordinary.

Leading him around the couch, she extended her hand in an invitation to sit. Before obliging her, he removed his jacket and folded it over a chair just left of the couch. As he moved, she could see the fine linen of his shirt pull tight over his shoulders. Moisture pooled between her legs. *Dear God.* Hannah's cheeks grew warm from embarrassment. What would he say if he knew? But he couldn't possibly.

He sat on the loveseat and rested his left ankle on his right knee, a man at his leisure. Meanwhile, Hannah was balancing on the edge of a wire, certain to fall.

She perched on the chair where his jacket was draped. He was supposed to enter the room and ravish her immediately, alleviating any need for thought or conversation. But the infuriating man never acted predictably. Prolonging the anticipation in this way made the whole prospect suddenly more illicit. What could he possibly want to discuss at a time like this?

'I'm not in the habit of seducing virgins.'

Ah. He wants to discuss the most awkward and embarrassing topic imaginable. Marvellous.

Hannah opened her mouth to try and form a response, but only managed a strangled squeak.

Thankfully, he continued, filling the silence with his deep voice. 'I don't want to frighten you or push you further than you wish to go.'

'I'm not scared.' But she was. And she hated the helplessness of it.

Killian smiled. 'Liar.'

'Ladies don't lie,' Hannah retaliated.

He chuckled darkly. 'I can agree you are most definitely a lady who deserves the utmost respect. So, I think it best to ascertain what your expectations are before we begin. And your under-standing of seduction. That way, we can avoid any false presumptions.'

This was completely unexpected. His elbow was on the armrest, his finger and thumb pressed against his temple and chin. His middle finger rubbed back and forth over his bottom lip. Hannah watched that finger like a snake might watch its charmer. Enthralled.

She collected her scattered thoughts and cleared her throat. 'I may be a virgin, but I'm not ignorant of what occurs between a man and a woman, Your Grace.' God forbid he think her innocent.

'Killian. It's what my friends call me. We are friends tonight, are we not?'

She would not describe them as such, but as no other word for their relationship sprang to mind, friend must suffice. 'Yes. Alright, Killian.' She stumbled over his name. 'As I was saying, I know the particulars of s-sexual congress.'

'Truly? I would love for you to tell me more about these particulars.' His voice was gravelled, and he shifted on the couch. Hannah was distracted by his movements. There was a noticeable bulge pressing against the placket of his breeches where none had been before.

Fascinating!

Hannah never let fear of the unknown stop her. She needed to approach this as she would a fight. Pretend confidence and move quickly.

Nerves got the better of her. She stood and began pacing.

'A man becomes hard and breaches the woman.' Hannah paused in front of him. She couldn't look at his face, so instead, she focused on his earlobe again. Until her traitorous gaze flicked down to his lap.

Good Lord!

She had no idea a man's appendage could grow so prodigious. Even through his breeches, she could ascertain the dimensions. The very idea a woman was meant to fit that inside herself was ridiculous. Her nipples budded, and she pressed her legs together against an unfamiliar ache.

She started to step back, but faster than a striking snake, he leaned forward and caught her hand in his own. He didn't pull her closer, but it was also impossible to retreat.

'Do you know what part of a man gets hard?' His fingers tightened around hers.

Hannah exhaled a breath as shaky as her limbs. In lieu of an answer, she gestured at his obvious erection.

'Oh, no. That won't do. I want to hear you say the word.' His pupils almost engulfed the green of his eyes. He shifted again. His thumb made a lazy circle against her palm.

She never thought talking about seduction could be as disconcerting as engaging in the act itself. It was both excruciating and arousing. The rhythmic friction of his thumb only increased the intimacy of the moment.

How on earth was she to answer him? She knew several words to describe the male anatomy, none of them proper. After a moment's deliberation, she settled on the most common.

'Cock.' It felt illicit in her mouth. 'At least, that is one of the terms, is it not?'

'Yes.' Killian hissed in a breath. This conversation was having an equally powerful effect on him. Good. She didn't want to be the only one flustered. He squeezed her hand again. 'And where does he place his cock in a woman?'

Hannah again recalled words never uttered in polite society. 'Her cunny. Or quim, I suppose. They are both the same, are they not?'

He clenched his jaw. 'Yes. Do you know that a woman's cunny becomes wet in preparation?'

Hannah's eyes flew to his in shock.

'Are you wet right now, Hannah?' Slowly, he pulled her close enough to press his lips against her palm.

She couldn't possibly answer him, but she felt his mouth move against her hand in a smile.

Insufferable man!

Before she could think of a cutting reply, he let her go. She should have moved a safe distance from him, but instead her hand dropped uselessly to her side. She was frozen. Ensnared by his gaze and the way his mouth moved as he spoke such illicit words.

'So, you understand the particulars of intercourse, but we are decidedly staying away from such activities. What else do you know about the pleasure found between two people?'

Hannah's brows drew close together. 'I don't understand. Do you mean seduction?'

He chuckled darkly. 'Isn't that why we're here? To practice the art of seduction?'

'Are you laughing at me?'

'No, I'm not. I'm just fascinated by the contradiction of a woman who is skilled with a blade, uses words like bollocks, cock, and cunny, but is ignorant to the myriad of pleasures that can be found in bed sport. You are an endlessly evolving enigma, Hannah. I find myself determined to discover your secrets.'

Hannah stiffened at the thought. 'There are some secrets best left in the darkness.'

'But isn't it our job to discover what's hidden?' Killian bit his lip.

'That depends. Sometimes, we hide things because it would be dangerous for others to find them.' She was revealing too much. But passion and fear warred within her, making it impossible to think clearly.

'And sometimes we hide things because we are scared to let our true natures be known. Is that why you keep to the shadows, Hannah?' His voice was soft, his green eyes delving too deeply into her soul.

What would happen if she told him? If she shared her most shameful secret? Could a man with his own demons understand hers? Doubtful.

Hannah squared her shoulders. 'I'm safe in the shadows. My secrets are mine alone. Isn't this night supposed to be about seduction?'

Killian lowered his chin in a slow nod of understanding. 'You're right. Of course. Forgive me.'

Hannah shrugged off the intensity of his stare. 'There is nothing to forgive. You asked me what I know about pleasure. I know kissing is quite pleasant. I was hoping we could do more of that.' She needed to take back control of this evening.

Sharing her body with this man was much safer than baring her soul.

Killian reached out and gripped both of her hips, moving her to stand between his spread legs.

Holy hell. Perhaps not.

Baring her body suddenly seemed just as daunting as throwing a light on her hidden depths. Bravado was quickly replaced by panic. Her breath came in rapid pants.

Killian's lips curled in a wicked smirk. 'Ah, yes. Kissing is quite pleasant. And there are so many places one can be kissed.' He raised an eyebrow and his gaze travelled from her lips to her breasts to lower, where the juncture between her thighs hid beneath two insignificant layers of flannel and cotton. 'Perhaps tonight, I can show you some new places to kiss.' His hands burned through the thin layers of cloth, scalding her skin.

Tingles burst every place his direct stare touched. 'Yes. Certainly. I mean to say. That would be quite agreeable. To me. I would agree. To that proposition.' She couldn't think. She had no clue what she'd just said. Why didn't the damnable man get on with things? If they were kissing, she could finally stop thinking.

'Kissing is much easier with proximity.' He licked his bottom lip and Hannah almost moaned. 'Will you join me?'

In a fluid display of strength and agility, he picked her up and placed her on his lap with her back against the armrest. Air whooshed out of her lungs in a rush.

She thought it was difficult to think standing between his legs but sitting on his lap completely destroyed her concentration. Her unbound breasts were hovering at his eye level. Her bottom was cradled against his hard thighs, where she could feel the growing evidence of his desire jutting upward. She wriggled in an attempt to stand, but he clamped his arm over her legs and clasped her hip.

'Don't. Move,' he growled.

Hannah froze as Killian took deep breaths through his nose.

'I am trying to keep control of myself, but if you continue to wiggle like that, I'll be lost.' He captured her gaze, and Hannah was almost swept away by the wildness in his eyes.

'I only meant to stand,' she whispered.

His words were a revelation. She had just as much control over him as he did over her. Hannah always imagined the man would hold command in sexual encounters. It was one of her biggest hesitations. But watching Killian tremble with desire, she felt a unique power, different from facing a man in battle, but just as potent.

He rubbed his thumb in slow circles against her hip. 'Yes. Of course. Is this too fast? Do you need to get up?'

His willingness to release her made her need to escape less imperative. 'No. I think I like it. You just startled me. I didn't expect you to want me on your lap.'

'I want you any way I can get you.' He moved his hand from her hip to her cheek where his fingers feathered over her scar. 'I wonder, will you tell me how you got this?'

Hannah froze. 'No.'

Killian's gaze leapt from her cheek to her eyes. He nodded. 'Ah. And now we're back to secrets. Some scars leave greater wounds on our soul than our skin. Later maybe?'

Never.

Hannah pressed her lips together and stayed silent.

His fingers delved into her hair, and he urged her face closer, pressing his mouth against hers.

Finally!

It was a relief to be pulled out of her mind and into a riot of sensations. This time, his kiss was far from chaste. He plunged his tongue into her depths. Hannah tasted whiskey and mint.

She twisted her torso to face him more fully. Resting one hand on his shoulder, she marvelled at the feel of his muscles as they flexed and twitched beneath her fingers. Her other hand drifted up, getting lost in his thick curls. She tugged gently and when he moaned, she pulled harder. This is what she craved. To stop thinking and just feel.

He sucked her bottom lip into his mouth, his bite sharp enough to flirt with pain. It was glorious. She gripped his head and scraped her teeth over his top lip.

'Straddle me.' He lifted her, creating space for her to spread her thighs on either side of his lap. Her shift crept higher, exposing her ankles, calves, and knees to the night as she complied with his request. The fire warmed her back.

He deepened their kiss. Strong fingers pressed against the small of her back, pulling her closer to him until the ridge of his cock rubbed her cleft. His rough cotton pants created delicious friction against her delicate core. Hannah gasped as he rolled his hips up. The only thing separating where he ground himself against her intimate flesh was his breeches.

He nibbled down her neck, across her collarbone. 'Will you remove your wrap?' Looking up at her, his eyes partially hooded and darkened by desire, Hannah was struck by his beauty.

She didn't hesitate. Stripping off her flannel wrap in a frenzy, she heedlessly threw it on the floor. Her shift draped off one shoulder. Looking down at herself: her nipples were smudges of dark pink, peaked against the translucently thin cotton. She should be embarrassed, but desire emboldened her, and she arched her back, offering her breasts to him like a sacrifice.

The raw hunger in his eyes reminded her, she was no sacrifice. She was a goddess, and he was in her thrall.

Killian dipped his head and sucked her nipple through the material. The contrast between his hot mouth and the wet cotton against her puckered flesh was overwhelming. Hannah moaned and leaned her head back, pushing harder into him.

He nipped and suckled until Hannah was sure she would fly into a thousand pieces. While his mouth was occupied with one nipple, his fingers dipped under the loose neckline of her nightgown and found the other. Demanding fingers pinched and squeezed, flicked and rubbed. Fissures of pleasure sparked and smouldered low in her belly, rippling out in waves. She rubbed her aching core against the hard flesh of his cock. Something sharp and sweet came alive.

Her world narrowed to his mouth, her breasts, his fingers, and her rolling hips. She was chasing something, pursuing it as ruthlessly as any criminal until ecstasy expanded in an explosion. She cried out, her breath coming in ragged gasps. Power and need coalesced in a conflagration of sensation that coursed through her, igniting every nerve ending in her body. Even her toes tingled. The pleasure washed through her in waves that slowly ebbed to a buzzing hum.

'What just happened?' Hannah whispered against his temple. She had heard of transforming religious experiences. Now she understood.

He pulled away from her. When she opened her eyes, he was watching her. Air sawed harshly in and out of his lungs, and his cheeks were dark with colour. 'You found your climax.'

An aching emptiness echoed deep within her, a poignant counterpoint to the pleasure effusing her body. 'That was... consuming. Amazing.'

She shifted and felt the hard ridge of his erection. *More.* Instinctively, she knew this was only a piece of something much greater. And she wanted it. All of it.

Killian pressed his lips together in a tight line and hissed.

Hannah was intimately acquainted with pain. She understood

how to deliver and endure it, so she recognised the signs in others. Awareness dawned. 'You're hurting. Oh, God. Did I do that to you?' She clambered off his lap and backed away. Her gaze locked on his lap, and she was horrified to see her wetness on his breeches. 'I'm so sorry.'

His smile was closer to a grimace. 'Don't be sorry. Watching you fly apart was...' he didn't finish his sentence but shifted again, wincing as he did.

'I must have done something wrong if you're in such pain.'

'You didn't do this. Well, perhaps inadvertently, but you don't carry the blame.'

'I don't understand. What happened?' Hannah was trained to inflict injury, but she didn't relish the idea of hurting someone unintentionally. Especially not Killian. Not now.

'It's not so much what happened, but what didn't.'

Hannah shook her head. 'You're speaking in riddles. Please, tell me plainly what caused this so I can avoid doing it again.'

'That's not possible.'

'Killian.' She infused her voice with a warning. 'Why are you in pain?'

He exhaled through clenched teeth. 'When a man is aroused, he grows hard. His cock fills with seed. If he doesn't, er, release it, there can be pain.'

How intriguing.

Hannah couldn't stop from staring at the juncture of his thighs where his placket strained to contain the hardened flesh. 'Can a man only release his, well, I suppose when he enters... I mean to say, can that only happen when he is inside a woman?' Hannah pressed her hand against her hot cheek. The things they said to each other! Madness.

Killian's face reddened, and she found a surprising measure of satisfaction in knowing he shared in her embarrassment.

'No. And if a man and woman are trying to avoid pregnancy, it's best for it not to happen inside a woman at all.'

'Truly?' Did other women know this? Hannah was full of questions 'How then do you find, er, release?'

'There are other ways.'

Bending to pick up her robe, Hannah wrapped herself in the warm flannel. She sat again on the chair. 'If there are other ways to alleviate your discomfort, we must explore them. You can't just sit here and suffer.'

Air exploded from Killian in a harsh laugh. 'How generous of you. I don't think you are quite ready for that. I shall retire to my room and deal with this alone.'

Hannah was suddenly very interested in knowing exactly what Killian might do to deal with his problem. 'I don't want you to leave. Not yet. You said you would stop when I asked, but I haven't asked yet.'

'You don't want to watch me frig myself, Hannah.'

She blinked. The image conjured by his words was equal parts forbidden and fascinating.

'When you were kissing me, something happened. You said I found my climax.'

'Yes. It can happen sometimes when a man plays with a woman's nipples, but more often when a man... well, there are other ways.'

'It was lovely. And powerful. And consuming. Will it feel like that for you when you release your seed?' Such mysteries she was unravelling.

Killian closed his eyes and clenched his hand in a fist. 'Similar, I would imagine.'

'Then, please, find your climax. And, let me watch.'

10

Killian had never been so desperate for release. His cock was harder than steel. His balls were drawn up and aching. Hearing her ask to watch him almost unravelled his control.

He flicked open the buttons on his placket, and his cock sprang free through the opening of his small clothes. He groaned at the release of pressure.

Hannah leaned forward. She bit her lip, and he almost spent just thinking about her mouth pressed against the pulsing head of his cock.

He gripped himself, hoping not to scare her with such a rude display. Her breaths were coming faster, and her eyes were fastened on where his hand held his hard flesh. Seed already seeped from the tip. Killian used the moisture to aid his task as he rubbed himself in firm, fast strokes. Seeing her consuming gaze fuelled his lust.

He was so close, it only took a few jerks of his hand. The burning coalesced in his spine, pulsing out in a powerful wave of pleasure as seed spurted on his belly and chest. Pressing his heels into the carpet, Killian let the heat consume him in searing flames that pulsed with his heartbeat as Hannah's eyes widened in wonder.

The crackle and pop of the fire blended with the sounds of their breathing. Killian closed his eyes, still riding on the ebbing tide. He had forgotten what peace felt like, but this echoed that old comfort.

'It's quite messy, isn't it?' Hannah's voice brought him back to the present.

He opened his eyes and laughed. 'Yes, I suppose it is.'

She stood and walked to the dressing table where a pitcher of water and shallow bowl sat. Pouring the water over a cloth, she squeezed out the excess water and brought it to Killian. Her hand shook slightly as she handed him the square of flannel. Her eyes flicked over to his cock, spent and softening.

'So, it just... deflates?'

Killian laughed again as he cleaned himself. The material was cool against his hot skin. 'Generally, that isn't something a man wants to hear, but yes. We would get very little done if it didn't.'

'Can it get hard again?'

'Oh, yes. But usually not immediately.' He put himself to rights, tucking his penis away before she could make any more observations.

This was an incredibly odd conversation to have and not something Killian had experienced before. Never had someone analysed every aspect so minutely. The women he bedded in the past were professionals, well versed in the act of fucking, and rarely interested in the details.

But Hannah made the details so important, granting each moment a new intensity.

This wasn't fucking. It was something else entirely. Killian had never seduced an innocent. He should feel shame, but he didn't. He was proud to have brought her pleasure and more than a little protective of her. If his guess was correct, she had just experienced her first orgasm, then watched him tug at himself like a randy schoolboy until he found his own release. This would be a vulnerable moment for anyone. 'Are you alright?'

Hannah didn't answer immediately. She wrapped her robe around her in a gesture that was becoming familiar to him. As though the piece of flannel were some kind of mythical shield keeping her safe.

'I'm... I don't know. When you kissed me earlier, it was wonderful. Everything sort of rose up to some kind of culmination. I had no idea I could feel that way. But then watching you do that just now created a new ache inside of me. A hollow pulsing.'

'Perhaps you ache to be filled as much as I ache to fill you.' And he did ache. Not in the usual places. This new pain emanated from his chest, thumping along with his heart, and echoing in that hollow vessel.

Hannah wouldn't meet his gaze. 'I think this has been quite enough flirtations for one evening. You should leave now. Please.'

'I fear we have far exceeded flirtation. Are you upset? Did I go too far?' He rose from the couch and walked to her, getting down on his knees and ducking to catch her gaze. The thought of hurting her was untenable.

Her eyes filled with uncertainty. She shook her head, and copper hair fell from her neat braid. Curls spilled around her face. 'No, I just need to think.'

He reached up and brushed his knuckles against her cheek, skirting the edge of her scar. 'I promised you I would stop when you asked. That will never change. Of course you want time. Take as long as necessary, but don't pull away. There is more, Hannah. So much more.' Killian had never questioned his course, but if she pulled back now, he wasn't sure what he would do. Need, desperate and fierce, surged through him.

A spark of curiosity brought the fire back to her eyes. 'More?'

'Infinite mysteries waiting to be solved.'

'Infinite is quite a lot.'

She couldn't refuse a challenge. So, Killian would give her one. 'I shall leave you with this secret, Miss Simmons. There is a delightful little treasure hidden in your quim. Find that pearl. I dare you. At our next meeting, I imagine you might have some new questions about all the ways a woman can find release.'

She narrowed her eyes. 'That's not possible. You are teasing me. How could I not know about a treasure in my... surely you jest.'

'See for yourself. If you are brave enough to explore.'

Hannah's eyes widened before she pressed her lips together and shook her head. He was certain he heard her mumble something close to 'insufferable man' before crossing her arms over her chest. 'Good night, Your Grace.'

'Good night, Miss Simmons. Sweet dreams.' He pressed a kiss against her lips, then rose and walked to her door.

'I won't do it, you know. Just because you dare me to doesn't mean I will.' Hannah's chin was up, and her arms tightened over her unbound breasts. Sitting in her chair with her hair around her shoulders and her wrapper pulled close, she was impossibly beautiful.

'Liar.' Killian grinned as he turned and opened her door, shutting it quietly behind him.

* * *

The next morning, Killian arranged a meeting with Lord Cavendale and his son. He would not run from his responsibilities any longer.

The butler showed Killian to Lord Cavendale's private study.

Lord Cavendale was behind his desk, and Alfred sat on a leather couch with an unopened book beside him. Both men rose upon Killian's entry.

'Lieutenant General Killian, welcome.' Lord Cavendale stepped from behind his desk to shake his hand. 'Would you like a drink? Coffee, perhaps? Or something stronger if you prefer. It's a bit early, but we won't judge.' He winked at Killian. For a wild moment, Killian was reminded of his own father. Grief and longing washed over him. He cleared his throat, attempting to regain his composure.

'Coffee would be fine.' Killian wasn't thirsty, but it would be a welcome distraction during what promised to be a difficult conversation.

'Williams, would you send up some coffee, please.' Lord Cavendale glanced at the butler, then gestured to the sitting area where Alfred stood stiffly, one hand clasped behind his back, the other tapping the book against his thigh.

Killian unbuttoned his jacket and chose a wingback chair in deep jade upholstery.

'Is there anything else, Your Grace?' The butler asked.

'Just the coffee,' Cavendale never turned away from Killian. 'I must say, we were hoping you would speak with us.' He sat in the brother to Killian's chair, leaving the leather couch for his son. Alfred sat last, placing his book on a dark oak coffee table separating him from Killian.

It struck Killian again how similar Alfred looked to Patrick. But he was also a copy of his father. Unfortunately, Alfred inherited his father's double-chin. Patrick had been spared that feature. Perhaps it would have developed over time if he had been given the chance to live long enough. Killian pushed down the guilt and focused on his task.

Lord Cavendale smiled at Killian, the wrinkles around his eyes deepening. 'Thank you for taking time to speak with us about such a painful topic. It may seem masochistic for me to want details, but sometimes imagination can be a cruel monster, creating the worst of scenarios.'

Alfred made a noise in the back of his throat like a choked cough. 'Please. Are you really thanking the man responsible for Patrick's death?'

'Alfred!' Lord Cavendale turned on his son, his mouth tightening as white brackets formed at the corners of his lips. His face grew red with anger or embarrassment, perhaps both.

Alfred couldn't be more different than his father in manner. Lord Cavendale was courteous and kind; his son was a battering ram.

Alfred glared at Killian, not bothering to mask his hostility. Killian knew anger and grief were twins born from the same pain. He couldn't blame Alfred for his disdain, but the man's rudeness still chafed.

'I won't sit here and pretend to be grateful to this man, Father. Unlike you, I hold no kind feelings toward a leader who failed to protect his men.'

The bullet hit its mark, and Killian clenched his hands to stop them from shaking. He had failed so many.

'Silence! I won't have any child of mine behave like a savage.' Lord Cavendale's voice shook as he gripped the armrest of his chair. 'I want to know what happened to my Patrick. Lieutenant General Killian has agreed to meet with us. Control yourself or get out.'

'I already know what happened.' Alfred stood and tugged roughly on his jacket. He strode around the low table, stopping several feet away from Killian. He jabbed his finger at Killian like a sabre. 'You, sir, are why Patrick is dead, and no amount of bills passed in the House of Lords for wounded soldiers will absolve you of your crime.' Unshed tears shone in the younger man's eyes.

Alfred's words were a guillotine severing Killian's hard-won composure. Both Alfred and his father deserved to hear at least some of the truth. Something to ease their pain. If Killian could offer a moment of peace, he must do it.

Rage and grief sometimes amalgamated into something else entirely. A raw need for revenge that would never be fulfilled. A madness with no cure, and he loathed for either of these men to embrace that monster. Killian forced his voice to soften. 'I do not seek absolution. But I would offer you some comfort if I can. Patrick fought bravely. You should know he died with honour.' The lie tasted bitter on his tongue, but he did not regret it.

Alfred's skin mottled red, contrasting against lips pressed so tight, they were a single white line. 'I don't need you to tell me that my brother was brave or honourable.' Alfred's voice broke. 'Patrick was always perfect. Even in death.' He cleared his throat and spun around. 'I'll take my leave.' He strode from the room without another word, slamming the door behind him.

Lord Cavendale wiped his hand over his mouth. 'Allow me to apologise for my son. Older brothers are supposed to be an example for their younger siblings. But Alfred followed along behind Patrick from the moment his younger brother could walk. I think Alfred's lost now, without Patrick to lead the way.' Lord Cavendale laughed, but there was no joy in the sound. Killian wished he could say something to help, but words failed him.

Lord Cavendale leaned back in the chair, his sharp gaze taking in details Killian wished he could hide. The sheen of perspiration on Killian's brow. The way Killian couldn't hold Cavendale's frank stare. The black halo of disgrace that covered him.

'Alfred is wrong about you, son.' Cavendale nodded at Killian in wordless affirmation. 'Patrick's death is not your fault. Poor

Alfred has always tried so hard to be the kind of man Patrick was. Tried and failed. When Patrick joined the military, his brother went out and joined one of those secret societies of all things. As if that was the same.' Cavendale tapped his fingers on the chair's arm. 'Don't let Alfred upset you, Lieutenant General. He doesn't understand men like us. Men like my Patrick.'

Killian couldn't imagine how difficult it must be to lose a son like Patrick and try to guide another like Alfred. He wanted to ease Lord Cavendale's embarrassment about Alfred's behaviour. 'Grief does strange things to people. And Alfred is right. It was my job to protect the men under my command. Including Patrick. I failed in my duties.'

Lord Cavendale harrumphed, an oddly comforting sound. 'Bollocks! I followed the campaign, you know. You did the best you could in an impossible situation.'

A footman entered carrying a silver tray laden with various pots and dishes. He set up the coffee, cream, sugar, and cups on the table and then exited.

Lord Cavendale poured two cups of steaming, black liquid. 'Please, join me.'

Killian leaned forward to take the offered cup, inhaling the rich aroma. Lord Cavendale's study was large enough to be comfortable without seeming ostentatious. Killian glanced to his left where three bay windows looked out onto the grounds. His entire body tightened. A distinctive leather boot, too small for a man's, poked out from underneath the forest-green curtains of the far-left window.

Impertinent woman!

Hannah must have been snooping in the study. She wouldn't have assumed Lord Cavendale to be conducting business so early with guests in his manor. All Cavendale needed to do was glance to his right, and she would be discovered.

Killian stood. Lord Cavendale raised a surprised eyebrow but was forced to join him.

Killian cleared his throat. 'I know you have questions about Patrick, but I would like to have this conversation when Alfred is present. You both deserve to hear the details. Perhaps I can speak to Alfred privately and ease his anger.' He grasped for a line of conversation that would get them out of the study. 'I have been told he has an interest in horses and that you have quite an excellent array of specimens in your stables. Major General Drake and I were hoping you would give us a tour. It might give me an inroad to winning over Alfred.' He gestured toward the door.

Lord Cavendale's eyes brightened. 'Clever idea! I admit, I hoped you and Alfred might strike up a friendship. He would benefit from your influence.' He clapped a hand on Killian's shoulder. Killian felt a strange warmth, something close to acceptance emanating from the older man. Lord Cavendale smiled at Killian, his crooked teeth lending an endearing quality to the expression. 'Yes, quite. I would be happy to show off some of Alfred's prime stallions. His hobby is an extravagance, but he keeps telling me there's profit to be made in quality horseflesh. Perhaps we can convince him to join us.' He stepped forward.

Killian glanced behind him. The boot disappeared behind the drapes. Just as he reached the door, he paused. 'I must return to my room to get my gloves. Shall we meet in the stables in fifteen minutes?'

Cavendale nodded his agreement, and they turned in opposite directions. Killian slowed his pace and listened to the older gentleman's boots echoing down the hall. When he could no longer hear them, he spun and retraced his steps. Moving swiftly, he snuck back into the study just as Miss Simmons emerged from the drapes.

'You sneaky little minx.' He shut the door behind him and

enjoyed watching Hannah's face transition from surprise to annoyance.

'How did you know I was here?' Her dark brows furrowed, creating a crease between them.

Killian's cock twitched to life. Ridiculous. To be aroused by a forehead wrinkle. 'Your boot was showing. And as you are the only woman I know who insists on wearing men's footwear, it was not difficult to determine your identity.' Tsking, he shook his head. 'Really, Miss Simmons. Such a disappointing lack of discipline.'

'I am the only woman you know who wears sensible footwear. Men shouldn't be the sole benefactors of adequate shoes.' Anger heightened her colour and quickened her step as she swished toward him. She was wearing brown. Instead of diminishing her beauty, the simple dress highlighted her trim figure and contrasted with the dramatic colouring of her red lips and pearl skin. 'I wouldn't have to hide if you didn't organise a meeting in Lord Cavendale's study.' She stopped in front of him, a finger pointed at his chest.

'You can't possibly be blaming me for this,' he sputtered.

'Why not? It's clearly your fault.'

'What exactly were you hoping to find?'

'Hah!' She dropped her accusatory finger and put her hands on her hips. 'Like I would tell you.' Her gaze dropped to his lips, and she licked her own.

Killian stepped closer, delighted when she didn't back away. 'Shouldn't you be focusing your attention on Lord Bradford? What do you think you'll find in Lord Cavendale's study of all places?'

'Did you not hear me the first time? I'm not telling you anything.'

'I bet I could find a way to convince you.'

Her breathing accelerated, and he watched her cotton dress expand and contract. He wanted to see her naked in the sunlight. To see every detail of her bathed in brightness as her body quickened with desire.

'I dare you to convince me of anything,' she refuted. She never backed down. He'd not met a woman so willing and ready to spar. It was intoxicating.

Killian raised an eyebrow. 'Speaking of dares. Did you take me up on mine?'

Hannah's skin flushed rose, and her eyes darted away from him. She bit her lip. Her citrus and vanilla scent filled his lungs.

He wanted to taste her mouth, to trace her full upper lip with his tongue. Instead, he settled for seducing her with words. 'You did, didn't you? You found your treasure. Tell me, did you play with that sweet little pearl? Did you think of me while you were touching yourself?' The image of her delicate, tapered fingers delving deep into the pink folds of her cunny almost destroyed him.

She returned his gaze and narrowed her eyes in a stubborn expression he was growing to crave. 'You are despicable.' She huffed out a breath. 'How did you know?'

'You can't resist a dare, Miss Simmons. And neither can I.'

'Now I know how to bring myself to culmination, what further use do I have of you?' She raised an eyebrow, her amber eyes flashing in challenge.

'Pleasuring oneself is akin to scratching an itch, don't you think? Quick, efficient, perfunctory. But what we create together, increasing the ache until it throbs, sharpening the pleasure until it cuts, fanning the blaze until it consumes...' He stepped closer with every incendiary word until they were a breath apart. 'I promise I can be very, very useful. I propose a new game for us to play during our next flirtation. It would seem you have details about Sarah Bright that I need. For every piece of information you share with me, I shall kiss, lick, suck, and nibble that sweet little pearl of yours. Interested?'

Her mouth fell open in shock. He took advantage and nipped at her bottom lip.

Footsteps echoed in the hall. They both froze. They turned in unison, their gazes on the door. There was no time to hide. If Lord Cavendale or Alfred returned to the study, they would be discovered. The footsteps approached the door, then continued down the hall.

Killian and Hannah exhaled loudly in shared relief.

Hannah took a large step away from him. 'We should leave. Separately. I'll go first.' Not waiting for Killian's response, she walked swiftly to the door. He admired the sway of her hips as she retreated. 'And yes, I might be interested.' Without a backward glance, Hannah opened the door and slipped out. Almost as if she were conceding a battle. Almost as if he won this skirmish.

Hannah dressed carefully for the mid-morning activities. They would be riding horses to a picturesque valley next to a river. The household staff would already be there, preparing a picnic for the party.

If Hannah ever wondered what outfit she would die in, now she knew. A borrowed riding habit from Ivy Cavendale's middle sister. Hannah was terrified of horses, and they loathed her. Every. Single. One.

'Miss, if you keep twitching your leg like that, I'll never finish. Please, could you sit still?' Poor Betty had to re-twist Hannah's hair for the third time. Hannah's frantic leg shaking threatened to exceed the limits of her maid's extensive patience.

'You have always been remarkably silly when it comes to horses.' Philippa sat on Hannah's bed, slapping a riding switch against her leather boots. She eschewed the respectable riding habit for a pair of split skirts, fitted vest, and tailored greatcoat. On any other woman, it would cause a scandal, but Philippa made the entire ensemble look quite dashing. She finished the outfit with a tall riding hat.

'Unlike certain duchesses, I was never given the opportunity to learn as a girl.' Hannah heard the sharpness in her tone. She hated feeling inadequate and sitting astride a horse, she wasn't just insufficient. She was woefully inept.

'Yes, and despite many attempts from a certain duchess to provide lessons, you never took the opportunity to learn as a young woman. So, this is what you get.' Philippa thwacked the riding crop against her boot again.

'Thank you so very much for your empathy.' Hannah ignored the precarious dip of her stomach.

'You're welcome. Now, did you learn anything from snooping in Lord Cavendale's study?'

Hannah would not blush. She refused to be embarrassed. She wouldn't think about her encounter with Killian in the study.

'You've gone quite flushed. What happened?' Philippa stood from the bed and narrowed her gaze.

Bloody hell!

'Nothing happened. Well, I was interrupted by Lord Cavendale, his son, and Lord Killian.'

'Really? Interesting. What exactly were they meeting about?'

For once, Hannah didn't want to share all her information with Philippa. Alfred Cavendale blamed Killian for his brother's death. And for some reason, Killian seemed to agree. She hadn't seen their faces, but she heard the accusation in Alfred's words and the shame in Killian's response. For reasons she refused to examine, she didn't want to share Killian's disgrace with Philippa.

Hearing the undisguised hatred in Alfred's voice as he hurled insults at Killian made her hope Alfred was the killer. She wanted an excuse to hurt him. What kind of woman wanted to hurt a grieving brother? Most probably a very bad woman.

Hannah forced her thoughts back to the conversation with Philippa. 'Lord Killian was speaking about Patrick, the youngest Cavendale son. Apparently, Lieutenant General Killian was Patrick's commanding officer and was there when he died. Alfred was incredibly rude about the whole situation. It's all rather complicated. It seems Alfred always held his brother in high esteem. He even joined some secret society when Patrick entered the military. Lord Cavendale did his best to make up for Alfred's ungentlemanly conduct toward Killian.'

Philippa tapped the riding crop against her lip. 'Killian?'

Hannah swiped at an imaginary speck of dust on the table. 'Lieutenant General Killian.'

'Hmm.' Philippa's gaze remained steady on Hannah.

Betty put a final pin in Hannah's hair. Hannah turned and smiled at her maid. 'Well done, Betty. Even with all my fidgeting.'

'You look ever so lovely in rose, miss. If you don't mind me saying. I don't know why you always wear such dull colours when...' Betty slapped her hand over her mouth, and her eyes widened.

'Don't worry, Betty. You're quite right. Miss Simmons may need to re-think her wardrobe soon. Especially now she's on a first-name basis with Lord Killian. I doubt the Duke of Covington will stand for his wife being shrouded in greys and browns.'

'His first name is Robert, as you well know. And I'm hardly a candidate to become his wife.' Hannah crossed her arms over the white bone buttons running down the front of her riding habit.

'Then you had better be very careful about how familiar you become with the duke, Hannah.' Philippa stepped closer, putting her hand on Hannah's arm. 'I don't want you getting hurt.'

Hannah bit her lip as a hot wave of embarrassment engulfed her. 'You are the one who spoke to me about the tenderness one might feel for another. You asked if I was interested in Killian, er, I mean, Lord Killian.'

Philippa pulled back her hand. 'Yes, and you told me you weren't the least inclined to find flirtations with the duke appealing. It seems your tune has changed.'

Hannah tipped up her chin and pressed her heels into the carpet. 'As has yours. Why are you so opposed to my interests?' She rarely fought with Philippa and hated when conflicts arose between them.

'Just be careful. Your heart is far more fragile than you think. Men can be cruel and careless when it comes to the tender parts of a woman.' Philippa glanced away, and Hannah thought of Lord Winterbourne. He had been so kind to her mother, but her suspicions about his treatment of Philippa grew darker.

'Is this why you've taken such a keen interest in your role as chaperone?'

Philippa shrugged. She looked out the window instead of at Hannah.

Hannah closed the distance between them. 'I'll be careful, Philippa. I promise. This is not an engagement of the heart. I just have questions he is willing to answer. Is that so wrong?'

Philippa slapped the riding crop against her hand. 'No. It's natural. It's bloody well encouraged in men. Why shouldn't we be allowed our share of desire? If you only want a physical relationship with him, I encourage you to do it and feel no shame. But Hannah, I see how you've been looking at him. How he looks at you. Physical attraction can so easily turn into something more.'

Hannah shook her head. Philippa was worried for nothing. 'It won't. I promise.'

Philippa held Hannah's gaze. 'I hope you're right. Because if he hurts you, I'll kill him.'

Hannah didn't doubt Philippa's words nor the unspoken love prompting them.

'You won't have to. I'll kill him myself and save you the trouble. But Philippa, I won't let him hurt me.' Before she could think about it, Hannah leaned forward and hugged Philippa. The older woman stiffened in her arms, dropping her riding crop. Hannah breathed in the rich scent of jasmine and something darker, frankincense or sandalwood. She released Philippa and stepped back.

Betty gulped in a breath and dropped the brush she was holding. Philippa retrieved her crop, thwacking it against her boot for good measure. Hannah smiled before sighing dramatically. 'I suppose we should go downstairs so I can hurry up and fall off a blasted horse.'

'Indeed.' Philippa pressed her lips together. Hannah wondered if they trembled, or perhaps her patroness was just irritated by such an unexpected display of affection. Before she could decide if she'd cracked the duchess's impenetrable shell, Philippa turned and led the way out of Hannah's room.

11

The women had assembled in the entryway. Ivy and Millie made a beeline for Hannah. Upon their approach, Philippa excused herself and drifted over to where Lady Bradford and Lady Hastings were admiring each other's riding hats. Miss Annabelle Hastings stood with the older ladies looking a bit out of place amongst the matrons.

'Are you well, Hannah? You seem... off.' Ivy's perceptive gaze scanned Hannah's face.

'I don't frequently ride horses. Truthfully, I never ride them.' Hannah desperately wished she could continue never riding them for the unforeseeable future.

'There's nothing to it.' Millie's husky voice was full of confidence. 'The trick is to show no fear.'

'Right. No fear,' Hannah echoed.

'If you show them one hint of apprehension, they'll trample you flat in a heartbeat.' Millie smiled brightly at Hannah. Hannah tried not to be sick all over her borrowed riding habit.

The late-summer sun shone down on them. Fluffy, white clouds played in a cerulean sky. Honeysuckle and hyacinth sweetened the air. Bees buzzed in the blooms. It was a glorious day. If only Hannah wasn't trudging to her certain doom on the back of a snorting beast.

The gentlemen convened in the yard near the stables. Alfred Cavendale was talking to Lord Franklin St George. Hannah felt Millie stiffen as they passed the two gentlemen.

'Good morning, ladies. Aren't you all looking lovely this morning?' Franklin St George's stare lingered on Millie. Hannah narrowed her eyes, her lips tightening into a scowl. The nerve of him! While Hannah didn't know the details, it was clear he had some kind of history with Millie. And not a pleasant one. How dare the bastard look at Millie like he was assessing a new stallion he wished to buy.

His chin dissolved into his neck and his ears stuck out, but his posture and fine clothes reeked of money. He kept his head tilted up to look down his nose at everyone. Such a pose left his soft throat unprotected and vulnerable. It would be so easy to punch him hard in his gullet and collapse his windpipe.

'Laugh, Millie. Pretend I just said something devastatingly funny. Throw your head back and laugh.' Ivy followed her own advice and let out a hearty laugh.

Millie turned to them. 'It's fine. I'm okay.' But her glassy eyes and accelerated breathing told a different story.

'Then show him.' Ivy put more energy into her laugh, making Hannah worry she might have a coughing fit.

Hannah joined in, no doubt sounding like a braying donkey.

Millie looked at Ivy and Hannah, shaking her head. The corners of her mouth turned up in a slowly widening smile. 'You're both mad, you know.' Her laughter was forced, but it filled the courtyard with a low melody.

Franklin St George's eyes hardened. His mouth turned down in a sour frown.

Hannah's laughter grew as she watched the pompous ass glare at them. The ladies crunched past the two gentlemen on the gravel drive. She kept herself between Millie and Franklin St George, determined to completely ignore the men. Still, St George's malevolent glare burned through her back.

Groomsmen brought saddled horses from the stables. Hannah kept her eyes peeled for Betty's handsome stable lad but was distracted by how massive the horses were as they stomped around the yard.

The assembly began choosing their steeds in a flurry of activity while Lord Cavendale, Lord Hastings, and Lord Bradford watched from a distance declaring themselves too old and too tired to join the ride.

Millie selected a massive Cleveland Bay mare and swept into her saddle without any help from the groomsman. Her eyes flashed with passion as her horse pranced in a small circle.

'Tally-ho ladies! Let's show these men how real horsewomen ride!' Millie looked like a Valkyrie ready to sweep down and steal the souls of unsuspecting soldiers.

Ivy followed Millie's lead, settling into her saddle with confident grace. Hannah tried not to scowl.

Philippa caused a minor stir in her split skirts, but it was nothing compared to the gasps of the women as she mounted her horse and rode astride. Hannah didn't miss the censuring brow of Lord Franklin St George as he muttered something to Alfred Cavendale.

Philippa noticed as well. She trotted the black gelding close enough to spook St George's horse, almost unseating the vile man. Glancing at Hannah, Philippa winked.

A curly-haired steward with bright eyes and a charming smile led a brown mare toward her. The horse snorted, pawing her front hoof on the gravel, kicking up stones.

Bother and blast!

Hannah could swoon. Surely if she slumped to the ground, someone would pick her up before the horse stomped her to death. She could go back to the house and snoop around to her heart's delight while everyone else went on their bloody picnic. Capital idea.

She was moments away from doing just that when Killian appeared at her side.

'She's just as nervous about you as you are about her.' He was standing too close as he reached up and placed a steady hand on the horse's nose, rubbing the white forelock. Hannah watched his fingers and felt irrationally jealous. Of a horse.

'I doubt it.' Hannah straightened her shoulders.

'She's a good girl, aren't you? What's her name?' Killian asked the steward. He grasped Hannah's hand in his, guiding it to the horse's neck to stroke. He stood so close, the heat of his chest warmed her back.

'Starlight. She's a gentle mare, is our Star.' The young man's voice was low and smooth. Hannah wasn't sure if he used that tone to calm the horse or her.

'Patient with new riders?' Killian moved closer. The vibration of his words buzzing through her senses.

'Yes, my lord, she's sweet and strong is our Starlight.' The steward ran a hand down the horse's flank.

'And you are?' Killian asked.

The steward ducked his head. 'Sam, my lord. One of the stewards here.'

Hah! Betty's handsome stableboy. I knew it.

Hannah might be facing certain death, but she had guessed Betty's sweetheart. That was a real comfort.

'Grab a handful of her mane. Sam will hold her steady, won't you, Sam?' Killian didn't wait for Sam's reply. He put his hands around Hannah's waist. Before she could protest, she was suddenly looking down at him from the dizzying height of her horse's saddle.

Sam handed her the reins, and Hannah held each in a fist, pulling them high to her chest.

Killian's eyes widened in alarm. 'Have you never ridden before?'

Hannah's shrill laugh startled poor Starlight, who sidestepped nervously. Hannah dropped one of the reins to grasp the saddle. 'Of course I have. Twice.' She couldn't remember a single instruction from the lessons she had taken years ago. Lessons that ended in disaster.

'Dear God.' Killian grabbed the remaining rein from Hannah and retrieved the one dangling on the other side of Starlight. Hannah took the opportunity to grip the saddle with both hands. He turned to the group, now all astride and ready to leave. 'I think Miss Simmons's horse may need a new bridle. I'll wait with her, and we'll catch up.'

Major General Drake must have seen something in Killian's gaze. He wheeled his horse around to face the group. 'Excellent plan. Any of you gentleman interested in a little race?'

Alfred Cavendale and Franklin St George nodded their assent.

'I'll wager I can make the first paddock before you clear the grounds, Major General.' Millie winked at Major General Drake. Her horse leapt forward before he had a chance to respond. St George scowled at the Major General before kicking his horse into a gallop and following Millie.

Ivy spurred her horse down the drive toward the open fields in a mad dash of hooves and gravel.

'We can't let the ladies beat us, Major General. How could we live with the disgrace?' Alfred shouted to Drake before slapping his crop against his horse's flank. Major General Drake quickly followed, passing Alfred before they cleared the drive.

Lady Bradford, Lady Hastings, and Miss Hastings embarked together at a much more sedate pace. Their laughter faded as the trio disappeared down the lane.

Philippa wheeled her gelding around. Her horse was anxious to follow his friends, and Philippa's equestrian skills were on full display as she controlled the spirited mount.

'I'll catch up.' Hannah echoed Killian's words to Philippa. 'I'll be fine.'

Philippa glanced at Killian before returning her worried gaze to Hannah.

After a rare moment of hesitation while her horse danced in frustration, Philippa nodded. 'Make sure you are fine. I'll keep an eye out for you.' She turned her horse after the group. He whinnied and broke into a blistering run. Philippa leaned low over his neck, moving with the muscular animal as though they were one flesh. Her hat flew off, but Philippa didn't seem to care a bit. She was magnificent.

'Shall I get a new bridle, my lord? I'm terribly sorry. I didn't realise there was a problem.' Sam reached for the reins, but Killian shook his head.

'The bridle is fine. Miss Simmons just needs a few minutes to get used to her mount.'

'Ah. Of course.' Sam looked at Hannah and winked. 'No shame in being a little nervous, my lady. Why don't I take the reins and lead you around a bit?'

The lad was too handsome for his own good, but he had kind eyes and gentle hands. Hannah would put in a word for him with Betty. If she lived that long. Which was incredibly doubtful.

After ten minutes of being led around while Killian kept a

keen watch on her, Hannah thought she might make it to the end
of the lane without falling off her steed.

Don't show fear. Don't fall off. Don't die.

Hannah tugged gently on the reins and Starlight shifted her
gait, turning toward the drive. Hannah pretended she wasn't
surprised at all that her horse complied.

Killian pulled alongside her. 'You're a fast learner.'

She concentrated on keeping her hips moving with the horse.

'Did anyone tell you how lovely you look in rose? That dress is
almost the exact colour of your ni—'

'Must you always be so scandalous?' Hannah's cheeks heated.

Killian laughed. 'I was going to say your neck when you blush.
Like now. Why? What did you think I would say?'

Impossible man!

She decided to retaliate by remaining silent. It was a
masochistic punishment because a million retorts burned the tip
of her tongue.

'So, are you interested in my earlier suggestion? You share
your information, and I share my skills with your hidden pearl.'

Hannah waited a moment. 'After giving it some thought, I have
a better idea. Perhaps you should be the one sharing information,
sir. And for every question I ask that you answer, I will allow you
one favour.'

Killian's eyes dilated. 'What kind of favour?'

'Whatever you ask of me within the bounds of our agreement.'
Hannah exulted in his silence. It felt glorious to momentarily stun
the man. She had thought long and hard about his suggestion,
and it was a brilliant way to extort information. So, she would use
his tactics against him.

'What if there are favours you wish to ask of me?' He raised a
brow.

'If I want a favour from you, I will first answer your question, just as you suggested.' Her breath was coming fast.

'Tonight? Midnight?'

Hannah opened her mouth to agree when a shotgun blasted somewhere behind them. Starlight whinnied high and loud before breaking into a wild gallop.

Hannah screamed. She grabbed onto the horse's mane. Starlight veered right, leapt over a fence, and galloped toward the forest.

* * *

'Fuck!' Killian glanced behind him. A man on horseback raced in the opposite direction over the paddocks west of Everly Manor. He should follow the shooter, chase him down and determine the man's identity before beating him to a bloody pulp and turning him over to the local magistrate. But he couldn't abandon Hannah. It was a miracle she didn't fall off the horse when the damned animal vaulted the fence.

He spurred his stallion to follow her. She might be a fast learner, but she wasn't ready for a wild race through the dangerous terrain of the woods surrounding Lord Cavendale's mansion. Even a skilled rider would need to keep his wits about him dashing through the forest's low branches and uneven ground.

Killian could see Hannah clinging to her horse as the beast entered the copse of trees. Hannah somehow managed to keep her seat. She was holding tight to Starlight's mane, leaning low over the horse's neck. Her position would help Hannah avoid any low branches, but she would be flung over the mare's head if Starlight stopped suddenly.

Fear licked along Killian's nerves. Tightening his grip on the stallion's mane, he urged his mount on, dodging a low branch and leaping over a tangled root.

Thankfully, Starlight was an intelligent beast. Sensing the danger of pelting through the uneven terrain, she slowed down quickly to a trot. Killian pulled alongside the horse and her terrified rider. He tugged on the reins Hannah had dropped. Starlight came to a slow stop.

Hannah trembled. Her head was buried against Starlight's neck, her hands gripping the horse's mane.

'It's okay. You're safe.' Killian dismounted and ran his hands over Hannah's back, soothing her while surreptitiously checking for wounds. That shot had been too close.

Her face was pressed firmly against the horse's neck, muffling her voice. 'I'm fine.' Hannah's body quaked beneath his hands.

Killian gripped her hips to pull her from the saddle, but she clung to Starlight's back like a cat.

'Shh. It's okay. You're safe. I have you,' he crooned as he might to a frightened child.

Slowly, she released her grip, and he was able to pull her down. She fell against him, and he wrapped her in his arms. Orange blossom and vanilla blended with pine, soil, and horse. Her hair fell around her shoulders in disarray, soft waves tangling in his fingers as he pulled her closer.

'It's okay, Hannah. I'm here.'

Her whole body shuddered violently, but she didn't cry. Instead, she became impossibly silent and completely still.

Killian ran his hand over her hair, savouring the silky texture. 'Are you alright?'

The sounds of the forest enveloped them. A woodpigeon called from the tree above while wind rustled in the leaves.

'Of course.' Hannah pushed away from him, her cheeks pale, her eyes unnaturally bright. 'I didn't expect...'

'For someone to shoot at us? No. Neither did I. Are you sure you are unhurt?'

'I'm perfectly sound.' She swiped at her hair, regaining some of the tartness he found so charming. 'Despite being completely inept as my horse careened into the forest. Despite being totally useless as you rushed in to save me. Despite wasting an opportunity to chase after the bastard who shot at us.' Hannah's voice was sharp in the quiet woods. Starlight stamped a hoof, and Hannah flinched.

Killian shouldn't smile. He shouldn't laugh, but the chuckle rumbled up despite his best efforts to stay serious. Relief flooded him. If she was annoyed, she couldn't be too rattled. 'You don't play the damsel in distress very well.'

Hannah narrowed her gaze and pointed a finger at his chest. 'Because I'm not. I'm completely capable of taking care of myself. If it wasn't for the bloody horse taking off like a cannon.'

'Wonderful. Shall we pursue the shooter?' He raised his eyebrows and used his most charming smile.

Hannah's eyes widened, her mouth fell open in a silent objection. 'What about the picnic? The group will wonder what happened to us. Philippa will worry if we don't arrive.'

Killian shrugged. 'We'll hurry. We can follow the culprit and see if he heads towards the village or in another direction, then double back and meet the party as they return. We'll tell them it took longer to fix Starlight's bridle than we thought, and she took you on a bit of a wild ride.'

Hannah bit her lip. Her cheeks were as pale as the moon on a dark night. 'I can't. I can't ride.'

Killian knew well the fear of falling. But he also knew the importance of standing back up again.

If Hannah didn't get back on Starlight, she would hate herself for it. Worse, she may let the moment grow so big in her mind, it would paralyse her. She might never ride again. That would be a terrible waste. Because she enjoyed it, when she forgot to be afraid.

He chose his words carefully. 'You don't have to get on Starlight again. The gunman has probably escaped, so you shouldn't blame yourself.' He shrugged. 'Everyone is afraid of something. It's certainly nothing to be ashamed of.'

Her eyes darkened, and her lips hardened into a stubborn line. 'You're just trying to needle me into getting back on her.' Hannah stepped away from him and closer to Starlight. She put a tentative hand on Starlight's flank. 'You can't dare me into doing something I don't want to do.'

'I know. I'm not daring you. A lot of people are terrified of horses. You certainly aren't alone. Why don't I walk the horses back to the stable? We'll get you inside for a nice warm cup of tea?'

Hannah scowled at him. 'I don't need a cup of tea. I'm not a helpless ninny.' She turned back to Starlight. Moving to the horse's left shoulder, Hannah turned to face Killian. 'Help me up.'

Killian bit his lip to stop from smiling. His hunch played out. He gripped her waist and leaned closer. It would be so easy to steal a kiss. But in the quiet solitude of the forest, he didn't trust himself to stop at just a kiss. Instead, he focused on the shape of her waist beneath his fingers, her soft hair tickling his nose, and the intoxicating scent of orange and vanilla as he lifted her onto the saddle.

'Which way did he go?' Hannah's hands trembled as she adjusted the reins. Killian hoped it was her reaction to him and not fear of riding.

He quickly mounted his horse and turned him. 'This way. We'll go slowly until we're out of the forest. When we increase our gait, she'll lift her head, so make sure you tighten your reins. Keep your hands low and steady.'

'I know. Don't show fear. Don't fall off. Don't die.'

Killian craned his neck around. 'What was that?'

'I said, let's ride.' Hannah's voice was tight, but she wouldn't back down now that he challenged her courage. She was breathtakingly brave and maddeningly stubborn.

They made their way out of the woods, and when the horses were back on level ground, Killian urged his stallion from walk to trot to canter. He kept his eyes on Hannah, half expecting her to fall behind, but he was getting used to her proving him wrong.

Starlight might be gentle, but she was also swift. The mare and her rider kept pace with Killian and his horse. When he was convinced Hannah had regained some confidence and wouldn't lose her seat, he let his stallion have his head and galloped across the fields west toward the village.

He kept his gaze scanning the rolling hills for any signs of a rider, but the shooter was gone. They rode almost to the village without seeing any definitive traces of a man on horseback.

Killian reined his horse to a walk. 'Wherever he went, I don't think we'll find him.' Disappointment tasted bitter on his tongue.

'I wasted too much time in the forest. My stupid ineptitude...' Hannah's voice trailed off, and she clenched her teeth. Tears glittered in her eyes. Killian guessed it was frustration, not fear.

'It isn't your fault. When a horse is spooked like that, it's almost impossible to control. You mustn't be so hard on yourself.' As a Lieutenant General, he was used to being critical of his men when needed, but Hannah gave herself no grace.

'Why shouldn't I be? The world makes no allowances for mistakes, Your Grace. Neither can I.'

'Aren't mistakes inevitable? Expected, even? To castigate yourself for every misstep seems unnecessarily cruel.'

'Life is cruel to most. But how could you understand? People expect you to rise to the occasion, put forth your best efforts, and emerge victorious. So, you do. But society holds no such aspirations for women. And certainly not for me. They expect nothing from me because I am worth nothing in their estimation.' She swiped at a tear that escaped. 'Which is fine. It works in my favour, actually. But every time I fail, I prove them right.' Hannah turned her horse back toward Everly Manor. 'And that, I cannot abide.'

Killian trotted after her. 'You didn't fail. You've only just learned to ride. You had a pretty big scare today on Starlight but look at you. Cantering across the countryside like you were born in the saddle. Hardly a failure. If the world doesn't see you, that is their failing, not yours.'

I see you. But he stopped himself from making the admission.

Hannah looked across the field toward the sprawling stone mansion in the distance. A playful breeze lifted her copper hair, whipping it behind her like a cape. How could anyone overlook such a fascinating woman?

'I have failed in ways you can't possibly imagine.' She shook her head. 'It doesn't matter. I shouldn't have said anything.' Turning to face him, Hannah hid all signs of distress under a veneer of calm. 'Do you think the shooter doubled back to Everly? Could it be Lord Cavendale?'

'Cavendale?'

Hannah snapped her mouth shut.

'Do you have information implicating Lord Cavendale?' Killian instinctively recoiled from the suggestion. Sarah Bright had worked for Bradford. He was their lead suspect. Why was Hannah moving her focus to Cavendale? 'Hannah, someone is shooting at us. The stakes are only getting higher. What makes you suspect Cavendale?'

Hannah hissed out a breath. 'Alright. I shall tell you. But only because I don't have time to deal with a dead duke on top of everything else, and you are so obviously on the wrong track.'

Killian smiled. 'You don't want me dead? You do say the sweetest things.'

Hannah scowled. 'Do you want me to share what I know or not?'

Killian extended his hand in a gesture of encouragement for her to continue.

Hannah rolled her eyes. 'Sarah Bright was taking another job. With the Cavendale family. It's why I agreed to come to this house party in the first place. So, yes. Lord Cavendale is most definitely a suspect.'

This was potentially damning information, and the biggest break they'd had in the investigation.

He needed to speak to Drake.

If Sarah Bright was taking a position in the Cavendale household, it was entirely possible that at the very least, Lord Cavendale had information about the last two weeks of her life. It was equally possible Lord Cavendale was the shooter. Still, it felt wrong. And Hannah didn't know there were multiple murders. Nothing in his encounters with Lord Cavendale hinted at the kind of cold calculation needed to kill several women in cold blood.

Regardless, the prime minister would need to be informed. A message must be sent immediately. Killian and Drake had much to consider.

But he didn't want to focus on the mission. Killian wasn't ready to end his earlier conversation with Hannah. How did she think herself weak? Hannah had strength of will, intimidating skill, keen intelligence, and striking beauty. Yet she saw herself as a failure?

Some insecurities were too close to the heart. Discussing

them laid one bare and uncovered hidden vulnerabilities. Never before had he wanted to know a woman's fears or hopes or worries. But he desperately wanted to know hers. If only she trusted him.

Not likely.

Killian returned to the safer subject of murder. 'If Sarah Bright was going to work for the Cavendale household, I suppose it's possible he was the shooter. But Bradford or Hastings had equal opportunity, and at least Bradford is similarly connected to Sarah.'

Hannah shook her head. 'But neither of them has a motive. If Cavendale hired Sarah Bright and thinks one of us is aware of that, he has every reason to try and scare us off, or worse.'

Killian squinted into the sun before looking over the fields. 'Only if he is responsible for her death. And what motive would Cavendale have for killing an innocent maid? We don't even know for certain that she was going to work for Cavendale.' He exhaled heavily. 'We need more evidence. At this point, anyone here could be responsible, or no one. The shooter could just as easily have been a hired gun from London.'

Killian shouldn't share his information with her about the other murders. She was smart, brazen, and motivated. Giving her confidential information about their investigation would only make Hannah a more formidable opponent. He couldn't allow her to find the killer first and exact such vigilante justice. But he didn't relish the idea of her life being in danger either. The faster they solved this case, the quicker she would be safe from harm. And the more she knew, the better equipped she would be to protect herself.

Until she takes on another assignment.

Killian resolutely ignored the annoying voice in his head. When this case ended, her affairs would no longer be his concern.

Which was a huge relief. Not a devastating loss. 'I know something you don't.'

'What do you know? I shared my information with you. Fair is fair.' Eyes like amber in the sunlight flashed with anger. 'You won't tell me, will you?' Her lips turned down in a scowl.

There was another motivation for him to share his information with Hannah. 'I'll tell you what I know if you promise to honour our bargain tonight. You shared information with me, so I owe *you* a favour. If I answer a question of yours, then you'll owe me one in return.'

She glanced away. 'After everything that's happened today, you still want to play this little game?'

'Oh, yes. But it's hardly a game, Hannah.'

'What favour would you ask of me?' Her chest rose and fell, trapped in the high-necked riding habit.

He itched to unclasp each little white button running down her front. 'I'll tell you tonight.'

'You want me to promise something blindly? How do I know your information's even worth it?' She raised her brows and cocked her head.

'What about this: I shall tell you my information now. Tonight, I'll ask my favour, and you determine if the price is worth the reward.' He understood her need to keep control. As a man once imprisoned, he was acutely familiar with the fear of losing autonomy. This was new territory for Hannah. She was brave and curious, but she also needed to maintain command of the situation. He'd never thought about a woman's place of constant subservience. Putting himself in her world, the lack of personal control would be untenable. Of course she wanted the same freedom he had in most situations. She had every right to be angry and frightened if that liberty was taken away.

'What if I decide your information isn't worth the favour?' Her hand snaked down to pat Starlight's neck.

'Then you send me away unsatisfied.'

'And you would leave?'

Killian wished they weren't on horses. He wished he could pull her close and press his lips against hers. Reassure her with his body when words failed. 'I would leave if you asked it of me. I would stay. I would stop. I would press forward. All at your command.'

She took a shaky breath, then smiled. The ride had restored her complexion, her skin now honeyed from the sun. A new sprinkling of freckles kissed her nose like fairy dust. 'Alright. I'll agree to your terms. You're a terrible negotiator, you know.'

Killian was an excellent negotiator. In the House of Lords or on a battlefield, he was brutal. Fierce. But this wasn't business. It was something else. Something far more important. Far more precious.

'Will you share your information, or shall we put this game behind us?' She raised a haughty eyebrow.

'Sarah Bright isn't the only murdered girl.' Killian couldn't dampen the sense of triumph he felt when Hannah's mouth dropped open. 'Several more were found in Calais and Boulogne. We aren't looking for a man who has murdered one woman. We're looking for a man who has killed many.'

12

Hannah felt like she'd been punched in the belly. As information went, this was inflammatory. Multiple women found in coffins. If they couldn't find the killer, the repercussions would shake London's very foundation. Fear would spread through the city like a virus. And more innocent girls would die.

Bloody hell!

'I thought ladies didn't say words like "bloody hell".' Killian's lips twitched.

Hannah frowned. 'I didn't. Did I?'

His green eyes sparkled in the sunlight. 'You did.'

Shrugging, Hannah clucked her tongue and delighted in Starlight's quick response as the horse moved forward in a rocking trot. Once Hannah overcame her fear, she relished the thrill of asking a wild animal to follow her command. She couldn't help thinking of other wild animals who might do her bidding. One in particular. In the duke genus.

Killian caught up with her. 'While your conjectures about Lord Cavendale are sound logic, surely you agree he isn't the kind of man who could kill multiple women.'

'Men can be deceiving, Your Grace. How did you come by this information?'

Killian shrugged, 'You hardly expect me to reveal my sources.'

'Nor can you expect me to rule out a perfectly viable suspect.' She wasn't willing to cross Lord Cavendale off her list of potential murderers. Not yet. 'We should head back. I wouldn't want the party to worry about us.'

'I want to be clear about something.' Killian's eyes flashed dangerously.

'What?' Hannah's belly clenched.

'I'll ask a favour of you tonight, but I owe you one as well. Think on that.' He spurred his horse ahead of her.

Hannah took a shaky breath. What favour did she want to ask of Lieutenant General Killian? *To share his heart with me.* Impossible. She urged her mount to catch him.

* * *

The returning group of picnickers were gathered where the forest met the lane leading to Everly Manor.

Philippa galloped up to Hannah. 'What happened to you?' Her eyes quickly shifted from fear to anger.

'I am well, Philippa. I lost control of Starlight, but Lord Killian saved the day.'

Philippa didn't hide her scowl. 'Did he?' She looked between Hannah and Killian.

Hannah tamped down her sudden anger. 'Yes, he did.'

Killian's smile was deceptively easy. 'By the time Starlight stopped her run, we were nearly to the village. Miss Simmons kept her seat remarkably well. She's a fast learner and could be a fine rider with more practice.' Killian looked at Hannah with a hooded gaze. Her belly fluttered, and heat pooled low. Delicate skin chafed against her saddle as sweat trickled down the small of her back. She wondered what favour he would ask at midnight. She wondered, and she ached.

'Hannah excels at whatever she puts her mind to accomplish,' Philippa snapped.

Killian wisely reined his stallion back, allowing distance between himself, Hannah, and Philippa.

'We shall make sure not to leave you again, Hannah.' Ivy rode next to them, bringing her horse alongside Hannah's left while Millie guided her Cleveland Bay to Hannah's right.

Safely flanked by her friends and patroness, they returned to the manor.

* * *

It had been a long, arduous, dangerous day. Hannah happily retired early after dinner. She wanted nothing more than a short nap and long bath before her intended interlude with Killian.

Unfortunately, Philippa had other plans.

She swept into Hannah's room without a knock. Hannah was chin-deep in hot water. The staff kindly brought a copper bath to her room, and Hannah was determined to enjoy the luxury regardless of unwanted visitors.

Betty had been bustling around the room but froze, bobbing her head at Philippa in a surprised half-curtsey. 'Evening, Your Grace. You near scared the life out of me. I'll never get used to how you two move so silent like.'

Water slopped over the edge of the bath as Hannah twisted to watch the duchess.

Philippa walked past the tub and settled herself on the stuffed chair placed near a large window. She narrowed her gaze at

Hannah. 'Exactly what happened between you and Lieutenant General Killian today?'

Hannah sank back into the soapy water. 'Several things. But not what you think.'

Philippa punched the pillow next to her in an unusual display of frustration. 'Really? Well, do please enlighten me.'

Hannah tipped her head back against the rim of the tub. 'I will tell you everything if you tell me one thing.' She kept her eyes closed but heard Philippa's exaggerated huff.

'What?'

'Why are you so angry about my interest in Killian?'

'I already told you this. I don't want him to hurt you.'

Hannah opened her eyes, pulled her legs to her chest, and turned her head to face Philippa. 'And I already told you, my heart is not involved, therefore he cannot hurt me.'

Philippa stood abruptly, throwing the abused pillow across the room. 'You lied. You are lying. To yourself. To me. Probably to him. Anyone with eyes in their head can see you're falling in love with him.'

'And what if I am?' Hannah spoke the truth before she realised it.

Oh, God. What if I am?

Philippa fell back into her seat. 'He will hurt you.'

'You don't know that.'

'I know he is a man. A duke with no intentions to marry. A soldier with battle wounds that still bleed. The prime minister's detective bent on beating us to this killer. How could he not hurt you?'

'I don't know.' Hannah felt the water cooling on her skin. 'Maybe I will get hurt. Maybe it will be worth it.'

Philippa's eyes were haunted. Her lips trembled, and she

hugged herself in a rare display of vulnerability. 'It won't. Trust me.'

'Was he that awful to you? Lord Winterbourne? I know he was my father, but was he also a monster?'

Philippa closed her eyes, a single tear tracking down her cheek. 'He was no worse a monster than any other man. And yes, he was awful to me. But even if he had been wonderful, it would not have mattered. He was not the one I loved. He was not the one I wanted.'

Hannah wished she weren't naked in the cooling water. She wished she could offer her patroness comfort. Sanctuary from past grief. 'I'm so sorry.' Hannah's words felt woefully inadequate in the quiet room.

'So am I.' Philippa wiped her cheek.

Betty stood frozen by the closet. 'I'm right glad he's dead then, madam. If you don't mind me saying so.' She crossed herself but thrust out her chin in a small act of defiance. 'I don't think a man deserves to live if he hurts someone as kind and generous as you.' Her cheeks glowed pink as she turned to hang up the riding habit.

'Well said, Betty.' Hannah knew Lord Winterbourne loved her, but he also hurt the woman who had been Hannah's family for ten years. For that, Hannah could never forgive him.

'Get out of that water before you freeze, then tell me what happened today.' Philippa stood, retrieved the neatly folded towel sitting on the vanity table and held it out.

Hannah emerged dripping from the copper tub and dried herself before Betty helped her wiggle into her nightgown.

'First, you should know I did lose control of my horse. But it was only because someone shot at us.' Hannah watched Philippa's face transition from haunted memories of the past to a raging fury for the present. It brought Hannah some relief because facing the truth of her father's duplicity was not easy, but seeing Philippa vulnerable and hurting was impossible. She much preferred the duchess angry and ominous.

'Someone shot at you? Who? How? Tell me exactly what happened.'

Hannah sat in front of the vanity while Betty brushed out her hair. She retold the events of the morning, leaving out the deal she made with Killian to trade answers for favours later that night.

Betty plaited Hannah's copper curls into a long braid. 'I'll take my leave, miss. Unless you need anything further?'

'You seem in a bit of a hurry, Betty. Do you have evening plans?' Hannah couldn't stop the smile curving her lips.

Betty's blush flamed so brightly, her ears turned pink. 'Of course not, miss. I can stay if you need me.'

Hannah laughed. 'I'm teasing, Betty. I'm sure there's a handsome young stable lad waiting to eat his supper next to you. But I would heed Lady Philippa's warnings and guard your heart.'

Betty nodded vigorously. She bobbed a curtsey to Hannah and another for Philippa before she left.

Philippa leaned forward from her precarious perch on the edge of Hannah's bed. 'Exactly what was that about?'

'I think our Betty has a sweetheart.'

Philippa snorted. 'What is it with the country air that turns women into complete ninnies?' She waved away Hannah's attempted reply. 'Never mind. We have more important matters to discuss. Lord Killian told you they found other women? Dead in caskets?'

'Yes,' Hannah answered.

'Why would he share this information? It gives us an undue advantage, or at least puts us on the same level as the prime minister's investigators.'

Hannah shrugged, feeling uncomfortably conspicuous. 'I couldn't presume to guess at his motivations.'

Because he cares. About me. She tamped down hope. *Because he wants an upper hand in our game of flirtation. Far more likely.*

'Multiple victims. This changes things.' Philippa rubbed her finger against her thumb. 'The Queen must hear about this. Unless she already knows.'

'She wouldn't keep something so important from us. Would she?'

Philippa shook her head irritably. 'When it comes to Queen Victoria, it's impossible to guess. I respect her immensely, but I don't claim to understand her. Regardless, she needs to hear this information. I must go back to London. Perhaps we should both return. We can leave tonight.'

'No!' Hannah panicked. She couldn't leave. Not tonight. Who knew when she would get another opportunity to be unchaperoned with Killian?

Philippa's gaze swung to Hannah. 'Excuse me?'

Hannah took a breath. 'We still have work to do here. I don't want to abandon that when you could easily return to London for a night without me. You can speak with the Queen, and I can continue our investigation at Everly. Lord Cavendale is still a viable suspect. We know Sarah Bright was leaving her position with Lord Bradford to work for Cavendale. Even if he is not her killer, he may have important information about her last few days. Maybe he killed all of the girls, or maybe multiple killers are working together. I wouldn't put it past St George to commit such a heinous crime. I don't know. But I do know there are answers to be found here. I don't want to leave until we find them.'

'If someone shot at you, someone knows you are investigating this case. You are in grave danger.'

'We don't even know if the man was shooting at me.' Hannah stood, needing to expel some of her nervous energy. She paced from the vanity to the bed and back again. 'Killian is investigating this case as well. Wouldn't it seem more likely the gunman was aiming for him?'

Philippa tapped a finger to her lip. 'So, we're back to Lord Killian? Is solving this case the only reason you wish to stay? Sexual exploration isn't worth a broken heart, and it damn well isn't worth a bullet in your gut.'

Hannah paused near the little hearth of her fireplace. She swallowed, her throat suddenly dry. 'I've never lied to you,' she had omitted some ominous truths about the night her mother died, but she never outright lied. 'I won't start now. I believe there are answers for Sarah Bright's case here. But I have other reasons for wanting to stay. You told me not to be ashamed of my desires, so I won't be. I want to spend more time with Killian. This house party gives us a chance to be together without worrying about society seeing us and judging. Without the lords and ladies of the beau monde spreading their insidious gossip. I want this opportunity.' It was an uncomfortable admission, especially when she was still coming to terms with it herself. Hannah's lips quivered with nerves. But she wasn't going to stop. Not now.

'And you're willing to put your safety at risk for this?' Philippa's voice was steady, but her fingers tapped incessantly against the floral coverlet of Hannah's bed.

'I put my safety at risk every time I go on the streets to investigate a case. Every time I sneak into some lord's study to look for evidence. Every time I strap on my weapons and confront the kind of men we hunt. How is this different?'

'Because usually the fiends we are looking for aren't also looking for us,' Philippa snapped.

'I'll be fine.' Hannah tried to keep her voice calm, but she wasn't sure what she would do if Philippa forced her to leave.

Philippa rose from the bed. 'I should order you to come with me.'

Hannah's breath froze in her lungs.

'I won't do it, but I very much want to.' Philippa pursed her lips. She looked like she just sipped pickle juice.

Air filled Hannah's chest, and she couldn't stop the smile of relief. 'Thank you, Philippa. I know—'

'Don't thank me for letting you put yourself in danger. And don't tell me you know anything. Yes, you can handle yourself in a fight; however, I'm less confident you can keep your heart safe from someone like Lord Killian. But if I forced your hand, you would never forgive me. So here I am, powerless.'

Hannah took a step forward, but her patroness put up a hand, halting Hannah's momentum. The duchess let her arm fall to her side. 'And because I hate this feeling, I would never subject you to such impotence. I won't take away your choice. Even if you are making a terrible one.'

Hannah was too grateful to be angry. 'I'm sorry you feel powerless, but I want you to trust me.'

'I trust you. It's Lord Killian and the killer intent on murdering you that I have some doubts about.'

Hannah took heart from Philippa's small smile. 'Will you really leave tonight?'

Philippa raised a sculpted brow, black as a raven's wing. 'Eager to be rid of me?'

'No. Of course not, I just...' Hannah's voice trailed off.

'With so much at risk, there's no time to waste. Don't fret. I'll take my leave now, so you won't have to find a polite way of kicking me out to make room for your dashing duke.'

'That's not—'

'Stop before you break your promise and lie to me. I won't be gone long. Four days at most. Promise me you'll be careful.'

'I promise.'

Philippa pulled Hannah into an abrupt and awkward hug

before turning and walking to the door. 'You'd better be.' She didn't look back as she shut the door behind her.

Hannah wished she could reassure Philippa that nothing terrible would happen, but both women had seen enough of life to know there were no guarantees, and Hannah promised she wouldn't lie. Bad things happened all the time, which was why it was so important she savoured the beautiful moments while they lasted. Another night with Killian lay ahead. Tomorrow's dangers were impossible to predict, but the pleasures waiting for her on this night were a sweet promise she intended to relish while she could.

13

In Killian's experience, there was nothing quite as dangerous as indecision. On the battlefield, hesitating was the fastest way to ensure a bloody end. Decisive action was integral to survival. Even the wrong choice was better than no choice. But as he stood outside Hannah's door with sweaty palms, a hard cock, and a head full of questions, he couldn't bring himself to knock.

He wanted her more desperately than any woman in his past, present, and – he dared to guess – future. But she wasn't the kind of lady a duke married. She wasn't a lady at all. Neither was she a night flower or wanton widow he could bed without doing irreparable damage.

The problem was Hannah. She was courageous, intelligent, brazen, and beautiful. She was curious and innocent and far more fragile than she knew. She was everything he wanted and nothing he could have.

So, he stood outside her door, agonising over a choice that should be easy. *Turn around. Walk away. Leave her alone.*

Killian knocked.

The door opened far enough for him to slip inside.

'I wasn't sure you would come.' The fire blazed behind Hannah, illuminating the lithe silhouette of her body.

Killian's heart stuttered.

Dear God. I'm in love with her.

The revelation stole his breath and weakened his knees.

Fucking hell.

'You're beautiful.' Of all the thoughts in his head, it was the easiest to say and the least important.

She looked at the carpet. 'No. I'm nervous. I owe you a favour, but I still have no idea what you might ask.' She clasped her hands in front of her, fingers intertwined.

'I want to watch you.' It was the safest option. He thought of a million different ways to bring her pleasure, a thousand favours he could ask. But watching her kept a safe distance between them. And in this moment, he only wanted one thing. To see Hannah Simmons come undone in front of him. To watch her shields fall away as she lost herself to desire.

'I don't understand,' Hannah paused and swallowed. Her throat moved, and he wanted to press his mouth against the hollow of her neck. To feel her heart beating beneath his lips. To lick her soft, sweet skin. To taste her. 'Watch me do what?' Her voice was spiced honey coating his senses.

Killian forced himself to remain still. 'Everything I ask. You can refuse, of course. You can stop whenever you like, and I won't touch you. But I want to watch you.'

Hannah unclasped her hands, putting them on her hips. Her eyes darkened with a familiar emotion. Annoyance. 'You could ask me any favour, yet you want to just stand there? Telling me what to do and watching me do it?'

Killian bit his cheek and willed his body to remain controlled. 'No. I'm going to sit.' He pulled a wingback chair ten paces away from the fire. 'Here.' His legs couldn't possibly hold him when so much blood was diverted to other areas. He tugged up his trousers and sat. 'And watch you. As you *let* me tell you what to do.' She wasn't going to agree. He could see the fear cloud her eyes. 'But I don't think you will. You don't like following orders. Especially not mine.' Hannah couldn't resist a challenge.

Her bottom lip trembled, and Killian's world tilted on its axis. Perhaps he'd pushed too hard. He might very well be the biggest bastard in England.

'So, this is just a dare you know I won't take?' she asked.

Killian's heart raced. 'No. This is a risk I'm desperately hoping you will take. This will only work if we trust each other.'

Hannah's hands dropped from her side. She fiddled with the lace on the sleeve of her nightgown. Her eyes darted from the fireplace to the window, then back to him. 'Men want to take control. Is that what this is about? Because I won't allow that.'

Killian gripped the arm of the chair. He could feel the hard bite of wood beneath the velvet-covered padding. 'How can I control the wind or the sea as it crashes against the shore? I could never control the forces of nature comprising you.'

Hannah quirked her brow. 'I'm a force of nature?'

Killian's low chuckle seemed loud in the quiet room. 'Oh, yes.'

'You want to tell me what to do, but I don't have to comply?'

'Exactly. You'll always have control.'

She was so close to letting him past her defences. He could feel the war waging within her. He understood that battle and wouldn't force a victory.

Holding his breath, he waited.

When she threw back her shoulders and walked slowly to stand in front of him, Killian thought he might combust, the sparks showering her in his inferno of need.

'What do you want me to do?'

* * *

Hannah had never felt so powerful or so terrified. Lieutenant General Robert Killian, Duke of Covington, favoured lord of the Prime Minister of England, commander of men, devious detective, and renowned bachelor at the top of every lady's list, sat in front of her with his legs spread, his breathing erratic, and his eyes promising dark and wondrous things. He wanted to lead her down a path, but he offered Hannah the ultimate control. This was the power she chased. This was the promise of fulfilment her body yearned to discover.

Be brave, Hannah.

She thrust out her chin and clenched her hands into fists so he wouldn't see her fingers shaking.

I can walk away whenever I want.

But what if I want to stay? Forever?

It wasn't a question she was ready to answer.

'I want you to take off your nightgown.' His gravelled voice echoed in the quiet room. The fire popped behind her. A clock ticked the moments away.

Hannah's nipples hardened into twin points of concentrated sensation as the thin fabric of her nightgown shifted over her skin. She pressed her lips together, savouring the sharp pressure of teeth cutting into her mouth.

He noticed. His eyes dilated, and he adjusted his position in the chair.

What a proud display of masculine power. His muscled thighs jutted toward her, thick and long. He rested his elbow on the arm of the chair, his index finger pressed along the sharp line of his cheekbone, his thumb braced against a jaw as solid as the cliffs of Dover. Killian's middle finger rubbed over his full bottom lip. But it was his hooded gaze that caused her body to grow hot and liquid.

Hannah had undressed in front of countless women. Her mother. Betty. Even Philippa. It never mattered because her body was just a sexless thing carrying her from one task to the next. But his gaze made this fundamentally different. She was something new in this moment. Something desired. Something inspired.

'Last night, you didn't ask to see me. We kissed and touched. The whole time, I kept on my nightgown. Why do you want to see me naked now?' The idea that he could derive pleasure just from watching her undress was fascinating.

He leaned forward, resting both his elbows on his knees. 'I want to see you naked because I want to be the only person who knows what Hannah Simmons looks like without her armour.'

It was a good answer. Honest. Flattering. Disconcerting.

She only stood a few feet from him. This close, he would see every detail. Standing fully naked in front of him, the firelight illuminating all her flaws, ugly scars, small breasts, muscular legs. He would see it all.

Hannah faltered. This was vulnerability on a scale she couldn't measure.

His eyes convinced her. The earnest need. The unguarded desire.

She should have undressed slowly, seductively. But she didn't know how. Instead, Hannah bent forward, grabbed the hem of her nightgown, and in one quick movement, whipped it over her head and let it drop behind her. Frightening tasks were best handled quickly.

Killian exhaled a whoosh of air. 'Fuck me.'

Hannah giggled. She couldn't help it. The fire warmed her back, but her nipples tightened in the cool air between them, turning her giggle into a gasp.

'Look at yourself.'

'Why?' Hannah knew what she looked like naked.

'Because I want you to see yourself the way I see you.'

Hannah glanced down. Her skin was shockingly pale in the dark room. Her nipples tilted up, puckering in the cold air. They were dark coral, contrasting against the swell of her shell-pink breasts. She had a long scar running down her right arm where she was cut in a brutal knife fight against a viscount who murdered his maid. The healed wound shone pearlescent in the muted light. Her ribs were still purple from a left elbow Philippa threw in their last sparring match. Her right leg was peppered with crescent scars from shotgun pellets.

How did he see her? Certainly not a blushing maid or a confident seductress.

'I'm hardly a gently bred lady.' Hannah wouldn't break eye contact. He wanted to see her without her armour? Fine. He could look his fill at all her defects. She refused to be ashamed of her body. It might not be soft and lush. It might not be smooth and perfect. But she was strong and resilient and true.

Killian shook his head. 'No. Warriors can't be gentle. Do you want to know what I see?'

No.

Hannah swallowed her fear. 'Yes.'

'I see a fierce goddess with strength and scars borne from battle. I see a delicate woman who could destroy me with one swipe of her blade. I see someone meant to be free, who would fly on wings of light if she could.'

'Don't.' His beautiful words ripped holes in her heart, making her bleed. He saw too much, but none of it was true. He described a stranger, a far cry from the woman she was. She fought to keep her voice steady. 'I'm no goddess. I'm about as delicate as a steam train, and if I tried to fly, I would drop like a stone.

Men say any number of pretty deceits to seduce women. Don't lie to me.'

Killian's lips tipped up at the corners. His teeth flashed white in the shadowed room. 'I can't lie to you. It's a real problem.' He pulled his shirt out from his pants. 'You are full of treasures, Hannah. I won't take your gifts unless you give them to me.'

Killian began unbuttoning his shirt.

Alarm thrilled through her as he revealed more of his torso. 'What are you doing?'

'I'm warm.'

When he reached the last button, he pulled his shirt over his head and let it drop next to the chair. Hannah lifted her gaze from the white silk clumped on the carpet to take in Killian's naked chest. He called her a goddess, but Killian was the one who resembled the statues of Olympian heroes. Thick muscles flexed in his upper arms as he rested his elbows against the armrest. His nipples were dark, flat disks in a wide chest sprinkled with black hair. Hannah's gaze lowered to where his stomach separated into eight defined ridges of hard flesh. His hair was thicker below his belly button, creating a trail disappearing into his breeches.

'Bollocks,' she hissed.

'Yes. They are becoming quite a problem.' Killian's words were playful, but his voice was rough with need. 'You told me you found your pearl. Show me. Touch yourself for me.'

Hannah stiffened. 'I can't. That's not...' Her face grew warm as moisture pooled low. Just the idea of playing with herself in front of him was equally embarrassing and erotic.

'You can say no. If you don't want to touch yourself.' He shrugged, and his gaze lowered to the dark thatch of hair between her legs.

Hannah's core tingled. What she must look like to him, so exposed, so vulnerable? She ached to rub the tight bud of flesh pulsing with need. To feel the soft friction of her finger against that cluster of nerves. 'I want to.' Her voice was husky. She didn't recognise it.

'Then, touch yourself, Hannah. Touch yourself and let me watch you.'

This was not a moment for anxiety to steal her pleasure. She was a woman who rushed into dangerous situations when others might run away. She could do this. She wanted to do this. Blast and damn, she practiced this moment alone, in her room, the previous night and thought about Killian every scintillating second. This was her chance to show him what she learned.

Hannah let her hand trail over the dip of her waist, tickling the sensitive skin of her belly as she delved lower. Killian hissed in a breath. She had captured this powerful man. He was mesmerised. His gaze locked onto her pale hand as her fingers tangled in the hair covering her intimate flesh before dipping between the soft folds hiding her clitoris. She curled her index finger, brushing the pad against the tight bundle where sweet sparks of sensation coalesced. What a wonder that she could bring herself such pleasure. She never knew it was possible. Until he showed her. Closing her eyes, she moaned.

'Don't close your eyes. Look at me. Keep looking at me.'

His voice was a line holding her steady in a storm of need. She opened her eyes and locked her gaze with his. He was beautiful. His face tightened with desire. His full lips parted as his chest rose and fell in heavy breaths. Tightening his grip on the armrest, his muscles corded, the firelight creating shadows in the ridges and dips of his powerful body.

Hannah rubbed harder, her fingers growing wet from passion. She reached up with her free hand, palming her breast, then pinching her nipple. Killian exhaled a curse. She couldn't stop the slow smile, knowing her movements controlled his pleasure. It was a heady feeling to hold Killian in her thrall.

She focused on the sensation of her finger sliding over her bud as wave after wave crashed over her, sucking her deeper into a whirlpool of aching need. Knowing her desire only increased his, she grew bold, undulating her hips.

He unbuttoned the fall of his breeches, and Hannah almost lost her rhythm as his cock sprang out, thick, long, and hard.

'Don't stop.' His gravelled voice scraped over her senses. He wrapped his fingers around his shaft, pumping his hand down to the broad base where black hair hid the rest of him from view. His tip seeped a bead of liquid. Their bodies were weeping for each other.

She dipped a finger deeper, coating it in her slickness before returning to her nub in small, devastating circles.

She moaned, so close to the shining pinnacle.

'Let go. Come for me, Hannah.' His green eyes were almost black in the shadowed room. He bared his teeth like a feral animal as his hand moved faster.

Hannah closed her eyes and lost herself to the raging brilliance. She cried out and flattened her hand, grinding the heel of her palm against her clitoris, needing more. Wanting everything. Drunk on her own power and his devastating need.

Killian cursed in a voice full of awe.

As her orgasm dissipated, Hannah's legs turned to jelly. She dropped to the floor, the cold wood pressing against her hot thighs and bottom. She leaned on her arm and let the glory of her crisis echo through her limbs. But the ache remained, deep and hollow.

His hand still gripped his cock, but he wasn't stroking himself any more. Killian watched her as her breathing slowed.

Hannah cleared her throat. 'My turn.'

* * *

Killian watched sunsets in the Afghan desert that stole his breath with their beauty. He had seen crystal-blue water chase itself along white sand beaches. He stared in wonder as a red kite swooped from the sky only an arm's length away from him. Never had he witnessed anything more stunning than Hannah in the apex of her orgasm.

His brain needed to catch up with his ears. 'Your turn?' He still held his cock in his hand, hard and pulsing, demanding release.

'Yes. You told me to think on the favour I wanted. I've thought about it. I know what I want from you.'

Killian blew out a shaky breath. 'I'm not following.' He was having trouble organising his thoughts.

Hannah reached behind her, pulling at the scrap of material holding the end of her braid. She unwound her hair. Killian was a fool to not have asked her to do that from the start. Long waves of copper shone in the firelight. Her sweet nipples peeked out from the silky strands now covering her breasts.

'I want you.'

Killian watched in fascination as a blush ran down the length of Hannah's entire body. He rubbed his hand over his cock, revelling in the sensation and imagining her tight quim holding him instead of his rough hand. 'You have me. Here I am.'

Hannah pushed up from the floor, the muscles in her arms and legs flexing. Killian had seen his share of naked women in all shapes and sizes. But he'd never encountered a woman with the long, lean muscles Hannah developed by years of hard training. She was a warrior priestess, proud and primal. Her stomach was tight, her legs long and shapely. Her body was sleek and powerful and perfect. Killian wanted to kiss every scar highlighting her courage and pledge his skills in battle to keep her safe. But she didn't need his protection. She was his equal. The only woman he knew who might understand the sins and seduction of his violent life.

Hannah's gaze dipped down to his erection. The tip of her tongue rested in the corner of her mouth. Killian ground his teeth together, willing his body not to betray him.

'No. I don't have you. Not yet. I want to give you the same kind of pleasure you have given me. I want to have sex with you. Properly.' Hannah didn't break eye contact with him, but he knew it took something from her, to ask so boldly and risk so much if he refused her. But how could he ever refuse Hannah Simmons?

Time froze. Details dissolved until it was just Hannah's eyes locked onto him, her red lips parted, her pale body glowing. She was offering him the one thing he wanted more than air. The one thing he promised himself he wouldn't claim. 'No. I told you; I won't take your virginity and walk away.'

Hannah put her hands on her hips. It was a pose he was familiar with but devastatingly more effective when she was naked. 'You're going to renege on our deal? You asked me to think on what favour I wanted, and this is it. You aren't taking my virginity. I'm giving it to you. I don't expect marriage. I don't want your title or your money. I'm not some innocent young girl who believes in romance and love. But I want this.' Her lip trembled, destroying a bit of her displayed bravado.

Hannah was wrong. She was innocent in ways she didn't even know. Every woman dreamt of romance and love. At least, every woman Killian knew. More importantly, she *deserved* romance and love. He couldn't offer her that. His parents had expected him to marry well and continue the dukedom's lineage. He couldn't betray them after everything they'd given him and all the ways he had failed them. He could only give Hannah this moment. It wasn't enough. Not for her.

Hannah narrowed her eyes. 'I'm going to have sex with someone. I want to know what it is to join with a man. I want it to be you, but I'll find someone else if you refuse.'

Killian imagined Hannah naked like this with another man. A dirty, hulking brute who wouldn't realise how fragile she was. Who wouldn't treasure her or take his time. Rage washed through him, as potent as whiskey, burning in his veins. He pushed up from the chair and closed the distance between them, grabbing her arms to hold her still. 'You will not.'

'You don't get to decide what I do. Not now. Not ever.' Hannah pointed her chin in the air with a defiance he both hated and admired. 'You said you wouldn't force me to do anything tonight, and I will extend you the same promise. If you don't want me, you are free to walk away.'

Killian growled in frustration and tightened his grip. 'Not want you? How could any man not want you? You are all I want. My body aches for you.' He grabbed her hand and pressed it against his cock. 'Can you feel that? How hard I am for you? I could explode from my desire. For you. But I can't give you what you deserve. Don't you see that?'

Hannah smiled. She pulled her hand away from his hard flesh and cupped his cheek, a painfully gentle gesture. In the muted light, her amber eyes shone like the heart of a fire. 'You may not be what I deserve, but you are what I want.'

Damn his soul. He wasn't strong enough to resist her. 'Be careful what you ask for, Hannah.'

'I'm always careful. Do you agree to my terms? Will you grant me this favour?'

He bit out a laugh. 'I'm not granting you any favours by bedding you. I'm taking your innocence. I won't have you pay me for the privilege with the information you shared. I'm a blackguard and a libertine; don't make me a whore as well.' The brutal truth of his words echoed in the darkness. He pressed his mouth against hers in a kiss tasting of desperation.

She pulled away, cupping his other cheek to bracket his face between her hands. 'You are courageous and honourable and kind. You are taking nothing from me that I don't freely give. Don't paint this moment with shame.'

He would never be strong enough to deny Hannah. He couldn't give her a future, but if this night was all they had, he would damn well make it worthy of her. A moment she could look back on with joy. A memory they would both hold in the secret caverns of their hearts for whatever dark days lay ahead.

He softened his kiss, licking the seam of her lips and tasting her depths as she opened to him. Sweeping her up in his arms, he pressed her warm body against his. Striding to the bed, he lay her gently on the covers. She scooted back, making room for him.

Stripping off his breeches, socks, and boots, he climbed on the bed and stretched his body next to hers, naked.

'I want to touch you. May I?' Hannah bit her lip. Every question she asked flayed another layer from his scarred heart.

'You can do whatever you want.' Killian put both hands behind his head to stop him from taking control of the moment. If she needed to learn his body, he would give her time or implode from the effort.

He clenched his jaw against the sweet torture of her fingers feathering across his skin. She sat up, running her hands over his shoulders, down his chest. When she circled his nipples with her thumbs, he groaned, closing his eyes, and revelling in the pressure. Her soft touch was replaced with wet heat, and his eyes flew open to see the top of her head as she licked him.

'God, woman. You'll undo me before we've even started.'

Hannah's chuckle was low and sweet. 'A duke undone, scandalous.'

She moved her explorations lower, and Killian tried to think of anything but her breath tickling his chest hair, her hands bumping over his stomach muscles as she moved closer to his throbbing cock.

When she wrapped her strong fingers around his erect penis, her exhalation of wonder washed across his over-sensitised skin, and Killian wondered if he could die from pleasure.

'I didn't think it would be so hard and silky at once. How is that possible?'

Killian had no clue. He couldn't remember his own name, let alone explain the mysteries of the male body. His cock pulsed as she stroked him tentatively.

'Does it feel good when I do this?' Her eyes were huge, her brows arched.

'Yes.' Killian ground out, thinking of cold winters, wet dogs, three-day-old porridge. Anything but her pale hand wrapped around his ruddy flesh. When she squeezed, Killian jerked. He grabbed her wrist, holding her hand steady. 'You're killing me, Hannah.'

In a quick motion, he flipped them so she was beneath him. 'I wanted to give you control, but I won't last if you keep this up.' He pressed his mouth against hers, plunging his tongue into her dark wetness as his fingers found her slit, sliding over the soft folds, seeking her pearl.

She cried out, and Killian made slow circles with his finger, nipping her bottom lip. He needed her wet and ready. He had never ravaged a virgin, but he knew it could be painful if a woman wasn't already lost to her own pleasure. He wouldn't allow himself to hurt Hannah. Not now. Not ever.

Moving down her body, he sucked a ripe nipple into his mouth, swirling his tongue over the rigid flesh. Hannah cried out again, but he gave her no mercy. He nipped, licked, and suckled one breast, then moved to the other. Her body tightened beneath him. Slowly, he pushed his finger deeper into her cleft, feeling her intimate muscles clench. She was so goddamn tight. There was no way he could enter her. Not without a measure of pain. His soul ached at the thought, but it only increased his determination to make this moment right for her.

14

Drowning in desire, Hannah longed to sink deeper. Killian's mouth, hot and insistent on her breast, sucked her into the heart of longing. His finger quested further into her, burning sweetly as her body tightened around him. She didn't know how he would fit inside her, but she was determined to find out. There was sure to be pain, but she was well acquainted with suffering. Never had it been so glorious.

'I don't want to hurt you.' Concern created a crease between his eyebrows. His voice was strained as his arms flexed. Removing his finger from her core, he put both hands on either side of her head, pulling himself back and watching her. Hannah moaned at the loss.

She arched her body, widening her thighs to make room for him. Wrapping her legs around his hips, she trapped him, ensuring he couldn't pull away. Her core was empty and aching. She drew him closer to her, the steel ridge of his erection nudging her wet, slick flesh. His cock slid over her throbbing clitoris.

'I don't care if you hurt me. I want you. I need you.' *I love you.* Hannah bit her lip to stop the words. But it was true. She was in love with Killian. The realisation penetrated her with the power of a punch. And he was going to hurt her. Not tonight, not with what they shared in this moment, but when he left. She would be devastated. Philippa was right. Hannah had been lying. She wanted all of him, forever. But it was impossible.

So, she would settle for all of him now, and forever could bugger off. The beauty of this moment would dull the edges of that knife as it cut into her heart. 'Now, Killian. I need you now.'

He plunged into her, hard and swift. Something tore, and Hannah's body tensed. 'Bloody hell,' she hissed. He tried to pull out, but she clenched her legs around him. 'Don't move. Just let me...' Their breaths were ragged, and his body shuddered as they stayed frozen in the moment. His cock was huge inside her, forcing untried muscles to stretch and burn.

Slowly, her body began to relax, easing around his invasion. She shifted her hips.

'Fuck,' Killian groaned near her ear. 'I can't...'

'It's okay. I'm okay.' Hannah rubbed her hands down his back, feeling his muscles like granite. She tilted her pelvis as the bright burn eased to something softer, and Killian pressed a gentle kiss to her temple. Hannah tilted up again. He caught her rhythm, slow and steady. His cock slid through her tight channel, each thrust hitting something sharp and sweet in her centre. 'Yes,' she breathed.

Time evaporated into the plunging beat of his hips, the staccato whisper of their breaths, the slap of skin against skin. He pushed harder, faster, the pleasure of each pulse merging into a symphony of sensation. Hannah shoved up with her hips as he thrust deeper. She cried out, shattering into a thousand brilliant pieces. Her core clenched around him as her soul flew high and bright, a shooting star soaring into the ether.

He grew impossibly larger and pulled out of her at the last

moment, his hips still thrusting as he gripped himself and stroked down hard once, then twice. His body shuddered, and he pulsed his essence onto the sheets beside her.

Hannah fell back on her pillow, replete.

'Blast and damn,' she breathed. 'That was brilliant. Can we do that again?'

Killian collapsed next to her. His chest rumbled with laughter. 'Not yet.'

They lay together on the bed, and he reached over, twining his fingers with hers. 'Are you well?'

Hannah wanted to stretch like a cat. It wasn't what she imagined. She thought it would be soft and ethereal and sweet. But what they did was base and raw and vital. It was so much better than she dreamed. 'Yes, very. Are you?'

Instead of answering her, he stood and retrieved a cloth from her nightstand. Filling the bowl with water, he dipped the cloth, squeezed it out, and returned to the bed.

'Open your legs.'

Hannah felt suddenly shy.

He smiled and put a heavy hand on her knee, slowly pushing her legs apart. 'I want to tend to you. You must be sore. And there's blood.'

Hannah got up on her elbows and looked down her body where he gently laved her sensitive skin with the cold cloth. It was heavenly. The white cotton came away stained with blood. Not nearly as much as she'd shed when Philippa once broke her nose, but this was her maidenhead.

Oddly, she was more worried about him. She felt glorious, but he seemed too quiet. 'You didn't answer me. Are you okay?' Hannah asked, lifting her gaze to his, but he looked intently at the cloth. When she reached out and ran her hand down his cheek rough with stubble, he glanced up. His fingers brushing over a puckered scar on her thigh.

'How did you get this?'

Hannah smiled. 'An angry earl who failed at murdering his wife attempted to dissuade me from delivering him to a boat bound for the Americas.'

Killian's eyes darkened and his jaw twitched, but his hand stayed gentle as he skimmed it up her leg. His thumb rubbed over the peppering of scars on her thigh 'What about these?'

Scar by scar, he asked, and she told him, revealing her secrets far more slowly than she had her body. Because it was harder. And with each recounted tale, she expected judgment, disgust, or revulsion at the violence she had endured or exacted. But Killian just moved on to the next scar, his hands worshiping her, his eyes unfathomable pools.

'Will you tell me about this? Now?' His fingers brushed over the mark on her cheek.

Hannah wanted to recoil, but after the beauty of what they shared, and his eyes looking so vulnerable and desperate, she needed to give him something. It wasn't a treasure, but it was a hidden piece of herself she had shared with no one. Not even Philippa. Her darkest secret. The moment that made her a monster.

But she wanted him to know. Because if he could accept that part of her, then everything between them would change.

She moved over and pulled open the sheet for him to join her in the bed. He climbed under the covers and wrapped himself around her, his chest pressed against her back. It was easier to tell him like this, not having to watch his face, cocooned in the warmth and strength of his body. Hannah kept her voice soft, as if whispering the truth would make it less real. She was swept back to that night, ten years ago when everything changed.

* * *

Lord Smythe was already angry when he arrived for dinner. Hannah could tell by the stiff set of his shoulders and his clenched jaw.

Cynthia tried to send Hannah upstairs, but Lord Smythe told her to stay. He poured Hannah wine even though Cynthia said she was too young. When her mother reached over to take the glass away, he slapped Cynthia. Right across the face.

Hannah started crying, like a stupid, useless child. Hardly the protector her mother needed. But Cynthia smiled carefully around her split lip and said everything would be fine.

It wasn't fine.

'Your mother was once renowned for her beauty. There wasn't a duke, earl, or viscount who didn't want her. Did you know that?' Lord Smythe asked.

Hannah didn't know how to respond. She looked to her mother for help, but Cynthia was staring at her plate, her cheeks pale except for the ugly red mark of Lord Smythe's hand.

Hannah cleared the fear from her throat and spoke softly. 'I know she is as beautiful now as she ever was.'

Lord Smythe laughed. An ugly sound in the quiet room. The fire crackled in the hearth, and the clink of cutlery scraped against porcelain.

'The bloom is off her rose, but your flower is only beginning to bud.' His words slurred. Grease from the beef was smeared on his cheek.

'Perhaps we should send the child to bed, my love.' Blood trickled from her mother's mouth.

'No.' Lord Smythe drank deeply from his wine glass and licked his lips. 'She's not a child any longer. Fourteen is old enough to marry her off. That's what you wanted, right? But it's difficult to sell the daughter of a whore. Even one with conquests as lofty as yours.' He sneered at Cynthia.

Her mother put down her fork and carefully wiped the blood from her split lip. 'This is not a discussion we should have now. I think you should leave.'

Lord Smythe narrowed his eyes and cracked his knuckles. He twisted the signet ring on his pinkie around and around. 'You mean to dismiss me?'

Hannah picked up the dinner knife. She didn't know what she would do with it, but it felt better to have something sharp in her hand. Her heart pounded. Her breath came fast and hard. She would not cry again. She would not be a weak infant when her mother needed a fearless defender.

'Hannah, it's time for you to go to bed.' Cynthia's eyes were wild, even if her voice was calm.

'No, Mama. Not until he leaves.' Hannah pressed the knife against the folds of her skirt.

'You think you can send me away?' Lord Smythe smiled at Hannah. His eyes were glittering chips of obsidian, cold and hard. 'You're just like your mother. But I decide if and when I leave.' He surged to his feet, smashing his glass of wine on the table, and shattering the crystal. A shard flew fast and sharp, slicing Hannah's cheek. She didn't feel any pain, just the warm blood flowing down her skin. 'No woman dismisses me. Certainly no bastard child of a whore.'

Lord Smythe grabbed Hannah by the wrist, dragging her off her chair and pulling her close. His fingers dug into her skin, but she was numb. Time slowed. She tightened her fingers around the knife handle.

'You'll never be a proper wife, but perhaps I can teach you how to be as talented a mistress as your mother.'

Cynthia screamed, lunging forward, and trying to pull him away.

The baron shoved Hannah away and punched her mother hard in the face. The impact propelled Cynthia into the mantel with a sickening thump. She crumpled to the floor.

Hannah cried out and tried to reach her mother. Lord Smythe blocked Hannah's path. Before she could push past him, he grabbed a handful of her hair, pulling her back. 'You have more fight in you than your mother. I like that.'

His wet lips smashed against hers as bile burned her throat and panic beat against her chest like the wings of a trapped bird.

She couldn't think. She had to make him stop. She had to get to her mother. Gripping the knife in her shaking fist, she plunged the blade into his neck. Blood flowed hot and sticky over her hand as she pushed him away.

Lord Smythe looked at her with wide eyes. His red face turned paler with each heartbeat. A keening scream rent the air, but the baron wasn't making any noise. Her eyes widened in horror as pink froth bubbled from his mouth. The haunting cry continued, only hitching when she took a ragged breath.

'No, no, no.' Her voice was too loud, too sharp, too jagged. She was shaking. She needed to stop the blood from pouring out of Lord Smythe, but how?

He fell to the ground in a heap of fine black silk.

'No, no, no.' She tripped over the baron in her haste to reach her mother's still form.

Hannah rolled Cynthia over. Her mother's eyes were open and sightless. There was a gash on Cynthia's temple where she'd hit the mantel, the cut bright crimson against her pale skin.

This wasn't happening. This couldn't be happening.

'Mama. Wake up.' Hannah shook her mother's shoulder. Once

bluer than a cloudless sky, Cynthia's eyes were oddly opaque in the firelight. 'Please, Mama!'

Hannah wrapped her arms around her mother, rocking back and forth as the fire burned down to coals.

* * *

Hannah stayed silent for a moment, waiting for Killian to respond. But he didn't say a word. He just held her in his arms.

'I don't regret killing him. I would go back and do it again. I would make him scream.' Her voice shook, but Killian only tightened his grip around her. 'My soul is surely destined to burn for all eternity, and even then, I won't regret killing Raymond Smythe.' She thought she would feel guilt, or shame. But what filled her chest was overwhelming relief. A tear tracked down her cheek and she took a shaky breath. After so very long of keeping her worst sin a secret, she felt free.

'I wish you hadn't killed him.' His voice was hard and cold.

The bubble of joy growing inside her cracked at Killian's harsh words. Hannah tried to pull away from him. Now came the judgment. Now came the damnation and rejection she deserved. But he pulled her tighter against him, tucking her body into the hard shell of his own.

'I wish you hadn't killed him, so I could hunt the bastard down and kill him myself. Slowly.' His breath caressed her hair, and his violent words swept away her disgrace.

'You don't think I'm a demon?' She didn't want to care about his answer, but it meant everything.

'No more than I am. Or any human put in that situation. Not many have the courage to fight like you, Hannah. But we all hope for it. We all pray for the strength to do what we must when we must.'

'Thank you,' she whispered because it felt like a benediction.

'I think you should marry me.'

Hannah burst into laughter. 'You can't be serious. I bet you propose to all the girls who confess their murders to you.'

Killian loosened his hold so she could turn and face him. 'A duke doesn't say something unless he means it.'

Sitting up, Hannah took the blanket with her, tucking it under her arm. 'Why?'

Could he want her for her? Knowing her sins, her lack of pedigree, her scarred body and blackened soul? Seeing everything but still loving her?

Killian mirrored her pose, sitting next to her. 'Because I understand you, Hannah. And more importantly because I compromised you. I was a man of honour once. You may not have a father to demand I make good on my actions, but I had one who would expect nothing less of me.'

Ah. Well. That hurts more than I expected.

He wanted to marry her. Not because she shared the most vulnerable pieces of her past and risked her heart. Not because he wanted her. Not because he loved her. But because he didn't want to become a libertine.

Moments before, Hannah was filled with light. Incandescently happy. Then Killian opened his stupid mouth and ruined everything. Anger poisoned her joy. Of course he didn't want to marry her because he needed her. He didn't want to marry her because the thought of being separated was untenable. He didn't want to marry her because he was desperately in love. He wanted to marry her to avoid besmirching his warped sense of integrity.

'You are a bloody idiot,' Hannah fumed.

His shoulders stiffened.

Hannah ripped the blankets off, jumped out of the bed, and began to pace. In her anger, she lost all modesty.

His lips were pressed tight, and he stared at his knees. The bloody stubborn brute wouldn't even look at her.

'What is wrong with you?' Hannah came back to the bed, kneeling next to him on the mattress. She couldn't believe he was reducing this moment to something as cold and heartless as obligation.

Killian's eyes snapped to hers. 'Everything is wrong with me. The war took most of my honour, Hannah. It stripped me of everything noble. I came back knowing any valiant ideal or decent action I had taken in my youth was a lie. There was no good left in me. You have lived the last ten years thinking you were a fiend for killing a man who deserved death. But I know the beast that lives inside of me. That would claw and maim and consume anyone in my path, regardless of their guilt or innocence. When your mother was threatened, you fought and suffered and bled trying to protect her.'

'And I failed. I failed and she died.' Hannah felt the brutal edge of a blade that never stopped drawing blood.

'You didn't fail. But I did. I watched my men be tortured, starved, and killed. I watched them being chained like dogs. They made me witness every atrocity they committed, and I did nothing to stop it.' His voice was ragged. Tears streaked down his cheeks. 'I came home horrified that I still lived when so many better men died. I promised myself I would make what was left of my life worth their sacrifice. I would reclaim my honour. I would do whatever I must to become the man of worth my father raised.'

Her heart ached for him, and that tempered her rage. Hannah put both hands on either side of his face, kissing him gently. While her body carried a myriad of healed scars, his wounds were still bleeding beneath the surface.

'Killian, you cannot possibly carry the weight of so much blame. What happened in that horrible war resulted from stupid, powerful men making bad decisions. You are one person who did the very best he could in an impossible situation. You are the man of honour your father raised.'

He covered her hands with his. 'My father loved my mother with his entire soul. He taught me to treat women with respect above all else. Don't you understand that's why I am making this proposal? What kind of blackguard would I be to ruin you and not offer marriage?'

Something fragile and bright broke within Hannah. She let her hands drop and sat back on her heels. 'Ruin me? Because all that makes me worthy is my maidenhead? Do you truly believe that?'

He didn't say anything. But he also looked away from her. Unable to refute her words.

Hannah shook her head. 'And you wonder why I think you're an idiot. By not making this ridiculous offer, you would be the kind of man who understands you did nothing to me I didn't allow. You would be the kind of man who knows marriage offered from obligation does not honour your parents' memory. It does not honour me. What would your parents think about you marrying the bastard daughter of a hired mistress? A woman who pays her way in blood? A woman you only offered to marry because of a misguided understanding of valour?'

He threw back the covers, stood up, and walked to the mantle where the fire had burned down to coals. Hannah tried to memorise the curves and lines of his body. This might be her last chance to see him naked. Her last chance to see him so vulnerable.

'They would understand that sometimes we make sacrifices for the greater good. You are not the duchess they would have chosen, but neither am I their honourable son if I abandon you.' Desperation roughened his voice, but she no longer cared. His words fell like stones, each one breaking something new within her. He was decimating her with every syllable.

Because he was the duke she would have chosen. Not despite his flaws, but because of them. She wanted to marry him not for honour, or obligation, or some fucked up perspective on propriety. She wanted to marry him because she wanted him in her life, every moment of every day. She wanted to marry him because he understood the darkness inside of her, and she understood his. She wanted to marry him because she loved him.

But he didn't love her.

He was offering for her out of guilt and obligation. It wasn't enough. It would never be enough.

She blinked back sudden tears. 'I am not the duchess they would have wanted, but you're willing to overlook that to redeem yourself? You would make the sacrifice of marrying me to preserve the greater good of your own honour? Heavens, how could I possibly refuse such a romantic offer?'

'Marriage isn't about romance.'

'Well it bloody well should be! You are missing the point, Killian. A marriage forced upon us by duty and regret over one night of passion would destroy everything good between us.' Hannah's voice broke, and she hated the weakness. She wanted him to see the ugliness of his proposal. The brutal betrayal this was to her and what they had shared.

Killian flinched. He ran his hand through his black curls, his bicep flexing. 'I am trying to redeem myself. How can I do that by becoming a feckless rogue? By taking your innocence and abandoning you?'

Hannah laughed, though nothing about this conversation was funny. 'I've never been innocent, Killian. And your proposal is hardly honourable. If the beauty we shared together tonight ruins me in your eyes unless we marry, then consider me utterly ruined.

I am certainly not duchess material. And I refuse to marry any man who is only asking for my hand in order to ensure his own honour.' She struggled for breath and battled back the tears.

Killian stood frozen, like a stone carving of a tortured god. 'What choice do you give me in this? I will not be a worthless rake, but you won't marry me!' he roared.

'No. I won't. Because I have a much higher estimation of my worth than a sullied woman who needs to be saved,' Hannah threw back. Fighting was so much easier than acknowledging her pain. 'This proposal mocks what marriage should be. What your parents' marriage exemplified. It will only breed hatred and contempt between us. I asked you for tonight. You gave me this gift. Let's leave it at that.'

Killian laughed harshly. 'So, I just walk away?'

Hannah's heart shattered. *No. You stay. Forever. You marry me because you want me, and I want you and society and its expectations can go hang. You marry me for love, not this twisted version of nobility.* 'Yes. I think that's the only way forward.'

His shirt was still on the floor next to the chair. He walked to it, picked it up, and pulled it over his head. With an economy of movement highlighting his physical prowess, he collected the rest of his clothes and dressed in silence. Hannah should have re-donned her nightgown but couldn't bring herself to move from the bed.

Killian looked at her. The wind had picked up, wailing through the trees in a melancholy lament. 'Good night.'

There was so much she wanted to say. 'I won't forget this night, Killian. Or you.'

He smiled, but his eyes stayed distant. 'Liar.'

Killian turned, opened the door, and slipped into the hallway. The door closed with a quiet click.

* * *

Killian woke up too early. He wanted to remain in a state of unconsciousness indefinitely, but fate and the bloody footman had other plans. The insidious man knocked at seven in the morning, holding a silver tray with a letter sitting in the centre. Killian swiped the letter and slammed the door before returning to his bed.

The previous night went horribly wrong. First, it was indescribably perfect, then it was a living nightmare. And he was entirely to blame.

Insufferable idiot! She shared her deepest secret with me, and I fucked everything up.

Why did he make his proposal about obligation?

Because I'm too scared to make it about love.

There was nothing quite so horrifying as self-realisation on an empty stomach at seven in the morning.

Killian ripped open the letter and unfolded the paper. He scanned the poorly scrawled script before stopping to read it over again.

'Bloody fucking hell.' It was from the proprietor of the Crown and Bull. Young Billy Bright had paid the establishment a visit. He was looking for the barmy toff who liked to hang out near the shitters. He had important information to share. According to the letter, the capricious youth would return to the Crown and Bull one week hence at six in the evening. Killian checked the date on the letter. 'Fucking bloody hell!' It had been written four days ago. London was two days ride from Berkshire. Killian needed to leave immediately and ride hard if he were to reach the Crown and Bull on the morrow at the set time. Master Bright said he would stay for thirty minutes, and then he was leaving. According to the letter, the daft bastard – that was Killian – could go stuff himself if he wasn't there by the determined time. Killian guessed the owner of the Crown and Bull derived great pleasure in penning the mischievous lad's words verbatim.

Killian dressed and tugged on the bell pull. His valet opened the door a few minutes later. 'Wake up Drake. Tell him we must leave for London. Immediately.' Killian walked to the desk and pulled out a fresh piece of parchment. He wrote a hasty note. 'Give this to Miss Simmons when she wakes.' Killian almost shoved the man out of his room as he continued readying for what would be a long day.

* * *

Killian and Drake rode hard, changing horses three times at coaching inns along the way and sleeping for a few hours at a common lodging house near Bray before reaching London and the Crown and Bull.

The wooden beams were stained with over a hundred years of smoke from the hearth fire, cigars, and pipes. Heavy furniture with thick upholstery was crammed into the crowded room, making it feel cosy.

They were sipping their second round of pints when a dirty hand reached out and snagged Killian's glass.

'Caw, this running round after coves is thirsty work.' Master Bright slurped deeply before Killian relieved him of his pilfered beer.

'I received your note.' Killian kept the humour out of his tone with difficulty. The brazen boy slumped into an empty chair and eyed Drake's pint glass.

'Don't even think about it.' Drake's deep rumble would have scared the wits out of most children, but the boy just gave him a cheeky wink. Drake's lips twitched.

Before Killian could quiz the lad, their food arrived. The smell of warm bread and roasted pork inspired a hungry growl from Killian's belly.

The boy's eyes widened as large as saucers. He licked his chapped lips. Killian could see the bones poking through Master Bright's thin shirt.

He pushed his roast pork and potatoes across the table. 'Eat.'

The boy didn't wait for Killian to change his mind. He grabbed a spoon and dove into the food with alarming focus.

Drake raised an eyebrow at Killian. He knew better than Killian the demon of hunger clawing from a man's belly, consuming his heart, and picking away at his mind until every thought dissolved into a singular need to find sustenance.

The boy made quick work of the meal, picking up the plate and licking it clean. He plunked it back on the table, sat back in his chair, rested his hands over his full belly, and burped. 'Could'a used more salt, those potatoes.'

Drake's bark of laughter surprised them all.

'You called us here, Master Bright. What information do you have that's so important I raced pell-mell across England to answer your summons?' Killian raised an eyebrow at the boy.

'You told me to come 'ere if I 'ad any information. Well. I got some. If you don't wannit, I'll be on me way.' The boy started to stand until Killian put a hand on his shoulder. Both men noticed the lad flinch. He was a courageous child, full of piss and vinegar, but beneath the dirt were bruises and behind the bravado was fear. No one grew up on the streets of Bethnal Green without feeling the bite of a fist from someone larger and stronger, and Master Bright was still a small boy.

Killian slowly removed his hand. 'You needn't fear us. Drake might look like a monster, but he screams like a banshee if a spider crawls over his hand.'

The boy looked at Drake, his mouth quirked. 'I don't like roaches. Me mum says there's nuffink wrong with steering clear of creepy crawlies.'

'She sounds like a wise woman.' Drake nodded. He hadn't touched his pie. Instead, he wrapped it in a cloth and pushed it over to the boy.

His hand snaked out to the wrapped pie, and he slipped it off the table and onto his lap.

'Well, Billy Bright, what information do you have for us?' Killian's heart cracked a little as Billy bit his lip, assessing the men. Trust wasn't easy for the lad.

The boy puffed out his cheeks and exhaled loudly, a little man with the weight of the world on his slight shoulders. 'Sarah's friend, Penny, came round to see me mum and dad.'

'When exactly?' Killian leaned forward.

Billy scowled at him. 'I ain't no calendar, am I? It must 'ave been two weeks ago, Sunday, because Mum was doing the weekly bake. She always bakes our loaf of bread on Sunday.' One loaf of bread to feed an entire family for a week. It was no wonder the boy was small for his age. 'They thought I was asleep, but I wasn't. It's hard to sleep sometimes. So's I listened to 'em talking. Penny worked with Sarah before...' His chin quivered, and he cleared his throat. Drake scooted his beer closer to the boy, motioning to the glass.

'Have a sip, lad. Wet that tickle in your throat.' Drake looked over the boy's head at Killian. Killian knew what he was thinking. There had to be something they could do to help this young lad. Surely, they could find a job for Billy. Work that kept his belly full and his hands busy.

The boy took a small gulp of beer. 'Penny brung some of Sarah's things. I fink me mum 'oped she would find the necklace she gave Sarah, but it weren't there. But that's not why I came 'ere.'

Killian forced himself to remain quiet. Billy liked to tell a tale in his own time. He wouldn't appreciate being interrupted again.

'Penny told Mum and Dad summink that night.'

The suspense was killing Killian. Drake leaned forward.

'She said Sarah was excited 'bout an in'erview for a new job. Me mum and dad knew all that, but then Penny told 'em summink else.' Billy went quiet, drawing circles on the table with a dirty finger.

'What? What did she tell them?' Killian couldn't stop the questions from bursting forth.

The boy looked up, his ancient eyes shrewd. 'What's it worth to you?'

15

———

Hannah would not read the note. Again. The folds in the paper were becoming alarmingly thin. She could recite it from memory.

Killian had been gone two days. He wouldn't return for another two if his note was true.

Hannah pulled the parchment from her pocket and ran her fingers over the ink on the front. His long, clever fingers had formed six simple letters.

Hannah

She wouldn't think about what things those fingers had done to her.

Thank God Philippa had left the same morning Killian did. Hannah would never be able to hide her feelings, and she had done the one thing she promised Philippa she wouldn't. She'd fallen in love, putting her stupid heart and her fickle happiness in grave danger.

No good could come from this. Killian might hold her heart in his hands, but what future would they have? Their night together was transformational, but it was also a soul-rendering lesson in impossibilities.

For a shining moment, Hannah had thought perhaps she could have it all. Love, friendship, a family. But then reality crashed in right when he began blathering about making sacrifices for the greater good. Adding painful insult to emotional injury, instead of meeting with her the next day, offering profuse apologies and professing his undying love, the bastard beat a hasty retreat to London.

A single note didn't repair the damage. And yet Hannah couldn't stop wondering what was in his mind when he penned the insidious words capturing her thoughts and distracting her from the mission the blasted Queen of bloody England expected her to complete.

My dearest Hannah,

Last night was more than I could have hoped for and far less than you deserved. I must leave immediately for London on business, but I shall return the day of the ball and hope you will reserve a waltz for me. There is much we must discuss. Until then, I will hold you in my thoughts.

Killian

His damnable missive created a world of questions with no answers. What did he think she deserved? Would he offer it? Why did he return to London? Was it about Sarah Bright? What on earth did he wish to discuss with her? Most importantly, while she might engage his thoughts, did any part of her capture his heart?

Betty broke into Hannah's maudlin thoughts. She bobbed a quick curtsey, almost losing her cap.

'Good morning, miss. Miss Cavendale and Miss Whittenburg

are in the main salon if you'd like to join them?' The maid clutched her hands together over her crisp apron.

'You look worried, Betty. Is anything amiss?'

Betty untangled her fingers and smoothed her hands over her skirt. 'It's only... you don't seem yourself, miss. If you don't mind me saying.'

Hannah huffed out a breath and turned to the looking glass. Betty stepped closer and began twisting Hannah's hair in a neat chignon with tendrils framing her face. Hannah's cheeks were pale, her eyes were unfocused, and her brown dress was ever so... brown. 'I don't feel myself, Betty.'

'It's no wonder. After everything you've been through. Do you miss him?' Betty immediately slapped a hand over her mouth. She spoke through her fingers. 'It's only I know I shall miss Sam terribly when we leave. We've only known each other a few days, but it feels like forever. I can't imagine how hard it must be for you.'

After Hannah's night with Killian, Betty stripped Hannah's bed and laundered her linens. She would have noticed the blood. And known the cause. In a way, it was a relief for Hannah to be able to share her misery with someone.

Hannah smiled, but she felt a hundred years old. 'Yes, Betty. I imagine I do miss him. The insufferable bastard.'

'Is he coming back?'

'He says so.'

Betty shook her head like a school marm scolding a naughty child. 'Lady Philippa will make him do right by you, miss. She'd shoot him dead before letting him abandon you.'

Hannah wiped the tear rolling down her cheek. 'That's just it, Betty. I don't want him if he must be forced.'

Betty patted Hannah's shoulder. In lieu of words, she clucked her tongue in a comforting sound. Hannah wanted to dissolve into a puddle of misery. But wallowing would accomplish nothing.

Hannah stood, brushing out her skirts. 'I'll be fine, Betty. Don't worry about me. Could you please let the ladies know I shall join them in half an hour? You can tell them I decided to have a lie-in this morning. There's work to be done, and I've let myself be distracted for too long.'

Betty nodded and bustled out of Hannah's room.

Hannah tucked her note away and straightened her shoulders. The men had gone on a hunting trip, and the other ladies were in the village shopping. The house was empty save Ivy and Millie. She might not get another opportunity to search the bedrooms. She would start with the most likely candidate: Lord Cavendale. Perhaps he kept some incriminating correspondence tucked away in his private chambers.

Hannah walked swiftly down the hallway. Alfred had a suite of rooms closer to his father, and at the far end of the eastern wing was Lord Cavendale's door. Before she was halfway down the corridor, she heard the unmistakable clack of shoes on the wood floor. If anyone found her in the family wing, there were sure to be questions. Questions she would struggle to answer. She ducked into Alfred's suite of rooms and quietly shut the door behind her.

Betty had been keeping track of the servants' schedules. This late in the morning, they should have completed their tasks in the bedrooms and be having their breakfasts or working in the public areas of the house. Part of being good at Hannah's job was improvising when things didn't go to plan. She was already there. She might as well do a little snooping before she risked venturing back into the hallway. After Alfred's abominable behaviour toward Killian, she wouldn't mind finding him guilty of a crime.

Hannah crept deeper into Alfred's private domain.

The space was silent and still.

Hannah explored his sitting room first. It was organised more like a private office than a place to sip tea and read books. The activities of men differed greatly from women. So full of purpose and intent while the ladies were expected to needlepoint cushions and paint flowers.

Ridiculous! As if we aren't just as capable. More so in most cases.

Hannah used her irritation to heighten her focus. She searched his desk and found numerous papers, but after scanning them quickly, they were all related to horseflesh.

The drawers weren't locked and contained nothing more nefarious than a secret cache of aniseed drops in a linen bag. So, Alfred had a sweet tooth. Hardly criminal.

She moved on to his closet, then his bedroom. After twenty minutes of industrious investigating, she knew his valet neglected to dust the top shelves of Alfred's closet, and the young man had an alarming addiction to cravats. She counted at least thirty, all in varying shades of snowy white. Unless he was using them to strangle his victims, it hardly helped her cause.

She hadn't really expected to find anything. It was his father whom she suspected, and she was running short on time. Every stray creak or quiet shuffle could be a servant returning to the room or Alfred himself. What a horrible prospect. What if he got the wrong idea and thought she was there to propose an illicit assignation? Banish the thought. While engaging in physical intimacy with Killian consumed far too much of her mind, the thought of anyone else, especially Alfred Cavendale, made Hannah queasy.

Alfred didn't seem the kind capable of killing a spider, let alone several women. Still, that was no excuse for shoddy work. She would search his bedroom quickly, then move on to the real target.

His bedroom was undeniably masculine. The walls were

papered in a deep blue with a geometric pattern of dark-grey diamonds. Windows looked out to the expansive lawns. His bed was a mahogany beast dominating the room. Sandalwood, smoke, and a hint of lemon oil created a pleasant scent.

Hannah began with the nightstands, carefully shifting and replacing the objects. She moved on to the credenza sitting between two large windows. One of the drawers was locked, but it only took a minute with her hairpin to spring it. Her hand shook as she removed a velvet jewellery box.

Oh my God. The lily necklace!

She opened the box, and a jewel-encrusted locket caught the light. Hannah blew out a frustrated breath. This was certainly not the simple gold necklace Sarah Bright had been given by her mother. Hannah opened the locket and discovered a small picture of a woman who could have been Ivy's twin pressed into one side. The other side was empty. Lady Cavendale, Hannah wagered. She recalled the woman had died not long after her youngest daughter's birth. Alfred must miss his mother to keep her likeness in such a valuable memento. She carefully closed the locket and laid it gently in the box. Putting it back in the drawer, she picked up a folded parchment paper sitting next to it. The broken seal was unusual. The head of a crow, the body of a wolf, and the tail of a snake. Scanning the letter, Hannah's heart quickened.

Dear sir,

We shall endeavour to keep any evidence hidden as you requested for a compensation of five thousand pounds. We shall send a second note detailing the transfer of funds in a fortnight.

If whispers were to reach Scotland Yard regarding your connection to the tragic victim, a terrible line of inquiry might unravel what has been a lucrative investment for us all. While we hold loyalty to our brotherhood as paramount, under these regrettable circumstances, we would be forced to ensure the immediate elimination of any member who threatens the safety of our community.

We expect a prompt response acknowledging your receipt of this communication and agreement to our terms.

Sincerely,

No signature indicated who wrote the letter. Instead, there was a stamp with the same image as the seal. Hannah took a notebook from her pocket and copied down the letter. Before she could return it, the door to Alfred's study creaked open.

Buggering blast!

She hastily tucked the letter into her pocket, looking madly around for a hiding spot. Kicking aside the duster, she shimmied under the bed. If the valet had been neglecting the top shelves, the state beneath Alfred's bed was disastrous. Thick dust clogged her nostrils. She pressed the back of her hand against her nose and willed herself not to sneeze.

While the dark-blue duster almost met the floor, obscuring her from view, a small gap allowed her to see a pair of shoes stride into the room. Hannah held her breath. She had no room to fight were she discovered. If the shoes belonged to Alfred and he chose to lay down on the bed, she would be smothered. Hannah fought back panic.

The shoes stopped in front of the desk. Drawers slid open, then slammed shut. A wild shuffling of papers and muttered curses indicated whatever the man was looking for was not in the desk.

Is that because it's in my pocket?

Seconds ticked by like hours as his search became increasingly more desperate. He strode around the room, opening drawers and tossing the contents out before moving on to the next piece of furniture. Hannah's heart pounded so loudly, she was sure he could hear it. His shoes approached the bed as he searched one nightstand, then walked around the bed to search the other.

Don't look under the bed. Don't look under the bed.

Hannah couldn't reach the Queen Ann pistol in her pocket, the dagger strapped to her thigh, or the throwing knifes hidden in her sleeves. She was a sitting duck waiting to be discovered.

Another round of vicious cursing indicated his search of the nightstands came up empty. His shoes were right next to her head. For a terrifying moment, Hannah could imagine the man bending over, grasping the coverlet with his hand, and pulling it up to reveal Hannah's wide gaze and pale face.

Instead, he strode out of the room as quickly as he entered.

Hannah sneezed loudly, banging her head on the bedframe.

Bloody fucking hell.

She shimmied from under the bed and looked at her brown dress turned grey by dirt. It was nothing compared to the mess created in Alfred's room. If she were caught now, there would be no explaining herself. She rushed out of the room, through the closet, and into the sitting room. The door to the hallway was ajar. The mystery man certainly didn't care about hiding his trail. She poked her head out of the door and glanced down both hallways. Empty.

Glancing at her reflection as she walked past a window, her hair was a nest of tangles dulled by a layer of dust. She made a hasty retreat to her room, breathing a sigh of relief as the door closed behind her.

Reaching into her pocket, she fingered the vellum edge of Alfred's letter. She was wrong about Lord Cavendale. Alfred was now number one on their list of suspects. The note was damning, but it wasn't irrevocable proof.

Looking down, Hannah sighed at the horrific state of her dress. 'Betty's going to kill me.'

But Philippa would be thrilled. They were one step closer to solving this case.

* * *

Killian fought between admiration and infuriation with young Billy. The boy was going to skin Killian for a significant sum and, in the process, ensure his sister received justice. Not bad for an eight-year-old boy who was more bones and scabs than anything else.

'How much is your information worth? Name your price, Billy. I could give you my purse right now. But it will only last you a few months. Maybe a year if you're careful.'

Billy's eyes grew wide. 'A year is more than a lifetime 'ere. No guarantees I'll live that long anyways. I reckon your purse would be 'nuff to loosen my lips.'

Drake made a gruff sound in the back of his throat. 'What about a job? Not as much upfront, but it would give you a steady income. A place to live. Food in your belly three times a day.'

Killian's eyes widened as he looked at his friend. Drake was not cruel, but neither was he kind. His offer was out of character for the war-hardened man.

Billy's laugh was high-pitched, and his whole body shook with mirth. 'You're just as loony as your friend. Nutters, the lot of ya. No one's gonna give me a job. Not for a bit of information 'bout my sister.'

'I would.' Drake looked just as surprised by his words as Billy.

He blinked furiously before continuing. 'You could start tomorrow.'

Killian raised an eyebrow. It would appear underneath Drake's scarred skin was the oozy middle of a cream puff.

'Caw!' Billy threw a thumb at Killian, then Drake. 'It's a wonder you don't both end up in the Red 'ouse if you ain't careful.' He shook his head like an old man disgusted with the frivolity of youth. 'Can you even imagine? Billy Bright working for a cove like you? Not likely.'

Drake leaned down, so he was eye level with Billy. 'Would you steal from me?'

Billy sat back in his chair. His throat bobbed as he swallowed. He stuck his chin in the air. 'I'm no thief.'

'Would you ever lie to me?'

Billy's brows came down, creating a wrinkle above his nose. 'I ain't no liar neither if that's what you're tryin' to say.'

'Do you promise to work hard and not laze about?'

The boy sucked air through his teeth. 'Me dad didn't raise no layabouts. I ain't 'fraid of a day's labour.' He crossed his thin arms over an equally scrawny chest.

'Then you sound like the exact man I need.'

Billy opened his mouth, then closed it again. His eyes darted from Drake to Killian and back again.

'What do you think, Billy? You tell us your information, and Drake here will give you a job.' Killian rested his hand on the table. It might be a mad plan, but the idea of this boy sleeping in a soft bed with three meals waiting for him every day filled Killian with an unfamiliar warmth. Perhaps the world was not quite as hopeless as he feared.

'Would I get to send the money 'ome? Me family depends on wot I bring in.'

'Your wages would be yours to do with as you please, though I hope you would put some away to save,' Drake answered.

''Ow do I know you ain't fibbing?' His eyes narrowed in suspicion.

Drake straightened. 'I give you my word as gentlemen.'

Billy snorted. 'That ain't worf nuffink.'

'You will soon learn it is worth very much indeed. But I will also give you this.' Drake twisted off the signet ring on his pinkie and held it between his thumb and index finger. The candlelight glinted off the emerald set into a thick, gold band. 'This ring was given to me by my father. It has been passed down for generations in my family. It is very important to me. I leave it in your hands as a token of my honour. You'll return the ring to my butler when you come to my house tomorrow to begin your new job.'

A thrill of alarm coursed through Killian. Maybe the boy was right. Maybe Drake was a barmy toff. That ring had survived with Drake through the war. He swallowed it when they were captured to ensure its safety. Killian knew how precious it was to his friend. 'Drake, perhaps...'

Billy's gaze was captured by the ring. Drake reached over and took one of the boy's hands, turned it palm up, then plunked the ring into his dirty appendage.

Billy swallowed. 'W-wot if I fence it?'

'You said you don't steal, and you don't lie. So, tell me now, are you going to steal my ring?'

Billy stared at the ring, then looked at Drake and blinked his owlish eyes. 'I'm no thief, nor no liar neither. Your ring is safe with me.'

This was a terrible idea. Even if the boy was honest, putting such a valuable possession into his hands was like balancing the ring on the edge of a ship's railing. One dip of the tumultuous waters surrounding young Billy's life, and it would be gone.

'Then share what you know about your sister. Think on my offer, and if you accept, bring the ring to my address tomorrow. I won't be there, but I will leave instructions with the butler.' Drake rattled off his address and made sure Billy knew exactly where to go. 'If you don't want the job, bring the ring back, and I'll compensate you with money. Whatever sum you feel is fair. Cook will give you a meal before you leave. What say you, Master Bright?'

Billy wrapped his small fingers around the ring and squeezed it. 'I say you're one daft cove, but I'll think about your offer. I need to talk to me mum and dad. They depend on me, you know.'

'You would get one day off a week to see your family. But if that is not amenable to you or your parents, fine. Return the ring, and I will pay you for your information.'

Billy nodded, and with the deal done, he heaved another world-weary sigh. His skinny chest deflated like a wine bladder emptying its contents. 'I know 'oo killed my sister. When Penny came to see my parents, she told 'em Sarah was s'posed to go for an in'erview at another gentleman's 'ouse. The man's son was doin' the in'erviews 'imself. A real poncy toff 'e was. So says Penny.'

Killian leaned forward. 'Who was it, Billy? Who was interviewing Sarah?'

Billy tucked the ring into his pocket and looked at Drake, then Killian. 'Lord Alfred Cavendale.'

16

Hannah tried not to think about Killian's return on the morrow. Assuming he made true on his promise to be back by the ball.

Despite her better judgment, she was lost in love with a man who could never offer for her. He needed a duchess, and she needed to remain a wallflower. A future was impossible. But her ridiculous heart refused to be swayed by her mind.

Stupidly, she had promised Ivy and Millie to accompany them to the village and visit the dressmaker. The two women insisted on finding something for Hannah in time for the ball. Both Ivy and Millie agreed any frock in a shade other than brown or grey would suffice.

Their dim view of her drab outfits was beginning to remind Hannah of Killian. Although almost everything did. The low sound of masculine voices at the dinner table. The scent of bergamot from her tea blending with the leather couch she sat upon. The dark green of the forest so similar to his eyes.

Unforgivably sentimental!

She could stare down the barrel of a gun without a flutter. Battle multiple opponents of greater strength and weaponry with fierce abandon. Dance with the Devil and escape unscathed. But now, the sight of black hair and a sharp jawline had her in a dither. How far she'd fallen when the very mention of Lieutenant General Robert Killian inspired her pulse to race, her lungs to freeze, and her body to burn.

'Hannah, are you ready? You look a thousand miles away.' Ivy swept down the front steps of Everly Manor and linked her arm with Hannah's.

Millie was right behind her, red hair flaming like a torch in the mid-morning sun. 'I'm dying to see you in something jewel-toned.' Millie's dimples winked in the sun.

Four hours later, Hannah felt far more exhausted than after any training session with Philippa. She couldn't believe the number of silks, satins, and velvets they'd draped over her during the course of the morning. In the end, Ivy and Millie convinced her to purchase no less than five dresses and an incomprehensible number of underthings. She blushed to imagine what Killian would think if he saw her in such froth and frills. All but one of the dresses would be sent to Philippa's house in London upon completion.

The final gown was being rushed over on the morrow just in time for the ball. It was a buttery cream silk with daring bronze stripes perfectly matching Hannah's copper hair. Hannah insisted the sleeves be altered to allow for easy movement. The dress-maker raised a perfectly darkened brow when Hannah also requested for each dress to include large pockets.

Lady Philippa had sent a message. She should be returning by early afternoon, so Hannah wasn't surprised to see a note on her table when she entered her room after taking leave of Ivy and Millie. Philippa requested Hannah join her for afternoon tea in Philippa's room.

Hannah was desperate to show her Alfred's letter.

Philippa sat on a high back chair near the fireplace. Her room had windows revealing the beautifully landscaped front gardens of Everly Manor. Sunlight streamed through the window, tea steamed on the low table in front of Philippa, and the scent of buttery shortbread blended with rose and lavender. It was a genteel and delicate backdrop to discuss dark and deadly deeds.

'I heard you were out shopping with Ivy and Millicent. I must say, it is good to see you developing friendships. Those two seem worthy companions for you.' Philippa poured Hannah's tea.

A bubble of warmth filled Hannah, and she smiled. 'Yes, they are.'

'Our enterprises require we keep so much hidden, but in rare circumstances, life provides us with people who respect the need for secrets, or even better, who can be entrusted with them.'

Hannah sat. 'I would not be willing to put either of them at risk by exposing our secrets. Speaking of which, I have news.' She dipped into her pocket and produced the letter.

Philippa placed her tea on the table and reached for it. Her eyes scanned the words. 'Intriguing. Where did you find this?'

'In Alfred Cavendale's bedroom.'

'The author does not name a recipient. Just "Dear sir". Maddening, is it not?'

'I assume that given its location, the "sir" referred to is Alfred.'

Philippa nodded. 'Certainly a logical assumption, but not definitive. He may have come into possession of this letter by other means. We must also assume the "tragic victim" is Sarah Bright, although again, with no names mentioned, this is just conjecture.' Philippa rubbed her thumb over the seal. 'My conversation with the Queen was rather enlightening. She was not surprised by our revelation. Indeed, she shared intelligence about a new secret society that bears this seal. They consider themselves creators of their own destiny. A group of men with God complexes and more money than sense. Pathetic, but like all men who have been granted too much power, potentially very dangerous.'

Hannah sipped her whiskey-laced tea and sputtered. It was almost completely whiskey. Philippa's visit with Queen Victoria must have gone badly indeed.

'She shared something even more dire. These men are not just killing women. They are selling them for trade.'

Hannah leaned forward and felt a crease form between her eyebrows. 'What do you mean? Trade for what?'

'What value is given to a woman of no means besides that of her body?' Philippa's voice was hard, her syllables clipped. 'They are being sold into the flesh markets of Europe. Girls from country towns lured into London by wealthy lords to interview as maids, only to be drugged and shipped across the channel in caskets where they are sold into slavery.'

It could not be true. Hannah recoiled, pushing back into her chair. 'Surely she is mistaken!'

Philippa shook her head. 'Queen Victoria is never mistaken. Certainly not about something as serious as this. These men are dangerous. They are making obscene profits and gambling with their lives if they are caught. Which means they are also desperate. They will kill anyone who threatens their enterprise. Didn't you overhear Lord Cavendale saying Alfred was the member of a secret club? If he is one of their brotherhood, we must consider our next steps very carefully. To take out one of their members is to enrage the entire pack and bring them down upon our heads, Hannah.'

'Are you suggesting we walk away?' Hannah's stomach clenched as bile burned up her throat. Retreating for fear of retribution while young girls were being sold into slavery was unthinkable.

Philippa stood and paced to the window. 'Absolutely not. But I won't risk your life either.'

'I can take care of myself, Philippa. You trained me to do just that.'

Philippa turned, and Hannah saw something she'd never seen before in her patroness' eyes. Fear. 'You cannot defend yourself against this brotherhood, Hannah. Not alone.'

Hannah stood and walked to Philippa, grasping her hands. 'I'm not alone. I have you.'

'Even together, the risk is dire.'

Hannah bit her lip. For ten years, Philippa had provided for Hannah, protected her, trained her, and in her own way, loved Hannah. But Hannah had never been completely honest with Philippa. She shared her darkest secret with a man destined to break her heart. But she had never shared that truth with Philippa.

They were playing a dangerous game. She and Philippa might not survive this mission. She didn't want to go to the grave with any deceit between them.

'Philippa, there is something you should know. About the night I arrived on your doorstep. The night my mother was murdered.'

Philippa squeezed Hannah's hands. 'Tell me.'

'My mother didn't kill Raymond Smythe that night. I did. I murdered him.'

Philippa could still surprise Hannah. She smiled. 'Darling girl, don't you think I knew that the moment you arrived?'

'But you never said...'

'You weren't ready to tell me. I was happy to wait. Do you remember the letter I wrote? The one that brought you to my house?'

Hannah nodded.

'My relationship with Lord Winterbourne was not ideal.' Philippa cleared her throat. 'Your mother provided him with things I could not. But she also gave me an invaluable gift. She kept him distracted. Attentions he would have forced upon me, she readily accepted. When I wrote to your mother upon his death and promised to continue the allowance he had given her, it was because I was grateful to her. And when I offered my help in a time of need, I truly hoped she would accept my offer. But I understand why she didn't. She was a proud woman who didn't want to be beholden to her lover's wife.'

Hannah shook her head as a terrible truth emerged. 'You would have helped us if Mama asked. She never would have had to take up with the baron if she accepted your offer.'

'Yes. That is true. And she may have lived. You would never have murdered the baron. But you also wouldn't be where you are now, Hannah. Only fire can forge steel. The hotter the flame, the stronger the blade. That night, you learned something invaluable about yourself. That you have the strength to do what must be done to protect the innocent.'

'But I didn't protect my mother. I failed her.'

'You were just a girl, Hannah. And you stopped a monster. It is because of what you did that night I knew you had the strength, courage, and fortitude to be my apprentice. You are Lord Winterbourne's only heir, you know. You carry with you the best of him. And the best of your mother.'

Hannah couldn't swallow past the lump in her throat. 'You taught me well, Philippa. I carry the best of you with me as well. And that is how I know we will catch these bastards. They may have a brotherhood, but we have something far more powerful. We have each other. And we don't fail.'

Not again. I will not fail again.

* * *

Drake pulled up hard on his reins. His horse reared in protest. Killian nearly ran into his friend before wheeling his mount in a tight circle.

'You did what?' Drake roared, his deep baritone echoing across the rolling fields.

'Bloody hell, Drake!' Killian fought to control the stallion beneath him.

They were only a few miles from Everly Manor and had been riding like demons for a day and a half. Killian was consumed with warring thoughts. His mission and his passion.

How could he convince Alfred to confess without bloodshed? Master Bright's information was damning but not enough for a conviction in the House of Lords. He needed a confession or hard evidence to prove Alfred's guilt. Yet, when he tried to devise a plan, his thoughts invariably returned to Hannah.

How could he salvage the mess he'd made? Instead of plotting Alfred Cavendale's capture, he desperately tried to discover a way forward with Hannah. His inability to puzzle out a plan led Killian to admit his actions to Drake as they neared Everly. He hoped for sage advice. Instead, his confession prompted Drake's ridiculous overreaction.

I'd have been better off asking Master Bright.

'I knew I shouldn't have told you.' Killian calmed his horse with a steady hand on the animal's powerful neck.

'You slept with Miss Simmons? A lady. And a virgin? Are you mad?'

Killian clenched his teeth together. 'She would argue the first and offer no compunctions about the second.'

Drake shook his head, his scar blazing white against his

darker skin. 'Bollocks to that! You know better. You *are* better than this.'

Guilt curdled like oil and vinegar in his stomach. 'I did propose... afterward.'

Drake's laughter was as dry and harsh as the Afghanistan desert. 'I'm sure she loved that.'

'She did not.'

'Of course she didn't, you idiot! Why? Why do this? Why ruin her and heap another bowl of burning coals on your own head? I know you, Killian. You are no rake. You will spend the next twenty years berating yourself for this.'

Shame, anger, and frustration clamped around Killian's lungs like steel. He couldn't think. He couldn't breathe. He would trade his freedom for a prison cell again if only he could make this right. 'Because I love her!' Killian thundered in desperation. 'I love her,' he said again in a ragged whisper. *I love her.*

Drake swallowed. His horse stamped the muddy path. A bee buzzed a lazy trail between the men, chasing the scent of pollen. 'Love?' Drake spoke the word like a curse. 'What an asinine reason for such a horrific miscalculation.'

Killian only refrained from leaping off his horse and dragging Drake into the mud because it would delay his arrival at Everly.

'Did you profess your love?' Drake asked.

Killian tipped his head to the sky. Fat white clouds skidded across a blanket of azure as deep and endless as his regrets. 'No. I may have mentioned sacrificing a proper duchess for the greater good of preserving my honour.'

'The greater good? Dear God, man.' Drake shook his head. 'It's no wonder she rejected you. I'm surprised she let you live. Well, what are you going to do?'

Killian turned his horse and urged him to walk. 'I don't know. That's why I'm telling you this. I wanted your advice.'

Drake fell into step with Killian, their horses plodding along; no doubt the beasts were grateful for a slower pace. The leather saddles creaked in a quiet rhythm as the afternoon sun warmed Killian's back.

'Run. That's my advice. Run as far and fast as you can from any woman who inspires an emotion as dangerous as love.'

Killian groaned. 'This is not helpful.'

'Then you shouldn't have asked. I'm the last person who should give advice about love.' Drake traced a finger over his scar. 'I would rather cut out my heart and eat it raw before letting another woman into my life.'

'Sheer poetry, Drake.'

'Thank you. Do you really want my advice? Are you ready for it?'

Killian raised an eyebrow at his friend. 'I'm scared to hear it, I think.'

'You should be. You have always held yourself to the highest standard. It's why your peers hold such regard for you. But it's also why you will never truly be happy. No man could live up to the expectations you place upon yourself.'

'The least I can do for my parents is live a life of honour.' Killian needed to prove that he was still worthy, even if it meant giving up his happiness.

'There is no honour in the love of a woman. But neither is there honour in a marriage built on duty and guilt.' Drake stared at Killian. His jaw clenched. 'If you believe in the lie of love, and are willing to risk your soul for it, maybe you'll find happiness. I doubt it, but I suppose it's possible.'

Killian looked into Drake's eyes and saw the yawning blackness of despair. His heart bled for his friend, and his concern grew. 'My parents' love was not a lie. It was action. It was sacrifice.

It was joy. And yes, it was also pain. But that only made it more real.'

Drake shrugged. 'Well, there's your answer, then. I can't imagine your parents would want you to sacrifice the kind of love you saw between them for a blue-blooded miss you will grow to hate. I don't think your Miss Simmons is worth the risk, but it's not about what I think. It's about what you believe. Even if what you believe is wrong.'

Hannah's face filled Killian's mind, and his heart stretched painfully. 'I know Hannah is worth every risk. She fights like an avenging angel, faces off against insurmountable odds without a hint of hesitation, shows more courage than any soldier I've known, and could best us both with a blade or a gun. She's insufferably stubborn and wickedly bright. I may be wrong about everything else, but I'm not wrong about her.' His conviction grew stronger with every word.

'Calm down. If she is as skilled and deadly as you describe, Miss Simmons will likely destroy you. A pity, that, because I won't be able to gloat about being right.' The corner of Drake's mouth ticked up in the ghost of a smile.

'I would rather be destroyed by her than live with anyone else.' As Killian spoke the words, he realised something.

I am an idiot.

His parents lived a life that exemplified the most honourable emotion, the highest ideal, the only thing that mattered. Love. They would have wanted him to marry whomever he loved, regardless of her pedigree. But even if they disapproved, it would have changed nothing. He loved Hannah. How could he imagine joining himself with anyone who wasn't her? It would be turning away from the sunlight to live in unending gloom.

'Thank you, Drake. Your advice has been invaluable. One day, I hope to return the favour.'

Drake snorted. 'I would rather be boiled in oil and spread on toast than listen to your advice on love.'

Hannah had taken up permanent residence in Killian's heart. Now, he just needed to convince her to move into his house and rule there as his duchess.

Killian spurred his horse into a canter. 'Make haste, Drake. I have a ball to attend, a lord to arrest, a waltz to dance, and a proposal to make.'

17

Hannah scanned the ballroom and resisted tugging up her dress. She didn't remember the neckline dipping so scandalously low at the modiste's. She brushed her hand against her skirt, taking comfort in the hard outline of her dagger. Hannah lived on the fringes of the crowd, never capturing the centre of attention. But tonight, she was trapped in the crosshairs of society's notice. It was distinctly uncomfortable.

'Don't look now, but I think the Earl of Plynth is heading this way, and his eyes are glued on you, Hannah,' Ivy spoke behind a glass of ratafia.

'Oh, dear. He's a notorious rake and a terrible dancer. Mind your slippers. He will tread all over your toes.' Millie hissed before popping a strawberry into her mouth.

'You'll be missing your boots tonight,' Ivy agreed. 'Although, those heeled slippers are lovely, Hannah.'

Hannah grimaced. 'Not lovely enough to be worth the blisters.'

They had positioned themselves in front of the refreshment

able, hoping to avoid the eligible gentlemen looking for a distrac-tion from quiet country evenings. The Everly Ball was a highly anticipated event. Everyone who was anyone jumped at the chance to wear their finest and preen in front of each other after weeks of absence from London's feverish social calendar. Hannah, Ivy, and Millie were happy to watch the show but had no interest in being participants.

Regrettably, the Earl of Plynth had other plans.

'Forgive my impertinence, Miss Ivy Cavendale, Miss Millicent Whittenburg, but I beg an introduction to your lovely compan-ion.' He tipped forward at the waist, nearly burying his nose in Hannah's breasts. Grasping her hand, he pressed his wet mouth against her callused knuckles.

Hannah endeavoured not to gag. The man had been availing himself of his own refreshments, judging by the sour scent of gin on his breath.

'This is our dear friend, Miss Hannah Simmons.' Millie flicked her fan in a gesture as vicious as a rapier parry, nearly taking off the earl's nose. He stumbled backward. Hannah wiped her hand against her skirt.

The Earl of Plynth regained his equilibrium and stepped closer to Hannah. His eyes remained glued to her humble cleav-age. 'Allow me to prevail upon you for a dance, Miss Simmons. If your card is not yet full?' He spoke directly to her neckline.

Hannah didn't even have a dance card, let alone names to place upon it. She was out of her depths. 'I...' Words failed her. It would be far easier to punch the man in his solar plexus than devise a clever evasion.

'This dance is spoken for. Miss Simmons promised me the next waltz.'

Killian's deep voice reverberated behind her and sent shivers of awareness across her skin like a warm breeze. Judging by her thwarted dance partner's wide eyes, Killian's tone sent different shivers through the Earl of Plynth.

'Err, of course. Forgive me,' the gentleman sputtered as he hastily spun and walked away.

Hannah turned to face Killian, her body tingling with awareness. He stood tall and proud in a black dress coat. A crisp, white shirt and equally snowy cravat highlighted his sun-darkened skin. His vest was embroidered with deep-green stitching echoed in the shade of his eyes. Hannah's mouth went dry. Her belly clenched.

'Damnation,' she breathed.

'Oh my. What a useful trick to rid someone of unwanted company,' Millie whispered, loud enough for Killian to hear.

Major General Drake, who stood just behind Killian's left shoulder, snorted rudely.

'Shall we?' Killian reached out his hand to Hannah and clenched his jaw.

'Oh my, indeed,' Ivy murmured.

Killian grasped her fingers and placed her hand in the crook of his arm, gliding through the crowd to the dance floor.

Hannah's face heated. 'Everyone is looking. I don't... you know I can't dance.'

'I know you move like wind through the leaves. Follow my lead, just this once. I won't let you fall.' Killian squeezed her fingers and spun her to face him. He placed her hand on his shoulder and clasped her other in his own warm grip as his right hand drifted down to her waist. They stood frozen, suspended in time, waiting for the music to begin.

Murmurs rose around her. She glanced over her shoulder as Lady Hastings whispered behind her fan to Lady Bradford.

'What are you doing, Killian? A duke does not dance with a wallflower.'

Killian stretched his mouth into a wide grin. His teeth flashed white in the glittering lights and his eyes sparked with heat. 'A duke does whatever he damn well pleases. And you are no wallflower, my dear Miss Simmons. You are a jungle of wicked thorns and wild blooms.' He leaned close to her ear. 'A man could get lost in the colour and scent of you.'

Hannah pressed her lips together to hide their trembling.

Insufferable, perfect man!

How she had missed him.

The whispers around them grew in fervour, but the strains of the strings drowned the gossips out in a melodic swell.

Killian's arms hardened to granite as his body moved forward. Hannah almost crashed into him. 'Keep your frame tight, and let your feet flow, Hannah. Remember our dance lesson on the terrace? Read me like you would in a fight. Predict my steps and match them with your own.' His forest-green gaze burned into hers, and she was lost.

She stopped thinking and let herself slip along the swells and dips of sound and motion. When he spun, she twirled. When he stepped with his left, she followed with her right. Their bodies created a rhythm of advance and retreat, give and take, rise and fall. Their movements as ageless and endless as the tides.

'I missed you. Every moment that I was gone was a bleak eternity,' Killian murmured against her cheek.

Hannah was too full of emotion to leave space for words. Relief. Anger. Confusion. Desire.

Love.

But he had abandoned her. 'Why did you leave?' Perhaps she sounded desperate, but she needed to know.

'I received a message from Sarah Bright's brother.'

Hannah missed her step, but Killian lifted her from the floor, keeping their bodies in sync.

'Billy Bright? He sent a message?' She struggled to keep her voice low as her feet skimmed over the marble slabs.

Killian swirled them to the edge of the dance floor. He leaned closer, his lips tickling her ear. 'Not here. Come with me.'

Hannah knew what it would look like. The Duke of Covington leaving the ballroom with a woman who lived on the goodwill of her patroness. If they exited together, people would notice. Assumptions would be made. Accusations would be hurled. She couldn't melt into the shadows when standing in the centre of society's censure. If the beau monde believed she and the duke were involved in a tryst, her anonymity would be compromised. Right along with her hypothetical virtue. While she couldn't care less about the latter, she was deeply invested in the former.

The music reached its crescendo, then eased into silence as the dancers slowed to a stop.

Hannah knew the perfect place to meet where no one would be watching. 'The library, just past the ladies' retiring room. Five minutes.' She curtsied to him and turned away, walking back to Ivy and Millie with her head held high.

'Dear lord, I thought the floor might catch fire from the sparks flying between you two. You've set the gossips' tongues wagging. Just look.' Millie nodded toward Lady Hastings whispering furiously to her daughter, Miss Anna Hastings.

Ivy huffed out a breath. 'I wish Anna Hastings did not have her cap set so firmly in my brother's direction. With a mother like that, family gatherings will be unbearable.' Ivy bit her lip and her pale-blue eyes clouded.

'They can go suck eggs,' Hannah hissed. 'I need your help, ladies. I am meeting Lord Killian in a few minutes. Will you join me on a trip to the retiring room?'

Millie's dimples emerged. 'You wicked woman! A scandalous

iaison with the delicious Lieutenant General? Of course we shall accompany you.'

Ivy clasped Hannah's shoulder. 'Are you quite certain you know what you're doing?'

'Of course.' Hannah tried to fill her smile with confidence.

I've no bloody clue what I'm doing.

'Alright.' Ivy grasped Hannah's hand. 'To the retiring room.' She led the way, staying close to the edges of the crowd.

* * *

Killian strode out of the ballroom, wound up the stairs, and turned right. He didn't have to wonder which door led to the ladies' retiring room. The shrill sound of feminine laughter and a pervading scent of lilies and pearl powder emanated from an open door halfway down the corridor.

He walked swiftly past. The next door was closed. If Hannah was right, it led to the library. Killian turned, leaning his back against the thick, mahogany wood. She would be along soon. He was happy to wait for her.

Hannah didn't keep him in suspense. He checked his watch as three women walked toward him: Hannah, Miss Ivy Cavendale, and Miss Millicent Whittenburg. Only a foolish man would refuse to admire such a variety of feminine charm. Killian was not a foolish man.

Hannah moved like a cat. Sleek, economical, deadly. Killian had touched every inch of her body, but she was still a mystery to him. One he hoped to spend a lifetime trying to solve.

He had thought his heart was going to stop when he first saw her on the ballroom floor. If there had been any doubt about his love for her, that moment would have confirmed the truth. She was the only woman for him.

His overtaxed heart stuttered as she strode closer. Her dress was sinfully crafted. The cascading confection of bronze silk and cream lace encapsulated her body like an embrace. She shone like a woodland creature caught in moonlight. Always draped in colours of the earth, she transcended into a wild thing of myth. The ache in his chest grew exponentially and his body hardened as he imagined all the ways he could separate her from her gown.

'My lord, I believe we have important matters to discuss.' Hannah nodded to her companions. Miss Millie winked at her while Miss Ivy glanced at Killian. Her mouth tightened.

'Take care, Lieutenant General Killian. She is our friend, and we will protect her, even from someone as fearful as you.' Miss Ivy's voice was hard with determination.

Killian was surprised. The delicate woman had grit and courage. He nodded to her. 'I would expect nothing less, Miss Cavendale.'

'Hmph.'

Killian couldn't decide if the sound indicated approval or dismissal.

She turned back to Hannah. 'We shall wait for you in the retiring room.'

'I shan't be long.' Hannah smiled at her friends, then faced him. Her garnet eyes flashed with what he hoped was desire. 'Shall we?'

Killian didn't need further invitation.

He jerked down on the door handle and pulled her into the darkened library, shutting it on Ivy's gasp and Millie's wicked chuckle.

'I think your friends might challenge me to a duel after this.' Killian murmured against Hannah's soft hair.

She backed away from him. He couldn't see her expression in the shadows, making it impossible to gauge her emotions.

'You would lose.' Hannah's voice was strained. 'But I did not come here to discuss my friends.'

'Nor did I.' Killian pulled her close, pressing his mouth against the soft hollow of her neck. When she melted into him, he sucked and nipped his way to her earlobe, nibbling on the delicate skin.

'Stop. First, we must talk. There is information I have that you need to know. And you must tell me about your meeting with Billy Bright.' Hannah pushed him away, and he reluctantly relented.

'Of course. Forgive me. Being apart from you has ripped away my vestiges of propriety. I am raw and aching. But you are right. We should talk.' He backed up, because it was impossible not to touch her when she was within his reach.

He used the burning coals from the library's banked fire to light a taper. Walking back to the table, he fumbled for a lamp. When he adjusted the wick, he turned to appreciate Hannah in the soft light.

'What did Billy tell you?' Hannah's eyes were luminous.

Killian smiled and shook his head. 'I don't think so, Miss Simmons. You first.'

A line formed between her brows as she harrumphed. Killian never thought such a sound could be sexy, but she managed to stoke his fires with minimal effort.

'Fine. I found myself in Alfred Cavendale's room.'

'You just found yourself there? Like one might find a lost shoe or a misplaced ribbon?' Killian raised a sceptical eyebrow.

'Yes. Just like that. At any rate, I discovered a letter implicating Alfred in the murder.'

A jolt of adrenaline rushed through him. 'Do you have this letter?'

'Of course. I mean, not on me, but in my room.'

'And it implicates him by name?'

Hannah bit her lip. Killian had to force his eyes away from her red mouth and white teeth. 'Well, that's the thing. It never mentions his name. But finding it in his room is pretty damning.'

'Not enough to ensure conviction in the House of Lords.'

'You forget, I'm not bound by the House of Lords. If the Queen is convinced, that's good enough for me.'

Killian's jaw dropped in shock. 'The bloody Queen? Of fucking England? That's who you work for?'

Hannah squared her shoulders and lifted her chin. 'Perhaps.'

Killian noticed how the movement pressed her breasts against the neckline of her dress.

Get control, man.

But he didn't want to be in control. He wanted to let his heart lead him and damn the consequences.

'Fascinating woman!' Before she could deny it, he continued. 'You play a dangerous game, Miss Simmons. Letting one person make the ultimate decision about another person's life.'

Hannah tsked. 'Please. Men do it all the time. Besides, in this case, I agree with the Queen. As does Philippa, and I'm guessing as do you. That's four people. Five if we included Major General Drake. Do you deny that he would agree to our deductions?'

Killian resisted the urge to smile. God, she was clever. And brave. And fearsome. And driving him mad with desire. 'Five people hardly equal the entire House of Lords, or the justice system they have comprised.' He couldn't stop himself from arguing with her if only to see her eyes flash and her mind race to best him.

'They place a title of justice on a corrupt system. It does not protect the innocent or uphold the truth. I trust our judgment over a group of men driven by greed and a need for power any day.'

Killian was charmed that she included himself and Drake in her small circle of formidable women that included the *Queen.* Drake would never believe him.

Hannah crossed her arms in front of her and cocked her hip. 'Your turn. What did Billy Bright tell you?' She tapped her foot as he pulled his scattered thoughts together.

'Apparently, Sarah Bright had an interview for a job. With Alfred Cavendale. It does seem his name is coming up quite often.'

She shook her head. 'I think we'll only discover the truth by questioning Alfred.'

While Killian knew Hannah was adept at protecting herself, the idea of her being close to a monster capable of such heinous crimes made his skin crawl and his hands fist into weapons of protection. 'Leave that to me. If he is responsible for one death, he won't hesitate to commit another murder, especially a woman with as little social consequence as you.'

As soon as the words escaped, she flinched.

Shit. I am an absolute idiot!

He reached out and grasped her hand. 'Hannah, you know that's not how I see you.'

'Actually, sir, you made it clear the last time we spoke that is exactly how you see me.'

Killian could have cut out his tongue. 'I merely meant to say, men like Alfred would view you as a liability easily removed. I know that isn't true, but I won't put you in danger.'

'No, you won't. You won't put me anywhere because you don't make choices about my life, Lieutenant General Killian. Not now. Not ever.' Her voice was brittle, her eyes flashing daggers.

'I'm not trying to...' But he was. And he was going to lose this battle. Because she was right. Even if his goal was protection, he had no right to make decisions for her. 'I'm sorry. Of course, you get to make your own choices. But I would ask you to let me speak with Alfred first. If he reacts violently, I would feel much better being the target of his aggression than subjecting you to a man who is larger and potentially better armed.'

'It wouldn't be the first time. It won't be the last. And so far, it hasn't affected my success.' She blinked slowly. He wondered if the Queen taught her that move. 'But I'll agree to let you speak to him first on one condition. I'm certain he won't confess to you. So, you must turn the other way when I get his admission of guilt and deliver his punishment.'

'You don't want me to force your hand, but you would force mine?'

'I'm not forcing anything. Philippa has orders from the Queen, and we will exact justice on Alfred Cavendale. If I get his confession and you do not, you will not interfere. That is my condition. How confident are you that you'll beat me to the truth, Lord Killian?'

Not very.

But it just meant he must try harder. He would move heaven and earth if it kept Hannah from danger.

'I agree to your terms, but I have my own condition.' He didn't give her time to think or answer or retreat. Grasping her hips, he pulled her to him, crushing his mouth against hers in a kiss of desperation. Hunger. Need.

* * *

Hannah's first instinct was to pull away, but the moment their mouths met, she was lost to her own frustrated desires. He had only been gone a few days, but it felt like eternity. She knew how her body could feel with his hands touching her, his teeth scraping over her skin, his mouth sucking her sensitive flesh, and she wanted everything. All of him. Now.

Killian lifted her and plunked her bottom upon a conveniently placed desk.

He pressed his lips against hers, hot and hungry. His tongue tested the seam of her mouth before plunging in to taste and tempt. Hannah dove her fingers into his hair, revelling in his growl as she tugged. His scent consumed her. Mint, leather, bergamot, and spice.

'I missed you too,' she moaned against his mouth. It was easier in the dim lamplight of the lonely library. To admit her feelings. To reveal her weakness.

'I want you. Now. Hard and fast. If you don't want this, tell me. I'll stop.' His voice was raw with need and tripped along her senses like lightning and fire.

'Don't stop.' She bit his lip and unleashed a demon.

Killian's hands were everywhere. His fingers dipped into the neckline of her dress, teasing her nipple before he pulled her bodice down and covered her other breast with his mouth. He pinched with his hand and nibbled with his teeth, scraping them over her budded flesh. Hannah almost flew apart. She gripped his head and pulled him closer. Mad with need, she grappled with his cravat, attacking the buttons of his shirt and vest to spread the material wide and expose his hot, hard flesh to her questing fingers.

'I don't want to be gentle,' he growled against her skin.

'I'm not fragile. I can handle roughness, but be warned, I'll give you back the same.' She grabbed his thick hair and fisted her hand. He hissed, turning his head to her forearm and nipping her skin before smoothing the bite with a kiss.

She felt wild. And free. And consumed. She pulled him to her and pressed her lips against his, licking and biting, drowning in the flavour of whiskey and mint and something uniquely Killian.

Rucking up her skirts, he spread her thighs wide with his hips. The granite ridge of his erection, trapped within his breeches, crushed against her lace drawers. A slit exposed her intimate flesh to the cold air. He slid his hand along her thigh, toying with the dagger tied to her leg with a silk ribbon.

'Fuck,' he groaned. 'Do you know how seductive you are, Miss Simmons? With your daggers and pistols? Knowing you could destroy me with a single thrust?'

She demonstrated her skill, rubbing her wet cleft against his covered erection. 'As could you, Your Grace.'

He fumbled with his breeches. Moments later, his unsheathed cock pressed against her entrance. Without warning, he plunged deep, gliding along her clitoris in a devastating stroke of friction. She cried out at the sudden invasion. Her body wept with joy.

He pulled almost entirely out before slamming back in. Deeper. Harder.

Hannah wrapped her legs around his hips. Killian reached beneath her, his unrelenting fingers digging into the soft flesh of her bottom. He pulled her to him. They were a frenzy of motion. His mouth feasted on her skin. Her moans melted into his groans. Skin slapped hard against skin. The desk creaked in protest of such abuse, but their bodies rejoiced as his ruthless rhythm drove her higher, sweeter, hotter, deeper into the abyss.

She imploded into a thousand jagged pieces of light as his cock stretched her taut flesh even tighter. Her body clenched around him. She felt his shudder of release as Killian plunged into her and held tight, pulsing in rhythm to her heartbeat.

'My God. Hannah.' His deep voice thundered along her nerve endings, intensifying the echo of her climax.

'Killian,' she breathed his name like a prayer. How could she let him go?

They stayed frozen in a desperate embrace until slowly Hannah's soul returned to her body. She loosened her grip and melted against him.

'We must talk.'

Hannah pressed a kiss to his chest as the laughter bubbled up. 'Talk? Now? I can barely breathe.'

He pulled away from her, and chill air raised goosebumps over her skin. 'I love you, Hannah.'

Time stopped. Hannah's heartbeat tripled; her lungs froze. 'What?'

'I love you. And I don't want to marry you because of duty.'

Hannah unwrapped her legs, and unsteadily balanced her weight on the ground. She pulled her bodice up, reclaiming some modesty.

He loved her, but he didn't want to marry her. Okay. That made no sense. But fine. She didn't want to marry him either. The bastard. 'At least we can agree upon that.'

Killian quickly buttoned his pants before gripping her shoulders. 'You don't understand. You said before that I was a man of honour. That the war didn't take anything from me. And I have spent the last four days thinking about your words. Thinking about you. I've reached a conclusion that will likely become a regular habit for me. You were right. You *are* right.'

Well, that was some small consolation. He wouldn't marry her, but at least she could remind herself on cold, lonely nights that she was right. She opened her mouth to reply, but he kept talking.

'I am a man of honour. But I don't want to marry you because of my ideals. Or my beliefs. Or my familial obligations.'

Dear God. He didn't have to beat her to death with it. He didn't want to marry her. Wonderful. She wasn't thick. She understood him the first time.

'I'm not asking you to marry me,' she hissed pushing into the anger. 'Marrying you is the last thing I want.' *Or the only thing.* But that was inconsequential.

Killian blinked. 'Well, that's unfortunate. Because I desperately want to marry you.'

Come again?

'Come again?' she asked.

'I want to marry you. Not for honour, not for duty, but because I love you, Hannah. Only you. And I can't imagine any kind of joy in my life if you aren't by my side.'

There was a loud buzzing in her ears. She shook her head. She couldn't have heard him correctly. Hannah's brain wasn't working. Her body still vibrated with the ecstasy of their union. Her heart stuttered at his declaration.

'I'm sorry, what?'

Killian's laughter was strained. 'I love you, Hannah. Please, marry me.'

She hadn't misheard that. He wanted to marry her. But could she actually marry him? What about her career? Her freedom? She felt like she was trudging through treacle and making no headway. 'I don't understand... what about Philippa?'

Killian's second attempt at laughter held more mirth. His dark chuckle stroked along her nerves like a silken caress. 'I don't want to marry the duchess, Hannah. I want to marry you.'

Hannah pushed him away, grasping at a safe emotion. Annoyance. 'Of course you don't want to marry her. I mean, what about my, er, relationship with Philippa?'

'That depends on what kind of relationship you're describing. Do you wish to marry Philippa? For a woman who is so opposed to scandal, that seems rather bold.'

Hannah scowled as panic licked up her veins and overwhelmed her heart. 'Impossible man! You're being ridiculous.'

'I'm being ridiculous?' He raised an annoying eyebrow, his sinful mouth curving into a lazy smile that Hannah wanted to slap from his beautiful face. He was enjoying this.

'Obviously, I don't want to marry Philippa. But she is my patroness. I have my mission to think of. How could I continue with my investigations if we were married? A husband controls his wife. Her finances, her housing, her activities, even her friends. I could never submit to the rule of a man, Killian. Not even a man I trusted. Not even you.'

Killian grasped her hand and pressed her fingers against his lips. 'Do you really believe I would expect obedience from you? Do not think me quite so naïve or so stupid. I value all my appendages and wish to keep them attached to my body.'

Hannah refused to laugh. This was not funny. 'You would let me continue with my work? Willingly allowing me to traipse into the dangerous night hunting violent men? You just asked me not to confront Alfred Cavendale because you were worried for me. That would change if we were married?'

'I asked you not to. I didn't command you. I didn't force you. I never will. I haven't thought out all the details. Of course, I don't want you wandering into danger alone, but you wouldn't be alone. Our goals are not so dissimilar. Besides, most marriages have some level of conflict. We can work out the specifics, but none of that really matters. There is only one thing that does. Do you love me, Hannah?'

Before she could answer, the door burst open. A gentleman stumbled into the library. A giggling woman in pink feathers and white silk traipsed behind him.

'Bollocks,' Hannah and Killian said in unison.

The besotted man was so intent on his conquest, he didn't

notice Hannah and Killian as they ducked behind the desk. The man swept the woman into his embrace, and they landed in a tangled heap on an unsuspecting chaise. Hannah couldn't help but note the library was equipped with incredibly accommodating furniture.

Killian and Hannah crawled along the shadowed wall to a door on the far side of the room. Killian reached up and slowly pulled down the handle. The door creaked open wide enough for Hannah to slip through. In a trice, he was standing next to her farther down the same corridor where they entered the library.

Alfred Cavendale alighted the top stair at the end of the hall.

'Bloody hell.' Hannah hissed.

Killian followed her gaze. 'Bloody hell is right.'

Hannah's hair was a mess, and her dress was dishevelled. Killian's own clothes were in a hasty state of disarray. She couldn't exactly confront a potential murderer looking like a common strumpet. If Alfred Cavendale caught them together like this, whether or not he was guilty of any crimes, it would be Hannah whose freedom would be lost. She wouldn't have a choice of marrying Killian or not. It would be decided for her by the gossips of the beau monde. Even worse, it meant Killian would be able to interrogate Alfred first. He would beat her to a confession. Which concerned her less than his safety.

There was no denying it. She loved the idiot.

'I must go. We will talk later. Please don't confront Alfred alone. If he is the killer, I don't want anything to happen to you.' Hannah wanted to say more. She wanted to tell him that she loved him. That she was terrified of trusting him, but even more terrified of losing him. That she couldn't imagine a future without him, but neither could she devise one where they might live together in harmony. There was no time. She needed to make a hasty exit before Alfred saw them together.

The ladies' retiring room was her best chance of escape. Hannah nodded to Killian and stepped away as he quickly buttoned his shirt and retied his cravat. She glanced back at Killian and then walked into the lily-scented room. If only she could read the expression in his eyes as easily as she deciphered the desire in his body.

Ivy and Millie rushed up to her in a flurry of silk and lace.

Ivy's hand fluttered around Hannah's falling curls. 'Oh, dear. I knew that dastardly duke was up to no good. How dare he take advantage of an innocent girl?'

Hannah pressed her lips together to stop the laughter. She was about as innocent as the Devil in a dance hall.

Ivy's hand curled into a fist, her pale skin almost translucent in the bright light from the blazing lamps. Her slight frame shook with rage. 'I'll kill him. Well, I won't, obviously. But I'll have Alfred challenge him to a duel.' Ivy chewed on her nail as her brow drew down in worry. 'No, then he'd just kill Alfred. Father would be a better choice.' She looked back at Hannah, her pale-blue eyes alight with the indignant fire. 'I'll have father challenge him to a duel.'

Dear God. If Alfred is the killer, what does that mean for my friendship with Ivy? How could she possibly forgive me for what I must do?

For a moment, Hannah wished Killian would confront Alfred. That he would bear the burden of justice and save her the cost of what would undoubtedly be her budding friendship with Ivy. But that was cowardly. And Hannah was no coward.

'Calm yourself, Ivy. Hannah hardly looks distraught. If anything, dear, you look like my cat after she's lapped up a bowl of cream.' Millie winked at Hannah. 'Let's just be glad no one else is here to see you. Never fear, we'll set you to rights, and then you can tell us exactly what happened.' She led Hannah to a vanity and pushed her into an overstuffed chair.

The women called over several maids who attacked Hannah's hair with the skill and precision of a military brigade. In moments, no one would guess Hannah had been madly kissing the Duke of Covington, in the library, with her dagger sheathed.

18

Killian forced himself to walk away from Hannah with the promise he would meet her in a few short hours and convince her to marry him or go mad in the attempt. Alfred Cavendale's timing was terrible, but Killian couldn't let this opportunity escape. Hannah may be worried for his safety, but he was a skilled warrior, and far better matched against a man of Alfred's size and strength than her. He couldn't allow Hannah to face a potential murderer when it was within his power to confront the culprit himself.

'Lieutenant General Killian! What a fortuitous happenstance. You are just the man I hoped to find.' Alfred extended his hand for a firm shake.

'Well, mission accomplished. Here I am.' Killian stretched his mouth in a fake smile.

'I must apologise to you for my egregious behaviour earlier. I still haven't recovered from Patrick's loss. Sometimes I am taken over by black moods. Please forgive me.'

Killian grasped for something to say. Did Alfred's black moods also include periods of murderous rage? Or had he been mistaken? Was Alfred just a grieving brother? 'Of course.'

'I hate to pull you away from the ball, but we had a stallion delivered to the stables. I would love to get your opinion. Allow me a chance to make a second impression upon you. Hopefully a better one, this time.' Alfred smiled. His face appeared younger when not creased with an arrogant scowl.

If Alfred Cavendale was the killer, Killian needed hard evidence against him. If he was innocent, Killian needed to clear his name quickly so they could find the monster behind these murders.

Looking critically at Alfred, he had the soft lines of a gentleman who spent more time drinking with his cronies at White's than engaging in nefarious crimes. But even a man like Alfred could overpower a much smaller individual. Someone like Sarah Bright. Or Hannah. Alone, in the stables, Killian could use any manner of persuasion to coerce the man to tell him the truth. And he needed the truth. Or Hannah would make good on her promise and put herself in grave danger. Really, he had no choice.

'I don't think the title-seeking mothers can blame us for a brief absence from their daughters.' Killian gestured to the stairs and followed Alfred down.

They strode out the front door, and Killian slapped Alfred on the shoulder. 'I've been thinking about our conversation the other day. I don't think your reaction was all that unforgiveable.'

Alfred tipped his head to the side. The son had inherited his father's profile. 'Really? Thank you. It's rare to find such understanding.'

Killian categorised the weapons on his person. He calculated how long it would take him to subdue Alfred and get a confession. 'You lost your brother. Someone you admired. Someone who may have been favoured by your father.'

Alfred's chin thrust forward, his lips hardening in the light of a full moon. He stopped a few feet from the barn. 'Did Father tell you that?'

Killian swallowed, sensing that he stood on a precipice. Anger seethed in Alfred's eyes. 'He hinted as much.'

Alfred barked out a laugh as he pushed open the stable door. Sweet hay, musty horse, and the pungent scent of manure enveloped them. 'Of course he did.'

For a large man, Alfred moved with deceptive speed. Killian saw the glint of Alfred's pistol in the moonlight as the man spun around, but he marked the man's movement too late to block the blow.

Killian's temple exploded in pain as the world went dark.

* * *

'Hannah, you look marvellous.' Ivy squinted at Hannah's hair then nodded in approval. 'Wonderful job, ladies.' She smiled at the maids in dismissal.

'Oh, bother.' Millie muttered a moment before Miss Anna Hastings and her mother swept into the room.

Hannah tried not to laugh as Millie silently gagged into her fan.

Lady Hastings pushed her daughter in the general direction of Hannah, Ivy, and Millie.

'Ah, Miss Cavendale, I was hoping we could talk. Privately. It is my wish to develop a much closer friendship with you.' Miss Anna's simpering smile made Hannah want to pinch the girl just to see a real emotion.

Ivy's shoulders grew rigid. 'There is nothing you can't say in front of my friends, Miss Anna.'

Miss Anna Hastings reached a pale hand to her powdered throat nervously twining her fingers in a delicate gold chain.

Hannah's gaze caught on the uncanny replica of an unfurling lily dangling in the hollow of Anna's throat.

Dear God. The lily necklace.

Hannah turned to Miss Anna Hastings. 'What a lovely necklace. Is that a lily? Pray tell where you found such a charming rendering?'

Miss Anna Hastings's eyes widened as she covered the necklace with her hand. She glanced at Ivy before looking away. 'I shouldn't say. It was a token of affection given to me by a certain gentleman who...'

'Dear God. It's Alfred, isn't it?' Ivy gasped.

'He asked me not to say. It is a secret, you see. But if he knew you approved, perhaps...' Miss Anna's voice drifted off as Hannah's world tumbled from its axis.

Irrevocable evidence that Ivy's brother was a diabolical killer. All of the pieces fell together in perfect symmetry.

Alfred was the member of a secret society that inspired fear in her fearless patroness. A society that threatened his safety when the body was found.

Alfred interviewed Sarah Bright for the service job at the Cavendale house.

Alfred gave Sarah Bright's necklace away to his sweetheart.

And Alfred came looking for Killian.

What if he knew of Killian's suspicions? What if he was intent on killing the only man Hannah could ever love? She had asked Killian not to confront Alfred alone, but had the stubborn man listened? Doubtful.

'Blasted hellfire!' Hannah hissed.

'I beg your pardon?' Miss Anna asked, aghast.

Hannah gripped Ivy's hands. 'I'm so sorry. But I must go.'

Hannah could only hope Ivy didn't follow her. She couldn't let he pale, delicate woman watch as Hannah killed her brother.

* * *

Hannah ran down the main stairs and almost crashed into Betty.

'Betty, what on earth are you doing here?' Hannah took in her maid's tumbled hair and wrinkled uniform. 'Is that hay in your apron?'

Betty's usually pink cheeks paled. 'I was in the... oh no!' She burst into tears.

Hannah didn't have time for her maid's histrionics, nor could she abandon the distraught girl. 'Are you hurt?'

'I must tell you something. And I know I'll probably get the sack for it, but... I was in the stables with... with...'

'Spit it out, Betty. I'm hardly going to fire you because you enjoyed a bit of fun in the stables with young Sam.'

Betty's eyes widened, and her mouth fell slack. 'How did you know? You're not going to dismiss me?'

'Of course not. But I'm looking for Lord Killian on an urgent matter. If you are well, I really must go.'

'But that's just it, miss. I came to speak with you about Lord Killian.' Betty gripped Hannah's arm as tears filled her eyes.

The swelling music in the ballroom dimmed. The glittering lights faded to grey. Hannah's blood froze in her veins. 'Tell me. Immediately!'

Betty paled further at Hannah's vicious tone. 'I saw him with Lord Alfred Cavendale. In the stables. Sam and I were in the hayloft when... oh, Miss Hannah. It were right terrible.'

Betty quickly explained that Lord Killian and Alfred entered the barn, then Alfred knocked Killian out, dragged him to a trap door and disappeared below the stables.

There was no time to waste. Hannah needed to save her duke.

'Betty, stay here. I must go.'

'Not to the stables, miss. Not by yourself. You wouldn't believe the look he had in his eyes. He's mad, I'm sure of it.'

'I must go, Betty. All will be well.' Hannah squeezed Betty's hand then turned and ran.

I will save him.

She had to save him, or nothing in her life would be well again.

Hannah raced out the front door, skidded on the gravel drive, and sprinted to the stables, all while cursing her delicate kitten-heeled slippers.

19

Killian regained consciousness in a slow, painful ascent. He ran through an internal assessment. Screaming headache. Arms and legs tied to the chair in which he sat.

Bloody freezing!

He kept his eyes closed and listened for any kind of sound. But there was nothing save the rush of his own breath.

Slowly, he opened his eyes. He saw little besides earthen walls, a flickering lamp, and a dirt floor. He could still smell the horses and manure, but a damp scent of earth pervaded. He must be in a cellar or some kind of tunnel.

'Alfred, are you there?' Killian's voice was a harsh rasp. It seemed odd to be calling for his captor, but he would rather face a threat than wait for it to sneak up behind him. At least Hannah wasn't with him. She was out of danger. For the time being. His biggest worry about dying was no longer being able to protect Hannah. Killian would gladly sacrifice his life if it meant keeping her safe.

'You seem to have gotten yourself into quite a pickle.' Hannah's voice was unmistakable in the quiet room.

No!

He twisted his neck and could make out the shimmer of her gown as she carefully walked closer. She kept her eyes roving the space behind him.

'You must leave, Hannah. Now. He could come back any minute.' Killian jerked on the ropes holding him hostage. He willed her to leave before Alfred's return.

'Then hold still so I can cut you free faster. I told you not to confront him alone. Insufferable man.' Ignoring his entreaty, she hunkered down beside him. Her dagger was already out and ready. When she placed her hand on his ankle, the weapon strapped there dug into his skin. She pulled up his pant leg.

'Hey! That's my dagger. From the first night we met.'

'I know. By all means, take it. There's no time, Hannah. Go now. Please.'

She narrowed her eyes at him. 'I will take it. Later. When you come to my room at midnight. Now hold still. I'm not leaving without you.' She began cutting the rope holding his leg to the chair.

'I rather think neither of you shall be leaving. More's the pity.' The deep voice echoing in the dark spaces didn't belong to Alfred. But it was Alfred who came into the circle of light. His pistol was trained on Hannah.

'Drop your knife, Miss Simmons. Now.' Alfred's voice was flat. He blinked rapidly, and his hand shook.

Killian strained his muscles, desperate to be free from his constraints. Desperate to protect Hannah. Desperate to do anything other than sit helplessly while someone threatened his love.

Not again. I cannot endure this again.

He would go mad. If he couldn't get free and use his body to shield hers, he would lose his sanity right along with his useless life.

The heavy thunk of Hannah's dagger hitting the floor reverberated through Killian like a thunderclap.

'Leave her alone, Alfred. She has nothing to do with this.' Killian had created some give in the rope with his struggles. He pulled harder.

'That's simply not true.' The same voice from before echoed in the darkness.

Lord Cavendale stepped into the dim light and joined his son.

'No!' The raw pain shocked Killian.

Lord Cavendale smiled, a chilling expression that didn't reach his eyes. The man had been nothing but kind to Killian. Blinded by his own grief and guilt, Killian had imagined Lord Cavendale to hold the same qualities as the father he lost. He had been so very wrong.

Lord Cavendale's icy tone matched his glare. 'Actually, a resounding yes, Lieutenant General. You are as wrong about this whore as you were about me. She is working for the Queen. Some kind of rogue detective, if my informants can be trusted... which I assure you, they can. And you, Lieutenant General, on a mission from the prime minister. My idiot son here seems to have gathered the notice of some very important people indeed.'

Alfred glanced at his father. His eye ticked. 'I told you I caught him, Father. See? Everything is going to be fine.'

'If you are involved, nothing ever seems to be fine. Dead maids, blackmail, and now this. Your failures are ever-increasing.'

Alfred ran a hand through his hair, tugging hard on the strands before smacking himself. 'I already told you, the maid was an accident. The greedy cow must have drunk too much of the tea. She was only supposed to have a few sips, not the whole damn cup.'

'You poisoned her?' Killian asked.

'No.' Alfred shook his head. '*No!* It was just to make her sleep. To get her in the casket and across the channel. But I've handled it. Haven't I?' He turned to Lord Cavendale. 'Haven't I?' Spittle flew from his mouth. 'You think I can't manage things, but I've sorted this. I caught the great Lieutenant General Robert Killian; does that not prove my worth?' His eyes darted from Killian to Hannah, his gun wildly following his gaze. 'And let's not forget, Father, you aren't so perfect yourself. Who missed his shot when we were on our picnic? A perfect opportunity, and you couldn't hit either of them.'

Before Killian or Hannah could react, the older gentleman pulled his own weapon. 'The only mistake I ever made was to sire you.' He shot Alfred in the back of the head. Blood sprayed across the earthen floor as Alfred collapsed to the ground.

'Fuck!' Killian said right before Hannah muttered her own curse.

Lord Cavendale toed the body with his boot before exhaling heavily. 'It's a shame, really. Alfred was never very bright. Always a disappointment. Our hopes rested in Patrick, but... you know how that ended, Lieutenant General Killian. Don't you?' Lord Cavendale turned to face Killian. His eyes glittered with concentrated rage, and the same madness Killian had seen in Alfred moments before he smashed a gun into Killian's temple.

Hannah's hand disappeared into her skirt. Before she could pull out what was certainly her pistol, Lord Cavendale lunged forward, grabbed a handful of her hair, and yanked her close to him, spinning her so her back was pressed against his chest.

Killian's heart leapt into his throat as he watched Hannah reach behind her, grabbing the back of Lord Cavendale's neck in both hands. She bent forward, using her bottom to push him off balance as she pulled his head down, over her shoulder. She bent further, gravity aiding her as he flipped over her back and slammed onto the dirt floor. She began tearing at her skirts, no doubt trying to find her weapon-filled pocket. Cavendale snagged her ankle, pulling hard. Hannah fell to the ground in a heap of bronze silk. Before he could crawl on top of her, she kicked out, her heeled slipper cutting a gash into Cavendale's cheek. The man changed tactics. Instead of attacking her, he stood and scrambled back to Killian.

Killian felt the cold metal of a gun barrel pressed against his temple at the same time Hannah pulled her weapon free of her skirts, aiming it at Cavendale and cocking the pistol.

'You might be an excellent shot, my dear, but I don't think your chances are quite as good as mine at hitting the mark.' Cavendale's raspy laugh wasn't nearly as chilling as watching the blood drain from Hannah's face.

'Do it, Hannah. Shoot him. He'll kill us either way.' Killian knew Cavendale would likely shoot him before Hannah's bullet reached its target, but it didn't matter. Nothing mattered except saving her.

'Drop the gun, Miss Simmons. Or I will shoot him.'

Hannah bit her lip. She looked from Killian to the mad man standing behind him. Killian knew the moment she gave up. A tear streaked down her cheek as she dropped her gun.

Realisation washed over Killian like sunlight emerging from a cloud. She loved him. In this moment, he wished she didn't. He wished she would sacrifice him to save herself.

'Full of surprises, aren't you, Miss Simmons? I must say, your disguise as a dowdy wallflower was convincing. Kick the weapon out of the way.'

Hannah followed his orders. Cavendale moved quickly for a man of his advanced years. He kept his gun trained on Killian as he drew closer to Hannah. 'Women are far too delicate creatures for such violence, my dear.'

Killian's stomach clenched, and he pulled harder on the ropes. Hannah spit into Cavendale's face. Lord Cavendale slapped her hard across her cheek. The crack of his hand meeting her flesh echoed through Killian's body. She careened across the floor, falling in a heap next to Alfred's still form.

Roaring in rage, Killian struggled harder. The bindings cut deeper into his skin. Hot blood flowed from the lacerations on his wrists. The sticky fluid made the ropes slippery.

Lord Cavendale strode over to Hannah, kicking her hard in the side. She curled in on herself and whimpered.

'Touch her again and I swear you will die screaming.' Killian was reduced to empty threats and the whisper of madness as he continued to tug at the ropes, his wrist slipping more with each pull.

'Exactly how will you manage that while tied to your chair? Doomed to watch her die, just as you watched my Patrick die. Useless. Impotent. Completely powerless. When I end your miserable life, it will be a mercy you don't deserve.' Lord Cavendale kicked Hannah again. She cried out, writhing on the floor, her arm crashing into Alfred's dead body with a dull thump.

Lord Cavendale turned to Killian. 'Alfred got himself involved in something much grander than his poor little mind could fathom. He was supposed to bring me that letter from the secret society he was so excited to join, but the idiot couldn't find it. He was never very bright. Took after his mother, I'm afraid.'

Hannah turned her head and looked at Killian. In the dim light, her expression was shrouded, but he could see her hand reaching for Alfred.

Not for Alfred. For his gun. Wickedly smart woman!

'Is the society involved in what happened to Sarah Bright? We know there are multiple victims. Who is behind this?' Killian prayed he could keep the man talking. Every second Cavendale focused on Killian was another second Hannah could use.

Lord Cavendale laughed. A chilling sound in the dark room. 'You know nothing about the society's true motives, Lieutenant General. But never mind. I should thank you. You've given me the perfect solution to my problem.'

'Exactly what problem is that?' Killian kept his face impassive while he worked the ropes at his wrist.

Almost there...

'Alfred, of course. He was becoming an embarrassing liability. But now...' Cavendale's gaze drifted to Hannah. 'Alfred must have stumbled upon the two of you in a lover's quarrel.'

Hannah froze as Cavendale knelt and brushed his hand over her cheek.

'Stay away from her!' Killian wrenched harder, ignoring the pain of rope tearing against his skin.

'Dear Miss Simmons was hoping to blackmail you into marriage. While she's certainly a lovely distraction, an illegitimate daughter grasping for a man so far out of her reach is no match for a duke.' Cavendale's gaze stayed locked on Hannah. 'In your rage, you killed her.' His hand drifted down to Hannah's throat.

'Get your hands off her, you filthy piece of shit!' Killian screamed.

Cavendale's fingers made indentations in her skin as he squeezed. Hannah tried to pull away, but Cavendale put the gun to her temple. 'Ah-ah. Miss Simmons. Don't move. Where was I? Oh, that's right. Lieutenant General Killian kills you. But not before Alfred valiantly tries to save your life. He fails, of course.' Cavendale tightened his grip. Hannah wheezed desperately. The insane lord kept talking. 'But he mortally wounded you, Lieutenant General. And for his trouble, you shot him.' Cavendale glanced back at Killian. 'I haven't ever killed anyone. Well, besides Alfred just now. It's fun, isn't it?' He returned his gaze to Hannah, dropping his gun to strangle her with both hands.

Killian wrenched his left arm free. He pulled Hannah's dagger from his ankle holster. The sudden movement drew Cavendale's attention. Realising the threat, he let go of Hannah, scrambling for his pistol and aiming at Killian.

Killian flung the blade through the air.

The gunshot exploded.

But it wasn't Cavendale's gun.

The man flew backward and landed heavily on the floor. Half of his head was gone.

Killian barely noticed the knife hilt buried directly in Cavendale's chest. He only saw Hannah.

She held Alfred's smoking pistol in a steady hand. Blood was sprayed over her face. She wiped at it, smudging the gore against her cheek. Her hair was in disarray, and her dress was ruined. He'd never seen a more beautiful woman in his life.

She slowly pulled herself into a sitting position, wincing as she cradled her ribs.

'Are you alright?' Killian needed to reach her. To hold her in his arms. He used his free hand to work frantically at the knot holding his right wrist to the chair.

'I've been better.' Hannah's voice was ragged. She stood up slowly. Stepping over Lord Cavendale's body, she paused to reach down, grab the dagger, and pull it from the dead man's chest with a swift jerk and a hissing breath.

Wiping the blade on her skirt, she walked over to Killian. Carefully lowering herself to her knees, she continued cutting the tie binding his ankle. 'I told you I would get my knife back. You have a steady aim, even with your left hand. It would have saved me.'

Killian stopped trying to untie his wrist. He brushed a tangle of hair away from her face and lifted her chin with his finger. 'But not me. He would have shot me before he fell. You saved my life.'

'Of course, I did.' Hannah's amber eyes filled with tears and her lips trembled. 'I love you, Robert Killian. I'm so very glad you aren't dead.' She reached for him, crushing her mouth against his.

For a moment, the world distilled to Hannah's soft lips, her sweet warmth, her salty tears, and the scent of orange and vanilla.

He pulled away to look at her. 'You say the sweetest things.'

* * *

The next few hours were a flurry of surreptitious activity. It seemed prudent to keep as much hidden from the guests as possible. With the help of Drake and Lady Philippa, they were able to move both bodies into a cold room in the kitchen cellar. They created a story of murder/suicide for the public. It would not look good for the family, but it was better than the truth. After Hannah cleaned up and carefully re-donned her grey gown, it was decided she and Lady Philippa would break the news to Ivy.

Hannah dreaded the moment. As horrific as the evening was, telling Ivy both her brother and father were dead seemed impossibly cruel. But Hannah would not shy away from it. It was her duty. Even in a situation such as this, taking a life was never clean. Innocent people were always hurt.

Hannah asked Millie to join them in Hannah's room. Ivy would need support, and Hannah doubted she would accept any comfort from Hannah once the truth was shared.

Lady Philippa was vehemently opposed to giving any details. It was troubling enough Cavendale knew about Hannah's work with the Queen. They didn't need to create any more suspicion when Ivy could be told the same story as the rest of the beau monde. But Hannah insisted. She would share as much as she could without betraying their relationship with the Queen. Ivy deserved to hear the truth.

Ivy sat pale and silent through Hannah's retelling of the evening.

'Are you sure Alfred was responsible for killing a maid?'

Hannah nodded. 'He admitted it to us. It was accidental. He only meant to drug her, but...'

'Why would he drug a maid?'

'It would seem he had improper intentions with the young lady.' Philippa gave enough information to let Ivy form her own conclusions. They would not be the correct conclusions, but neither would they be wrong.

When Hannah told her about Lord Cavendale shooting Alfred, Ivy shuddered as if she felt the bullet that ended her brother's life.

'Father killed Alfred?' Ivy's pale skin drew tight around her lips. Millie sat next to Ivy on Hannah's bed and gripped her hand.

'Yes. I'm so sorry, Ivy.' Hannah bit her cheek, refusing to let the emotions surface.

Ivy's pale gaze flitted from Hannah to Philippa, finally landing on Millie. 'I should say I can't believe he would do it, but...' Her face crumpled, and she leaned into her friend. Millie wrapped strong arms around Ivy as she dissolved into quiet sobs. It was several minutes before she was able to speak again. 'And Father, he's dead too?'

Hannah nodded.

'How did he die? Lord Cavendale?' Millie asked.

It was the question Hannah most dreaded.

She swallowed. Straightening her shoulders, Hannah blew out a shaky breath. This was the moment she destroyed her shiny new friendship with Ivy and Millie. But she would not lie to them.

'I shot him. He was going to kill us. I had no other choice. I'm so sorry, Ivy.' Her voice broke despite her best efforts, and a tear tracked a hot path down her cheek. Not for the death of Lord Cavendale. But for the pain his loss brought to her friend.

Ivy pulled away from Millie. 'You shot him? Not Lord Killian?' Her icy-blue eyes were red-rimmed and widened in shock.

'Yes. Well, Lord Killian was tied to a chair, and your father was not in his right mind. I...' Words failed Hannah. How could she justify murdering her friend's father? Even if the man was a monster?

Ivy leapt from the bed, and Hannah ignored her instinct to protect herself from the inevitable attack. Whatever Ivy did, Hannah would take it. She deserved it.

Ivy flung herself at Hannah, hugging her so tight, Hannah's ribs screamed in protest. 'Thank you,' Ivy whispered the words. Hannah froze, too astonished at first to return the hug. When she finally did, Ivy's thin body shuddered against her.

Ivy pulled away. Her nose was red, and her eyes were swollen but she held her head high.

'I think I shall go to my room, now. I need some privacy.' Ivy reached a hand to Millie. 'Walk me there?'

Millie nodded but lingered a moment after Ivy left. Her sharp gaze raked over Hannah. 'I won't share stories that aren't mine to divulge, but I will say some losses are actually gains. A lucky shot, Hannah? I had no idea you were so well-versed in the use of a pistol.'

Hannah tipped up her chin and shrugged.

Millie's dimple emerged, and she winked before following after Ivy.

'That was interesting,' Philippa remarked. 'Those two are far more than they seem. I like them. And I don't usually like anyone.' She stood, brushing out her skirts. 'I shall also take my leave. I must send a message to the Queen. She will want to know about your cover being blown.'

Hannah wasn't ready to contemplate what that meant.

Philippa approached Hannah, running her fingers over the bruise on Hannah's cheek. 'I'm very glad you are safe.' She sniffed then stepped back. 'Another mission accomplished, though not as neatly as we hoped. It's nearing midnight. I'm sure you'll want to be alone.' She raised an annoyingly perfect eyebrow at Hannah 'Or at least, not with me. Give my regards to Lieutenant General Killian.' She stretched her mouth in a Cheshire grin before floating out the door.

20

Fifteen minutes remained until midnight, but Killian couldn't wait a moment longer. He left his room and almost crashed into the Duchess of Dorset as she exited Hannah's.

Shit.

'I, uh, was just... um...' *Heading to your ward's room to ravage her.*

'Lord Killian. What a surprise.' Lady Philippa narrowed her gaze, making him squirm like a schoolboy. 'I was determined not to like you. Men, in general, are among my least favourite things. But you've proven me wrong. Which never happens. Don't ruin things now.' Philippa took a step closer to him, and he forced himself not to retreat, knowing she would see it as a sign of weakness. 'If you hurt her, I will kill you. Slowly and with great relish.'

Killian cleared the fear from his voice. 'I know. I won't hurt her. Ever.'

'I'm inclined to believe you. May wonders never cease.' She strode past, frankincense and jasmine lingering in her wake.

Killian exhaled a breath he wasn't aware he was holding. *That woman is more terrifying than any man I've ever met.*

Killian opened Hannah's door. Betty was helping Hannah with the buttons of her dress. The maid squeaked when she saw Killian.

'Oh.' Hannah's eyes warmed, and Killian's heart expanded to stretch his ribs. 'You're early.' She turned to Betty. 'I think you can retire for the evening, Betty.'

'Yes, miss. Of course.' She curtsied and rushed past Killian, pausing at the door. 'I'm awfully glad you weren't hurt, sir.' Her cheeks rounded like apples as she smiled. She dipped another quick curtsey, her hat bobbing madly as she bustled past.

Killian crossed the room and wrapped Hannah in his arms. He propped his chin on top of her head and held her, breathing in her scent. Soaking up her warmth. Revelling in the strength and softness that made her so unique.

Hannah sighed and sank into him. For a time, they just breathed together.

'May I undress you?' He needed her skin against his. Their bodies intertwined. Her weight holding him onto the earth's surface, so he didn't fly away in all the 'what if's' that could have taken her from him.

'Please. Only, carefully.' Hannah smiled, her cheek stained purple from the night's violence.

Killian feathered a kiss against the bruise. 'Always.'

He moved behind her and took his time with the buttons of her dress. When he slid his hands beneath the fabric to push it over her shoulders, she sighed as the weight fell away. He untied her skirts and pushed them down, helping her step out of them before gazing his fill at Hannah in nothing but her shift and corset. With each breath she took, her breasts pushed against the boned cotton.

'God, you are beautiful.'

Hannah bit her lip. Killian fell impossibly deeper.

Turning her, he broke his promise to remain gentle, tackling the silk laces tied in a perfect bow.

Killian leaned forward and pressed open-mouthed kisses where her neck met her shoulder, savouring the salty flavour of her skin.

She gasped when his teeth sunk into her flesh.

His cock demanded immediate fulfilment, but his heart needed to spin this moment out forever. Stepping back, he began unravelling the ribbons. Each tug elicited a sigh of pleasure from Hannah.

The stiff material fell away. He gripped her shoulders, turning her to face him. Hannah started to lift her hands, then winced. Killian captured both her hands, halting her movement. He leaned forward and pressed a kiss against each wrist where Hannah's pulse beat madly.

'Do you have any particular attachment to this shift?' He glided his fingers up her arm and tripped along the neckline. Her nipples hardened beneath the thin fabric, and he clenched his jaw. She was destroying him in delicate degrees.

'No.' Her eyes glittered with mischief, daring him to make the next move.

'Good.' He ripped the flimsy material in two, the pieces floating to the floor in a heap. She was completely naked, save for the pistol strapped to her thigh, the throwing knives secured in a clever leather holster around her forearm, and the dagger on her ankle.

Hannah put her hands on his vest. 'Why am I the only one naked?'

'You're hardly naked. You could wage war like this, a fearsome Lady Godiva. I'm not sure whether to be scared or very, very aroused.'

'Both.' Hannah laughed softly, and the sound caressed his senses.

Killian helped her remove her weapons before quickly stripping off his own clothes.

She had vicious bruising across her ribs. Her left hip was scraped raw, and her elbow was bleeding.

'We killed him too quickly. He should have suffered for every injury he dealt you.' Rage overpowered Killian's lust as he remembered the desperate helplessness of watching Hannah suffer.

She ran her hands over his chest and down his arm to trace the bandage around his wrist. 'Indeed. He did not deserve such a merciful death. But revenge holds no comfort.' She pressed her palm against his heart. Catching his hand in hers, she moved it to her own chest and pressed it flat between her breasts so he could feel the steady rhythm. 'This is our sanctuary. This is our benediction. This is the grace we seek and the only vengeance we need.'

Helpless to resist, Killian pulled her close, pressing his mouth against hers, questing her depths, tangling his tongue with hers, seeking an absolution only she could provide.

* * *

Hannah broke their kiss and lead him to her bed. She wanted him inside of her, to feel his powerful body surrounding her, healthy and vital and strong. She needed the heat and friction of him to know it was real.

He helped her under the covers then climbed in after her, holding his weight on his arms so her ribs wouldn't be crushed. She opened her legs, and he settled between her thighs, easing into her body like an ocean wave. He rocked slowly, and she sank into the pleasure, glory made sharp by their love.

'Stop me if it hurts.' Killian's forest-green gaze burned into hers.

'Never.' She tipped her pelvis and flexed internal muscles, cradling him in her depths.

'Marry me, Hannah.' He thrust into her, his words falling against her skin like rain on wildflowers. 'I know this isn't how a proposal should be made, but I can't live without you.'

'Who determines how a proposal should be made? And you never have to live without me.'

When he froze, Hannah nudged him with her hips, but he stayed still.

'What are you saying?' His dark brows pulled together, a wrinkle forming between them.

'What do you think?' She pulled his head down and kissed him. 'I'm saying you have proven my fears unfounded, Lieutenant General Robert Killian.' She pushed up with her hips, ignoring the pain in her ribs. 'I'm saying I trust you with my freedom.' He refused to play her game, staying resolutely frozen, hard as granite and just as immovable. She grew more determined. 'I'm saying, despite your title, your money, and your position in society, I will marry you anyway.' She clenched around him, silently demanding friction. The insufferable man remained still.

'You'll marry me?' His muscles shook from the strain of holding his weight above her.

'I won't if you don't bloody well ravish me properly.'

Killian's lips curled in a smile. 'Liar.'

He thrust into her. Hannah gasped as he found that gloriously bright place hidden deep within her core.

'Of course I'll marry you, Killian. I can't live without you either. I love you,' she managed before words were lost in the eloquent language of their bodies merging, the symphony of heartbeat and breath, the divine magic of two souls weaving into one.

ACKNOWLEDGMENTS

Writing a book is mostly a solitary experience, but publishing a book takes a group effort. I wanted to first thank my writing group for their support, skills, and endless supplies of tissues for the many rejections I received while learning the craft. My greater writing community – particularly, the Pacific Northwest Writer's Association – for providing tricks, expertise, and comradery along with classes, pitch sessions, and a host of talented authors willing to support newbies on their journey. Liz and Meghann, for reading every word I've written – even my dismal first attempts – and cheering me on along this twisting path. My 'write till we die' team – Lisa, Lyssa, and Jana – for all the support, commiserations, and celebrations. Gerri Russel, for her wealth of wisdom, generosity with her time and experience, and huge heart that shows in her writing and her support. The charmingly irreverent and immensely talented Damon Suede, for teaching me so much about the technical craft of writing and, more importantly, the magic that transforms words into worlds. My amazing agent, Katie Reed, for believing in this story. My patient and kind editor, Megan Haslam, for making my words shine bright. The Boldwood Books team, for taking on this project and running with it to places I could never reach on my own. My family, for always believing in me. My soulmate, best friend, and life-long traveling partner (aka husband), for taking on the cooking, cleaning, and dog-watching while I tapped away on my laptop. And finally, the readers, for making this entire adventure possible. A heartfelt and immense thank you!

ABOUT THE AUTHOR

Darcy McGuire is a high school counsellor who grew up in the wilds of New Zealand but happily settled in the Pacific Northwest. In between dodging territorial geese, gathering duck eggs, taking the dog for long walks, Darcy loves writing about fierce female protagonists who may dodge daggers and bullets but never seem to escape Cupid's Arrow.

Sign up to Darcy McGuire's mailing list for news, competitions and updates on future books.

Visit Darcy's website:

Follow Darcy on social media here:

instagram.com/authordarcymcguire

Letters from
the past

Discover page-turning
historical novels from
your favourite authors
and be transported
back in time

*Join our book club
Facebook group*

https://bit.ly/SixpenceGroup

*Sign up to our
newsletter*

https://bit.ly/LettersFrom
PastNews

Boldwœd

Boldwood Books is an award-winning fiction publishing company seeking out the best stories from around the world.

Find out more at www.boldwoodbooks.com

Join our reader community for brilliant books, competitions and offers!

Follow us
@BoldwoodBooks
@TheBoldBookClub

Sign up to our weekly deals newsletter

https://bit.ly/BoldwoodBNewsletter

Made in the USA
Middletown, DE
25 June 2024

56291824R00157